MIRROR

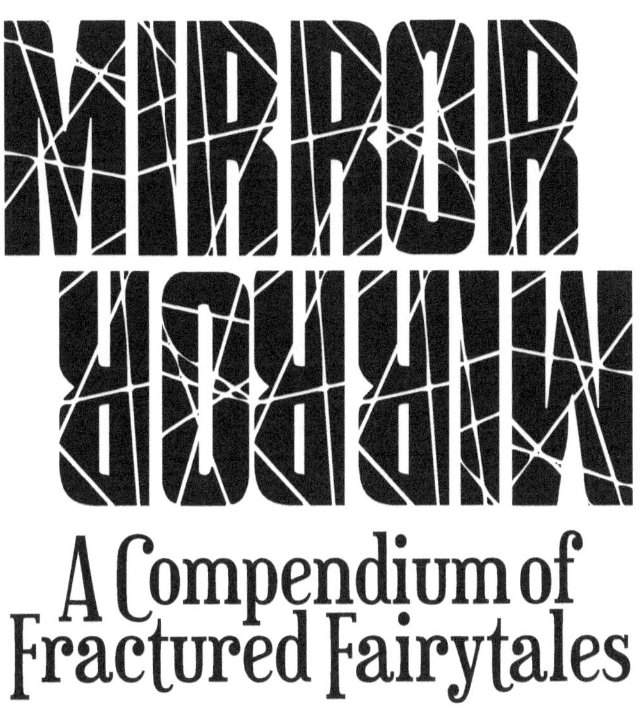

MIRROR MIRROR

A Compendium of Fractured Fairytales

Edited by
Emily Barnett Kudeviz

FRACTURED
MIRROR

For my family
and everyone who grew up
enamored by fairytales

Table of Contents

Foreword
Emily Barnett Kudeviz

Fairy tales have staying power. A conglomerate of stories told over generations and generations, fairy tales pull from different cultures and times. Even today we are seeing fairy tales infiltrate our culture with the remakes of "Snow White," "Beauty and the Beast," and "Rapunzel." We are infatuated with the stories, marketing everything from fairy-tale princess wedding dresses to birthday cakes and backpacks. Fairy tales "attract us because they contain what we lack: characters who struggle and demand to live in truth, wounded characters who want to be whole and wholesome" (Zipes, "Speaking the Truth with Folk and Fairy Tales: The Power of the Powerless", 248). These stories capture us with little effort it seems, but as we see with other literature, fairy tales are more than what is on the page.

Throughout the years different groups of people have collected, written, and arranged fairy tales, such as Charles Perrault, Jacob and Wilhelm Grimm, Hans Christian Andersen, Andrew Lang, and Madame de Villeneuve. Sometimes these fairy tales come with a moral or lesson, such as Perrault's versions ("Little Red Riding Hood" is one), and many of these stories help guide readers, especially children, in the act of growing up. While this aid in transition from child to adult, in and of itself, is not necessarily a problem, assimilation through stories does have the potential to box children into predefined paths and gender stereotypes.

With newer renditions of these tales, particularly tales involving beasts (especially of the bridegroom variety) and "witches" (also seen as evil stepmothers), we are seeing an attempt to disrupt the predefined paths of childhood. We are seeing a push back against the 'proper' performance of femininity and an attempt to embrace the "Other," in this case freedom from restriction. These retellings complicate the relationships between child and beast, innocence and adulthood, acceptable behavior and unacceptable behavior.

Fairy Tales as Teachers: A Pathway to Conventional and Subversive Lessons

Fairy tales are tools of civilization, a way to teach and cultivate the desired behaviors and morals of a good citizen. In the 1690s, with the rise of Perrault and a plethora of French woman writers (such as Mlle. Marie-Jeanne L'Héritier, Mlle. Catherine Bernard, Mme. d'Aulnoy, and, Mme. Durand), we began to see a shift towards fairy tales being constructed for children specifically. These stories were tailored, "for the most part to express their views about young people and to prepare them for roles that they idealistically believed they should play in society" (Zipes, *Fairy Tales and the Art of Subversion*, 29). These are powerful tools. In fact, they were, and still are, "considered as one of the vital socializing elements in Western civilization" (Zipes, *Fairy Tales and the Art of Subversion*, 34). And, being as the education of children tends to the more conservative side, fairy tales have been subject to "discreet inquiry and censorship…to guarantee that fairy tales were more or less constructed to follow the classical pattern and to reinforce the dominant social codes within the home and school" (Zipes, *Fairy Tales and the Art of Subversion*, 34).

The power that fairy tales have is because they are subliminal. Instead of sitting children down in a classroom or nursery and telling them how they should behave, literature, and specifically fairy tales, do that same task subtly. In fact, what makes fairy tales so effective is that "they convey values and expectations which are always evolving, in the process of being formed, but—and this is fortunate—never set so hard that they cannot be changed again, and newly told stories can be more helpful than repeating old ones" (Warner, "Monstrous Mothers", 19). Many of these stories "show the powerless moving toward a position of power, the poor finding wealth, the beautiful but impecunious marrying well" (Webb and Hopcroft 316). They present princesses who receive a husband when they are virtuous and kind. They present young men who use cunning and trickery to gain riches. They present protagonists who receive happy endings when they are able to assimilate and villains who succumb to horrible ends due to their preconceived vices. By reading or hearing these stories, children begin to absorb the "right way" to behave, and thus, the civilizing power of these tales is enacted.

That is not to say that all fairy tales are ones which adhere to the status quo. Alison Lurie, in her book, *Don't Tell the Grown-Ups: The Subversive Power of Children's Literature*, argues that fairy tales are "among the most subversive texts in children's literature" (16) as they often "support the rights of disadvantaged members of the population against the establishment" (16). In fact, education authority Sarah Trimmer called for caution against fairy tales in the later 18th century, as they "taught ambition, violence, a love of wealth, and the desire to marry above one's station" (Lurie 17). Zipes, in his article "Speaking the Truth with Folk and Fairy Tales: The Power of the Powerless", expresses something similar to Lurie's ideas, writing that these tales "tend to sympathize with victims and underdogs and are replete with compassion and justice, even if such 'values' were not evident in the societies in which the tales were told and written" (248). However, he also argues that many tales do reinforce patriarchal views and have been simplified for children.

While both Lurie and Zipes present important points, if we consider the popular fairy tales that we grew up with

("Cinderella", "Beauty and the Beast", "Snow White") then we are faced with a handful of stories that do try to civilize our children. We are presented with stories that "reflect the taste of literary men who edited the first popular collections of fairy stories for children during the nineteenth century" (Lurie 20), and that taste includes very specifically the stories that they then rewrote to "make them suitable for Victorian children" (Lurie 21). These tales were then bowdlerized further by the Walt Disney Company and others until the stories that remained with us were the ones that stripped fairy tales of any subversive tendencies they once had.

But, this quality of fairy tales is also subversive, as we are seeing in more modern renditions of the stories. While theorists such as Bettelheim and writers such as Perrault looked at these stories as way to cultivate exemplary citizens who embrace the adult norms, revisions of fairy tales also have the ability to subvert them, providing children with ways in which they can "overcome oppression" (Zipes, *Fairy Tales and the Art of Subversion*, 174). Philosopher Ernst Bloch, for instance, explored the ways in which fairy tales positioned how the "underdog, the small person, uses his or her wits not only to survive but also live a better life" (Zipes, *Fairy Tales and the Art of Subversion*, 174). Fairy tales have the ability to offer those with no power a chance to imagine, and even jump start, change (Webb and Hopcroft 316).

It is the timelessness of fairy tales that make them a perfect canvas for subversion and revision. That is not to say, however, that every revision of a fairy tale will change or subvert the tale. Some are merely faithful retellings. A quick search of picture books of "Beauty and the Beast" revealed a dozen or so beautifully rendered versions of the classic tale, all without any surprise or twist. These versions include *Beauty and the Beast* retold by Samantha Easton and illustrated by Ruth Sanderson, *Beauty and the Beast* retold by Mahlon F. Craft and illustrated by Kinuko Y. Craft, and *Beauty and the Beast* retold by Cynthia Rylant and illustrated by Meg Park.

But, others, take the themes and structures we know and present alternative paths. For instance, author Neil Gaiman's and illustrator Chris Riddell's *The Sleeper and the Spindle* takes the familiar tales of "Sleeping Beauty" and "Snow White" and surprises readers. Instead of being rescued by a prince, Beauty is rescued by a queen. The accompanying pen and ink illustrations accented with gold also seem to offer a nod to the more classical artistic renderings of fairy tale art. So, while this rendition provides a familiar casing in both structure and illustration to more traditional versions of fairy tales, it eschews the conservative leanings of them, providing children with the idea that women can save their own kingdoms, women can save each other, and women don't need the love of someone to survive.

Like Gaiman's story, many modern retellings of fairy tales tackle difficult subjects. If fantasy and fairy tales are a way to face the difficult demons in our lives, modern authors are looking beyond the rigid ideologies of what makes a good citizen and instead taking on the topics of "child abuse, drugs, sexism, violence, and bigotry through their transformation of the traditional fairy tale motifs and plots" (Zipes, *Fairy Tales and the Art of Subversion*, 189). It is because of this that fairy tales are still immensely important in our society.

This Collection

Which brings me to this collection, *Mirror, Mirror*. Putting together this collection of tales has been a joy and a challenge. We received so many wonderful submissions that covered a wide expanse of original material, stretching from the beloved favorites of "Cinderella" and "Sleeping Beauty" to more obscure tales such as the Portuguese story "The Lady with the Goat Feet," the Indian tale "The Demon with the Matted Hair," and a retelling of one of the oldest Welsh fairy tales about Elidyr.

Each story in this collection strives to present new ways of looking at fairy tales, updating them, re-envisioning them, turning them on their heads. I have carefully curated this collection to represent a breadth of writing styles and opinions, and the fourteen authors represented here all bring something unique to the compendium, a little something extra that adds to the staying power that are fairy tales.

I hope that you enjoy this collection!

Works Cited

Easton, Samantha. *Beauty and the Beast*. Illustrated by Ruth Sanderson, Andrew McMeel Pub, 1992. Print.

Gaiman, Neil. *The Sleeper and the Spindle*. Illustrated by Chris Riddell, HarperCollins, 2015. Print.

Lurie, Alison. *Don't Tell the Grown-Ups: The Subversive Power of Children's Literature*. Boston: Back Bay Books, 1990. Print.

Rylant, Cynthia. *Beauty and the Beast*. Illustrated by Meg Park, Disney-Hyperion, 2017. Print.

Webb, Caroline and Helen Hopcroft. "'A Different Logic': Animals, Transformation, and Rationality in Angela Carter's 'The Tiger's Bride'." *Marvels & Tales: Journal of Fairy-Tale Studies*, vol. 31, no. 2, 2017, pp. 314-337.

Zipes, Jack. *Fairy Tales and the Art of Subversion*. New York, NY: Routledge Classics, 2012. Print.

Zipes, Jack. "Speaking the Truth With Folk and Fairy Tales: The Power of the Powerless," *Journal of American Folklore*, vol 132, no. 525, pp 243-259.

The Turtle on the Lily-pad
Sonia Focke

The lily-pad ripples on the surface of the lake
making the tiny amethyst turtle dance.

I. Na-apia

The peaty, heady scent of the swamp fills their nostrils; the cool black mud oozes between their toes. Their harpoons catch on the pliant stalks of papyrus, rustling the leafy umbels like a thousand strings of beads.

Two sisters pick their way towards a gathering of trees, a tangle of twisted brown limbs and thorns, smelling sickly-sweet of overripe fruit and echoing with the calls of monkeys and hoopoes fighting above them.

They have just reached it when Maia pinches Na-apia's arm.

"What?" Na-apia considers pinching her back.

Maia thrusts her chin towards the Lake.

The Lake, Na-apia thinks, is not a proper lake like in the stories, with land on all sides and happy villages along its banks. It was more of a neutral ground between the swamp and the wood, a place not yet choked by papyrus and reeds nor colonized by roots and fallen branches, a place where the water came up for air and found mostly lily-pads and floating islands of moss and wild rice.

At first Na-apia thinks Maia is pointing to a pair of fine mallards, fat and sleek, gobbling at some fish or salamander between two open waterlilies, but then one of the floating islands grows a leathery head with a tiny snout like a shrew's and huge, yellow eyes that blink lazily in a patch of sunlight.

"Look at the size of him," Maia whispers into her ear. "He'll feed the whole village for a week."

Na-apia looks and clicks her tongue. "We should leave him for Sun Day."

Maia grabs her harpoon, tests its barbed tip of barren white bone. "He might be gone by then. No-one's seen him before this." She unbinds her red bark-cloth skirt and hangs it on an overhanging branch. "Anyway, he wouldn't even fit in the basin."

"Maybe he's a god." Na-apia picks up her own harpoon and winds its cord around her hand.

"Pffft. Whoever heard of a god taking the shape of the Enemy of the Sun?" Maia crouches low and crawls over the tangle of roots and moss along the bank. "I'll try and catch him in the neck."

"And how will we tow him on land?" But Na-apia takes off her skirt and follows Maia anyway. This might be their last hunt for a while. Na-apia watches the muscles ripple under Maia's dark skin, the moisture beading on her shaved head, and her heart swells in her chest. Yesterday, Maia was nothing but a tangle of chubby limbs, running away giggling whenever she got into trouble. Tomorrow, Maia will cast off the wilting flower collars that bump against her chest and put the first bead to her first real necklace; tomorrow she would take her First Spouse.

Maia creeps to a spot on the far side of the immense turtle and slips soundlessly into the water, holding her harpoon aloft so it won't splash. Na-apia does the same from his other side, shivering slightly as the cool waters of the lake embrace her, careful to make as little noise as possible as she untangles her legs from the stringy clutches of waterlily stems. She circles clumps of wild rice and rotting vegetation and sweet-smelling blossoms.

The Turtle on the Lily-pad

The turtle ignores them. This isn't the first turtle Na-apia has seen with moss or weeds clinging to their shell. Some are as small around as her splay-fingered hand, others as big as a potter's turn-tray. This one you could have stood four goats to graze on without them tangling their horns.

He paddles in place, sending ripples through the floating lily-pads, and sometimes Na-apia catches a glimpse of his huge, meaty flippers.

Maia is almost level with him. He briefly ducks his head under water and Na-apia fears for a moment he will dive, but he soon comes up again, a mass of uprooted waterlilies dangling out of his mouth, chomping languidly as his muddy tongue waves a single blossom back and forth.

Na-apia carefully angles herself to grab onto his shell and ram her harpoon into the meaty flesh of his legs, but Maia doesn't wait. As he dips his head down into the murky water again, she strikes.

The harpoon sinks into his flesh just where his neck connects to the tangled island of his shell. The huge creature bucks, his head shoots out of the water and his snout waves in the air in distress. Maia cries out in triumph and uses the shaft of her harpoon to pull herself up, swinging one leg over his back until she is astride him. Then, with a triumphant howl, she draws her knife from her belt and rams it into the back of his neck.

Na-apia throws herself back to avoid a huge, clawed flipper thrashing the water. She tries to find a vulnerable spot and throws her own harpoon. It sticks fast; the line pulls tight against her palm as she tries to avoid being dragged too near the still-thrashing flippers.

Finally they still and Maia holds out a hand, grinning from ear to ear. "What a dish for my husband!"

"Pfffft. No luck to you. Manakhuria hates turtle." Manakhuria had been her own First Spouse, until she finished her first five necklaces. He would take good care of her sister.

She grabs Maia's hand and pulls. The resulting splash is very satisfying.

Maia surfaces, spluttering. "What was that for?"

"Not waiting. We both have to be in the water to tow him, anyway."

It gets easier once they can stand, their feet sinking into the cool, slimy silt as they strain to pull the enormous carcass toward the bank.

The underside of his shell, a pale yellow bright against the lush vegetation on his back, scrapes and grinds over the tree roots. Na-apia is trying to prevent his flippers from getting caught when she hears the rush of water and sees the wave. She immediately leaps back.

Maia screams. Na-apia sees her fall back, drawn into the water by a reptilian head. Na-apia yells and tries to pull her harpoon from the turtle. She tugs, it resists, stuck fast. She sees Maia's head disappear under the water. Na-apia gives up on the harpoon and lunges.

She grabs Maia by the foot, pulling, pummeling the creature with her free hand and feet, screaming. The creature jerks back and she fumbles for her knife. As she draws it, it lets go.

Caught unaware, Na-apia falls hard in the shallow water, dropping her knife and pulling Maia along with her. Praise the Sun and River, Maia sits up, spluttering and gagging as she crawls up the bank. Na-apia pushes her along, scrabbling with her feet while frantically feeling for her knife in the silt. Her fingers encounter smooth rocks, slimy wood, tickling moss, but no knife.

The creature resurfaces and Na-apia sees that it is not a crocodile, but another turtle, even bigger than the first. Her shell is as big around as a hut, her eyes the size of winnowing baskets, rheumy and ancient.

"How dare you claim my prize?" Her voice sounds like gravel on a millstone.

Na-apia yelps and Maia, still heaving, snatches her hand and squeezes it, eyes wide.

Na-apia breathes hard. In the stories, the gods are made of gold and lapis-lazuli and speak with voices like an earthquake. They weren't the black of new earth, covered in moss, with a young persea sapling swaying on their shell.

She takes a calming breath. "She is my sister."

"And that was my mate she killed. She owes me a replacement."

Maia grips Na-apia's arm, squeezing so hard it hurts. She mouths a silent "no, no, no".

Na-apia strokes Maia's head. "My sister cannot breathe under water. She would not survive to be your mate."

The turtle snorts, her trunk-like nose quivering. "Is that any business of mine? Did she ask if I wanted my husband dead before murdering him? She will survive to my home and there she will be my wife."

"She will be Manakhuria's wife to-morrow. So, you see, she cannot marry you."

"Have the wedding gifts been exchanged? Has the wedding feast been eaten? Take her home, then. I will drink the lake dry. I will suck the water out of the swamp. You will have no fish to grill over the fire, no lily roots to eat, no papyrus for your mats."

Na-apia looks down at Maia, at the soggy, torn flowers of her collar, at the drops of water sparkling on the fuzz of her head like stars in a night sky. She thinks of their parents preparing the wedding feast. She thinks of her time in Manakhuria's house and the meals they had prepared together, how safe she felt in his arms.

"Take me instead."

A quick thrust of powerful flippers brings the turtle closer to Na-apia. She can smell the earth and water of her, feel the heat of her breath. "Does my husband's blood stain your blade? Does his death throes still ache between your legs?"

"Blood for blood. My mother's blood flows through both of us."

"Pfffft. Flesh for flesh, life for life—and bride for groom."

Na-apia shakes her head, thinking fast. "When Baboon first tries to bring back the Sun from the Far South, the Sun wanted the hearts of three young vultures. But he offered her his own because, like a sycamore, a heart grows better as it matures. A small sapling is not worth a fruit-bearing tree. Your mate was ancient; my sister is young and not yet a bride. My First Marriage is behind me and I am not yet promised to another. My heart is ready to bear fruit. Hers has only just produced its first flowers."

They stare at each other for three eternities, the woman and the turtle. Eyes bright and fierce, eyes ancient and hard.

Finally, the turtle says: "Hold your breath."

And she grabs Na-apia's arm in her mouth and drags her under.

Na-apia's lungs strain inside her chest. The cool water embraces her, squeezes her; the waterlily stalks snatch at her, catching her foot. But still she is dragged down, down, down, as the water grows heavy with silt, engulfing her. She gives a last, desperate prayer to the River and the Sun, and waits for her chest to burst.

But the water grows cool and caressing, and she can see the monstrous form of the turtle in a jeweled sunbeam and then the water releases her and there is air, real air and sunlight. She drinks it all in big gulps.

"Get on my back," the turtle says.

She turns to clamber on and gasps. The moss, the ferns, the persea sapling are gone. The turtle's shell is pure gold, gleaming so brightly it hurts Na-apia's eyes. It is inlaid in dusk-blue lapis, in fresh green malachite, in blood-red jasper, in pink amethyst. More stones dot the turtle's neck and head, others slide down her throat like a necklace, stark against the deep brown of her neck.

The turtle grunts impatiently. Na-apia swallows her questions and grabs onto the smooth shell, climbing on. As they swim to the shore, Na-apia surveys the world on the other side of the Lake.

The Turtle on the Lily-pad

It was a real lake, here, glinting under a bright golden sun, grasslands stretching out as far as the eye could see. No swamp, no little wood, but a scattering of trees and a village near the shore.

The village looks shockingly normal, round wooden frames hung with coloured mats, hunting equipment and shields hanging just outside the doors. The sound of children laughing echoes across the water along with the thump-thump-thump of mortars.

"Get off."

Obediently, Na-apia slides off the turtle's back into the shallow water near the shore. Pebbles massage the soles of her feet and small shrimp tickle her toes.

The turtle heaves herself out of the water. As it cascades over the stones of her shell, it leaves them gleaming in deep colours under the dazzling sun.

Children set up a cry, adults come running, all of them bedecked with gold and lapis and amethyst.

"Grandmother!" one of them calls, "where have you left Second Grandfather this time?"

"Second Grandfather is dead," the old turtle answers in her rasping voice. "This one will be sharing my hut, instead."

"My name is Na-apia," she says, standing tall to face them, aware that her skirt was still hanging on the branch on the shores of the other Lake.

"Your name is Other Wife," Grandmother snaps, "until I say otherwise. Now come."

Grandmother leads her to the village, past tall posts carved and painted with turtles, like a fence missing its basketry. As she walks, her heart too full to think, Na-apia sees the men and women bedecked with jewels, pounding tubers and milling grain, mending sickles and baking bread, and everywhere there are turtles flopping about, carrying baskets on their shells and dragging mats behind them. As she passes the houses, Na-apia sees that what she had thought were shields hung next to the doors are actually jewelled turtle shells.

The turtle called Grandmother leads her to a hut right at the edge of the village, then stands up on her two hind legs. She takes off her shell and as she hangs it on a leather thong by the door-post, she shrinks, her limbs grow thinner and longer, her head rounder, her nose flatter, her lips fuller, until a woman stands before Na-apia in the fullness of years, her limbs muscled but loose, her face lined. The eyes are much the same, reddish and rheumy and hard. She wears a gold cap set with stones on her head, a broad collar of lapis and amethyst across her empty breasts.

She holds open the door-flap and gestures for Na-apia to come in. Inside, the hut was much like her own, filled with baskets and mats and pots hanging from the rafters. But instead of a sleeping-mat, Grandmother has a little platform on legs for her blanket and headrest.

Na-apia squats down. "I need a skirt."

"You don't," says Grandmother as she grabs a piece of blue bark-cloth from a basket and ties it around her own waist.

Na-apia stares at her a moment, trying to judge her, then shrugs. "Pfffft. I don't care. Let the village think you cheap, to let your wife run around without a skirt."

Grandmother grunts but throws a red-and-green skirt in her direction.

Na-apia puts it on. "What should I do?"

"You make my meals. You keep this," she gestures at the inside of her home, "clean and tidy. What you do with yourself the rest of the day is not my concern." And with that she stalks out of the hut, leaving Na-apia to stare at the undulating door-flap as tears run down her cheeks. It feels as though her heart is seeping out with her tears, leaving her chest hollow and empty.

Grandmother has not come back by the time the sun had set, so Na-apia picks a mat from a pile and uses her arm as a headrest. She sleeps an empty, hungry sleep and wakes up feeling like a sucked egg.

Grandmother is lying on the platform, snoring, so Na-apia makes a meal by peeking into all the pots hanging from the rafters, rummaging through the baskets for tinder and rubbing-sticks and wandering around outside the hut until she finds the hearth. She makes rice-cakes and boils dried fish and sets them down inside. Grandmother is awake, but doesn't move.

Na-apia picks up some gourds and goes to the lake to get water and wash. She isn't the only one; men and women are chatting and greeting each other as tiny turtlets splash around in the shallows.

Na-apia marvels at the clearness of the lake. She wants to cry. The tears are there, somewhere, but her hollow heart is not full enough to let them out. She washes and fills her gourds and sits down at the edge of the lake, letting the cool water lap over her feet. What now? The house is tidy enough. She had put everything back where she had found it after making the meal. Does Grandmother have a garden? If so, it wasn't near the hut. Does she own a plot of land? Where was it? She had never liked working the land, though Manakhuria had shown her how. Did turtle-people hunt?

She turns to a man washing out his skirt. "What am I supposed to do?"

He chuckles. He has kind eyes. "Third Nephew and Day Cousin have been working Grandmother's earth since anyone can remember. Second Grandfather was too old for that. He mostly told stories to the turtlets, kept them out of everyone's way." Such odd names. Was everyone here named after their relationship to someone else?

"I'm no good at stories." She got along all right with children, but not for very long.

"What did you do in your village?"

The hunters are out but the old man tells her to stay in the village. There are things she needs to learn before she goes out.

"Rituals?" she asks.

He shrugs. And so she spends the day wandering the village, getting in everybody's way. She tries to explore the grass plains, but a lump of yellow fur the same colour as the grass stirs and a beak the size of her head opens in a yawn. It stretches limbs like a lion's, wings like a hawk's. There is a wide gash along its flank where something has clawed at it.

Na-apia takes a step back, bumping a passing woman's arm.

"It's only a Guardian." The woman clicks her tongue and keeps walking.

When Na-apia returns to the hut, Grandmother is still on her platform. Na-apia washes her empty bowl and replaces it with a mess of rice and beans. Her polite questions get nothing but grunts.

As she tries to sleep, the wind howls and cackles and hoots. Footsteps pitter-patter and the ground shakes, as though giant feline paws are tramping a path around the village.

This time, the tears come.

II. Other Wife

The tall grasses caress her shoulders, whispering in the wind. The high plateau of her world, a place of brush and lizards and jackals, here is filled with singing grass as far as the eye can see, while the far-away River, wider and sluggish and red with silt, feeds the Lake through a small rivulet filled with turtles and frogs and mudhoppers. It rains, here, though it is not raining now. Instead, a hot breeze rustles the grass, bringing tantalizing smells and odd dangers with it.

Na-apia feels a tap on her shoulder and turns around. A hunter called Little Uncle points to something beyond the cluster of boulders and brush where they have stopped to let Swift Cousin fill her gourds with milk. Na-apia carefully lifts her head over the grass and nods. The creature looks like one of the wild bulls from her world, but bigger, hunched like a boar and with a thick mane like a lion.

The hunters hide their packs and shells in a hollow by the rocks and start after it.

Na-apia savors the tingling in her limbs as she waits, the surge of elation as she strikes, the fear as the creature bellows and bucks, the long trudge as they follow its bleeding trail. Then Little Uncle comes up with the nets and poles and the skinning tools and they start butchering it, while Little Uncle circles around them waving the carved and painted Hunting Wand, chanting softly.

Na-apia can feel the hot breath of the Stalking Clan as they gather around their kill, eager to infest the meat and be swallowed with it, held back only by the magic oozing from the wand. Smaller prey are sown shut and taken back to the village whole, but the heavy cow-like creatures were too big, so they are hastily butchered and wrapped up in parcels of their own hide. Before her first hunt, Little Uncle made her squat down before him like a child and memorize a rhyme.

"Why do two-legs stay in town?
Because the Stalking Clan will hunt us down.
Why do hunters wrap their prey in hide?
Because the Stalking Clan will get inside.
Why do cooks use herbs dried or fresh?
Because the Stalking Clan will wear our flesh."

A low moan Na-apia thought came from the smoke-like figures of the Stalking Clan turns into a gasp. She looks up to see Swift Cousin clutching a long gash on her arm.

"The bleeding won't stop," she says. Na-apia thinks she can feel the Stalking Clan focus, like hounds pricking their ears.

Little Uncle hurries over, trailing magic from his wand. "Cover it up. Quickly."

The thick magic of the wand solidifies around them, keeping the Stalking Clan at bay. Na-apia looks at the wound.

The needles they use for the skins are too fat; she would only bleed more. Four Aunts, another of the hunters, tears a strip of bark-cloth from her skirt and wraps it around Swift Cousin's arm. They soon have the meat bundled into the skins and the skin bags stuffed into nets slung onto the carrying poles. They set off for the boulders almost at a run, but they soon slow down, for Swift Cousin is stumbling, Little Uncle's hand on her elbow. She collapses at the base of the boulders, hiccupping in pain.

"She should put on her shell." It is Four Aunts again, the largest one of them, as she shrugs into her own. Her face elongates and grows a snout, her neck thins and her limbs shorten and thicken to great flippers. The back right one has a jagged scar to match the one on Four Aunt's leg. The turtles are not very fast on dry land, but they can carry heavy loads and most of the dangerous beasts and spirits ignore them when they wear their shells.

"I don't have it with me." If Swift Cousin becomes a turtle, Swift Cousin would stop producing milk, so she leaves her shell at the village.

Little Uncle grunts. "You can have mine. It won't suit you well, but you should be turtle enough to be safe."

"No!" Swift Cousin clutches her arm, where the blood is already seeping through the bark-cloth. "I won't!"

"Silly girl! There are other women to nurse New Aunt. But none to be her mother!"

"Little Uncle," one of the men loading the meat onto Four Aunt's back points to Swift Cousin. "She won't survive the transformation. Not with another person's shell."

Na-apia follows his finger to Swift Cousin's arm, where a dense smoke is eating away at the bandages. Without thinking, she grabs the Hunting Wand from Little Uncle's hands and jabs it at the smoke. The Stalking Clan retreats with a hiss.

"Tss!" Little Uncle squats down and probes the wound. The edges are blackened and a tendril of smoke rises from it. "Only a little of the Stalking Clan got in. If we keep the wand tied to her arm, she might make it to the village. Grandmother will know what to do."

"But how?" asks the man from before.

Na-apia looks around, at the carrying nets and the heavy bags of skin and meat. "Four Aunts will have to change back," she hears herself say. "She is the strongest. I will help, because I have no shell. The rest of you, sew the skins together two by two and sling them over your necks, then put on your shells. Four Aunts and I will carry Swift Cousin in the nets, opened and strung between the carrying poles."

Four Aunts bobs her head, first right, then left, and turns back. She grasps one end of the carrying poles, Na-apia the other. Four Aunts is burlier, but they are about the same height.

Na-apia's legs are on fire and her chest feels as though she is being squeezed between the worlds again by the time they finally stumble past one of the village guardians, a mottled, pantherlike creature the size of a hut, with a long, snakelike neck that bends down to nuzzle Little Uncle as he passes. It bares its teeth and hisses when it catches sight of Swift Cousin, but Little Uncle barks a command and it shrinks into his open palm, nothing more than a carved jasper figure.

Na-apia stares but there isn't time to wonder, there isn't time to think. The Fence around the village tugs at Swift Cousin, holding her back, and Na-apia and Four Aunts stumble and pull until Little Uncle grabs the Hunting Wand from the wound and strikes the nearest fencepost with it.

The hold on Swift Cousin is gone in a blink and they all tumble inside. There is a sense of speed and dark smoke roiling towards the gap, but Little Uncle speaks another word and the Guardian springs from his hand, snapping up the Stalking Clan as it lands and gobbling it down.

Na-apia is on her knees, her eyes streaming as she tries to catch her breath.

"Other Wife, go get Grandmother!"

It takes her a moment, as it always does, to remember her new name. No-one ever goes into Grandmother's hut. But the Other Wife can.

She staggers to her feet and stumbles to the hut, pushing the curtain before her and leaning on the door post.

"Grandmother, come quick! Swift Cousin is hurt!"

Grandmother doesn't turn around. "So sew her up."

"The Stalking Clan got inside."

At this, Grandmother does turn around. The loose skin around her eyes tightens, but she turns back to face the wall. "Pffffft. Then you are all doomed."

Na-apia closes her eyes. They don't have time for this. "Not much. Please, Little Uncle said you would know what to do."

Silence stretches out, taut as a net full of fish. Na-apia opens her mouth to plead again when Grandmother mumbles, "Is the flesh black?"

"No. Just the lip of the wound. Grandmother, she has a baby."

"Well, and what did she go do that for? Children are ungrateful, needy things. Want, want, want, all their lives, and you give, give, give, and for what?"

Na-apia crawls to Grandmother's baskets and grabs the nearest one, pawing through it in the hopes of finding something, anything to help. Bark-cloth in patterns of red and blue, a small jar with malachite beads. She grabs the next one.

"What are you doing?"

"I am not sitting around while Swift Cousin is dying, or being taken over by the Stalking Clan, or whatever is happening to her." She finds a basket full of odd and wondrous things, the magic clinging to them like resin. She gathers it up and struggles to her feet.

"Stop."

Na-apia stops, then decides that she is not a going to let a selfish old woman kill Swift Cousin. She takes another step.

She hears a sigh. "The red basket with the blue ties. You need a medicine and you need spells. How's your memory, girl?"

The Turtle on the Lily-pad

When Na-apia reaches Swift Cousin, her breathing is shallow and irregular. The Hunting Wand is still on the wound, but the edges have started to crinkle and flake. The Stalking Clan is spreading its poison through her body, trying to take her over. Next to her, her husband Second Nephew holds a squirming, crying baby, trying to keep her on his lap as he squeezes his wife's hand.

Na-apia falls on her knees. She grabs jars with herbs and pastes from the basket and starts mixing them in a cup. She doesn't know what they are. Grandmother only said "the jar with the green lip", "the bird-shaped jar", "the red herb with the jagged leaves, no, the other one, you club-headed child." Her hands are trembling and she smears them on the lip of the cup. By the time she is finished, two of the jars are empty.

She scoops the mixture up with a finger and carefully dabs some of it on Swift Cousin's lips. She opens them slightly and Na-apia shoves the goo into her mouth and tries to remember the words Grandmother recited to her ("Tell me, child, are you strong enough to let it go?"):

"Stalking Clan, Stalking Clan, hear me say
You will not have my child today."

She feels something bubble inside her, deep in her belly. Her heart pounding, she goes on.

"Stalking Clan, Stalking Clan, listen well,
I will not bid my child farewell."

The bubbling sensation rises to her stomach.

"Stalking Clan, Stalking Clan, leave her be.
You will not take my child from me."

The magic rises into her throat like boiling, honey-sweet bile. It hurts. But as it starts to seep from her throat to her head, to her heart, to her shoulders, she feels its strength. The pounding in her head ceases, the soreness of her shoulders eases, she feels tall, she feels strong, she feels *alive*.

It fills her mouth with its viscous sweetness and for just a moment, she thinks: If I keep my mouth shut, if I don't utter the words, it will all be mine.

But Swift Cousin's baby mewls and twists in her father's arms, her face contorted in helpless confusion, still too young for tears, and Na-apia opens her mouth.

The magic spews out, gushing like a broken retainer wall. It spreads out from her mouth, seeking, searching, a maggot out of the ground. She chokes on it. She forces her mouth around its pulsating bulk, pushes her tongue through the thickness, and screams:

"Stalking Clan, Stalking Clan, hear my song.
You will leave my child and be gone!"

The magic twists and wriggles in her mouth, taking shape, two eyeless larvae that latch their round mouth-holes onto Swift Cousin's wound and start sucking, their almost-bodies rippling with the motion, the inky tendrils of the Stalking Clan filling their bodies with smoke. Na-apia can taste the foulness in her mouth; she gags and coughs as the two maggot-creatures keep sucking and pumping. Na-apia struggles to see through the tears streaming out of her eyes as she chokes the last of the magic out.

When the maggot-things are as black as a cloudy night, black as the silt brought by the River inundation, Na-apia speaks one last word.

"Go."

And the larva-creatures burst like ashes in a gust of wind, grey smoke riding the breeze. Na-apia puts her forehead down on the ground. It is dry, still warm from the day. Perfect. She closes her eyes and falls into the darkness.

"So you're not completely useless," Grandmother remarks.

Na-apia feels anger bubble in her chest. Who has been

keeping her fed? Who has swept and cleaned while Grandmother lay in bed all day? "Some of your pastes and herbs are empty."

Grandmother shrugs. "So fill them."

"I don't know what they are!" Na-apia yells at her. She takes a breath. There are more important things, now. "One of the fence-posts was damaged. And the Hunting Wand. And Little Uncle says the long-necked Guardian won't last much more than a month."

It wasn't just the Stalking Clan. They were mostly out on the plains. But you could see the others near the village sometimes, the swift-footed plants with roots that poked through flesh, the Long Moans and the Severing Mouths.

"Pfffffft. Then Little Uncle shouldn't have destroyed it. What, does he think I use the things as pestles?" Grandmother picks up the bowl and scoops some meat into her mouth.

"He had to, to bring Swift Cousin to safety."

"And he endangered the whole village for that. Let *him* repair it."

"But he doesn't know how!"

"Then maybe he should have learned when he had the chance, instead of when it is convenient for him. It is not convenient for me now. Did I birth him, to pick up after his mistakes?" And with that she pops a rice cake into her mouth and goes back to her bed.

Na-apia breathes through her nose. Then she stomps over to Grandmother and pulls the bowl from her hand. "I am hungry," she tells her. "Getting fat is for mothers with children and old grandfathers who tell stories and flint-knappers who make tools. Not for a lazy old woman who can't be bothered to keep her village safe!"

Grandmother sits up. "How many years? How long have they all been whining and pawing at me? Grandmother, my baby has colic. Grandmother, my knees hurt. Grandmother, there's a Drilling Mother growing out of my wrist. Phah!" She makes to grab the bowl but Na-apia dances back. "Ungrateful little bastards. Don't you ever have children." And with that she turns her back on Na-apia.

Na-apia feels bile gather in her throat. Evil, selfish, lazy, cruel…You don't deserve to eat my gruel…Hard-hearted, greedy, laggard, petty…My rice cakes won't be in your belly…

The lump rises. Grandmother should have left her in the other world. She would have seen her little sister married, would have laughed with Manakhuria about her first-bride foibles, would maybe have found somebody she likes as a Second Spouse. She would have added beads to her necklaces and, with them, memories. She would not be stuck here where no-one uses her actual name, where the children laugh because she doesn't have a shell, where demon creatures plague the night and lay siege to the day.

She opens her mouth only to realize that it wasn't phlegm, but magic that gathered in her throat and is now escaping in sharp, needle-like threads that lacerate the inside of her mouth. She snaps it shut, but not before one of the threads strikes Grandmother.

The old woman yelps and turns around, wide-eyed. With a few muttered words she snaps off the other strings. "Try to curse me, would you, child?"

Na-apia gags against her closed lips, trying to keep the magic from escaping. She claps her hands to her mouth, dropping the bowl. It shatters.

Her heart is racing but the magic subsides, drawing back from her mouth and slowly sliding down her throat, losing its sharp edges and settling like an oily puddle in her stomach.

She runs out, all the way to the lake, where she weeps and weeps as she tries to wash the blood from the open wounds in her cheeks and lips. Stupid old lady. Stupid magic.

She watches the turtlets paddling around, the gems on their shells twinkling in the fading sunlight, until a mother calls them in. Fishermen emerge from the Lake with their prey in their mouths, their strong flippers pushing the sand and pebbles behind them as they head toward the village. She looks at the depths of the Lake, remembering the unending darkness, the weight of the water all around her. She is stuck here, and it is not her fault. And the children and fishermen and the old man who comes down to wash out a basket are in danger, and that is a little bit her fault.

So, she gets up and returns to the hut. Once more she ransacks the pile of baskets with Grandmother's magica. The old lady sits up, but she merely glares at Na-apia, her mouth a thin line. This time, Na-apia looks for anything with the symbols she has seen on the warding poles.

She finds some carvings of turtles, and a wand with some lines like the pattern on the Hunting Wand. She grabs it all and goes looking for Little Uncle.

He is outside his hut, having food with his husband, a shy man about Little Uncle's age. Na-apia shows them her treasures. "That's a Gathering Wand," he touches the short stick with the lines. "Mostly against Drilling Mother and her children, and the Long Moans. But maybe some of these…" He looks up at the shy man, who ducks his head.

"Weaver Father would know."

"Pffffft. Then he shouldn't have gotten himself eaten by a crocodile. Come on."

They take the turtle statues to the damaged fencepost. With the help of Little Uncle's husband, they right the pole and examine the carvings. One of them is damaged, chipped. Someone has tried to re-carve it and fill in the paint. Little Uncle shrugs, embarrassed. "It was worth a try. I can use the wand, and I can command the guardians, but that's it."

Na-apia fingers the broken turtle. It is blue, its flippers pointing upwards, rings of concentric red circles, like an eye in an eye in an eye, dotting its shell. She feels the faint pulse of magic, slick and fatty against her fingers. She picks up two of the blue turtle carvings. On one, the shell-markings are square, like the golden ornaments the villagers wear on their chests. The magic feels thinner, like plant oil. The other has the concentric circles, and the magic feels greasy beneath her fingers.

None of them know if it will help, but they bind the turtle charm to the fencepost. Na-apia imagines she can feel the magic reach out to the other posts, weaving a mat of protection around the village, but she can't be sure.

That night, she sleeps with Little Uncle's family, and plans.

III. Guarding Wife

Na-apia still hunts, sometimes, when her legs ache to run and her breast to breathe in the grasslands air and her throat hurts from the burning of magic. But mostly she spends her days in a spot just outside the Fence, surrounded by Grandmother's magica, tasting their magic and trying to figure out how it all works. She finds out how to replicate two of the thick, oily pastes. She makes out what most of the amulets and wands do, though her attempts at making them fail. She manages a small amulet against mosquito bites, but she can't find the right rhymes for the more powerful wands.

She starts helping people, hesitantly, her heart beating like drums whenever she tries something new. The villagers are patient with her, carefully hopeful. The first time a spell of hers works, she clutches her necklaces and almost cries. Swift Cousin's recovery, this child's suckerfish bite—in her village she would have taken a special bead for that tenday, one of the bright glazed ones the traders bring from Neqaia, to commemorate the occasion. But her necklaces remain static. There is no leftover clay here to make tenday beads; Potter Mother makes long journeys to gather it from the edges of the River.

A few days later, Shy Husband comes by the hut and puts two carnelian beads into her hand.

She still can't measure the time on her necklaces, but now she has a new one with beads of carnelian and jasper and obsidian and amethyst. She cooks for Grandmother once a day;

she herself eats elsewhere, often with Shy Husband and Little Uncle, sometimes with Swift Cousin, New Aunt's cheek soft on her shoulder, her limbs dangling.

She is trying to set a bone. Every hunter learns how to set limbs, but the fracture isn't right, and Green Cousin howls in pain whenever he puts on his shell, though a well-set bone would heal with the transformation. She has found several pastes that join things together, but she isn't sure of the combination. The blue one and the one from the foot-shaped jar seem almost right, but the magic boiling up from her belly feels like spilt, thin gruel, spreading formless in her mouth. She tries to push it into shape, opens her mouth—

And jumps when a bony hand lands on her shoulder. "You'll only make it worse, like that."

With a muttered rhyme, Grandmother pulls the magic from her mouth like a rope, twisting it and kneading it until it is like slick clay, settling it around Green Cousin's legs and hardening it until it pushes his bones together with a crunch. Green Cousin howls, but Grandmother simply mixes some paste from a third bowl, one Na-apia never even considered, and lathers it onto his leg.

She turns back towards her hut, motioning Na-apia to follow. "They will all be at my door now, begging."

At the hut, she sits Na-apia down, takes a pot with a zigzag painted around its rim, and bangs it down between them. "This is softwort and tilapia scales and the red earth you find underneath the rocks that look like a wolf. Mix it in equal parts, and a tenth of rainwater. Against the Severing Mouths. You slather it on a wolf claw painted with a blue sun. The rhyme is this…"

Sometimes Grandmother teaches her all day, sunrise to sunset. Sometimes she gives her one lesson, then turns away, bored.

Some days Grandmother spends in bed. Na-apia learns how to make small amulets and mix the pastes, which herbs to add at the beginning or the very end, how to shape words to call the magic.

Once, when Na-apia is trying to carve a frog from a bone, Grandmother says, "You can bring your blanket to the bed if you want. Second Grandfather liked to sleep near the wall."

Another day, when Na-apia is throwing up the dregs of a spell gone sour, Grandmother remarks, "They call you Guarding Wife, now."

"It's still not my name," Na-apia points out, gasping.

"Pfffft. Names change. Are you the same person who came out of your mother's cervix? Now tell me why I am adding lilies."

One day, Grandmother comes upon Na-apia trying to make beads from clay she has begged off of Potter Mother in exchange for a mosquito amulet. Na-apia doesn't know if it is the New Year—in this world, the River's inundation doesn't reach the village. But she is tired of barely knowing how much time had passed. There are festivals here, of course—the Time of Rains, the Hatching—but they mean little to her. Between them, the days blur into each other.

Grandmother's hand on her shoulder is dry as reeds. "You want jewelry, you have only to say. I have enough." This is true. Three whole baskets full. Na-apia still doesn't know where the stones come from. All Grandmother will say is, "Shells stretch and grow."

"This is for my year-necklace. Every tenday a bead."

"Pffffft. Days are not worth counting." She squats next to Na-apia and fingers her necklaces. "What are these?" She rolls a bright blue bead in the shape of a hut between her hands.

"Wedding bead." Na-apia fingers a few more, painted, glazed, rolled-up bark-cloth. "My cousin's wedding. My first hunt. The first time I wore a skirt."

"And these?" she taps little turtles painted red and yellow.

Na-apia shifts uncomfortably. "Sun Day."

Grandmother takes her hand, clasping it in her wrinkled ones, an uncommonly tender gesture. "You were married? What happened?"

"Nothing. My First Marriage ended after five years, as it should. I was still looking for my Second Spouse."

Grandmother grunts. She watches as Na-apia forms her beads. "Second Grandfather—I didn't love him. But he was kind."

Na-apia starts burying the beads in the smoldering coals of the cooking fire. "Nobody likes being alone."

The sun grows heavy and golden as they watch the fire's embers. It is a special silence they have found, together.

Grandmother stirs. "You would have had a special bead for your sister's wedding?"

Na-apia nods. She had helped Maia make them, carefully painting on the round symbols for the huts, in the green of beginnings.

Grandmother gets up. "Well, come on. The Lake's not getting any warmer."

The slick mud feels good between Na-apia's toes. There is just enough water left to seep into the footprints she leaves behind. Perspiration clings to her skin as she picks her way through the swamp, clutching the scale from Grandmother's shell to her chest. She is still not quite sure why she is here, but it is real. The earthy smell of the swamp rises up in her nostrils, the papyrus rustles drily. The papyrus parts, and there is her own village on the plateau. There are no turtle flopping about, the shields next to the door don't sparkle, but the voices are warmer, the sound of pestle and grindstone sweeter. No Fence, no lurking Stalking Clan, no Drilling Mothers in the grass.

Na-apia runs. She runs until she reaches Manakhuria's hut, bursting through the door hanging, launching herself at the first figure she sees—Manakhuria himself, big and hearty and smelling of goose fat—and she is laughing, and she is crying, and he is calling for Maia and Maia is hugging her and there are her parents and everyone, everyone who matters is there.

They don't believe a word of what she tells them, not about the grasslands nor the hunch-shouldered bulls nor the antelopes with the strange horns nor the rabbit with the long feet. Not about the Fence nor the Guardians nor the Blood-Sniffers nor the Long Moans. Not about the turtle shells nor the magic.

But it doesn't matter. She hunts with Maia. She helps her father pound bark for weaving, and her mother harvest rice from the fields. And she laughs and laughs and laughs, one laugh for every tear she has shed in Turtle Village.

"Come on, big sister," Maia throws a fish-spear at Na-apia with a wicked smile. "Time to go hunting."

The swamp is almost desiccated, nothing but a few scattered ponds shared by desperate fish and hopeless shrimp. The Lake has shrunk, leaving tree roots naked and exposed, slimy under their feet.

"What are we hunting?" Na-apia calls. She stares at the Lake and wonders if Grandmother will come to take her back today. She didn't mention for how long Na-apia could stay, only thrusting her turtle-scale into Na-apia's hands and saying, "Call for me if you want to come back sooner."

How soon was sooner? Sooner than what? Na-apia doesn't miss Turtle Village, exactly. But sometimes she thinks of New

Aunt's tiny flippers in her hand, or Shy Husband's surprisingly loud laugh, and something tightens in her heart.

"What do you think we're hunting?" Maia tosses her head. "Tomorrow is Sun Day."

She has no concept of time anymore. Sun Day! Na-apia shivers, thinking of the last time they hunted a turtle. Grandmother probably won't come back for her today.

Please the River, let Grandmother stay home today.

The waters of the lake are murky; silt swirls around their ankles at every step. Some of the other hunters see a snap turtle and Na-apia relaxes. Snappers have beaks, not the almost prehensile trunk of Grandmother's family.

The snapper dives and disappears. Na-apia helps them look, the lily roots and lake grass tickling her fingers. Then someone points and exclaims: "That's a big one!"

Na-apia's heart leaps to her throat, but though it was big, big as a winnowing basket, it was not Grandmother. You could just about fit one goat on it, two if they didn't fight.

Na-apia stands back as the others capture it, their forked fish-spears pinning its neck against one of the big tree roots. Maia dances back to her and jabs an elbow in her ribs. "Friend of yours?"

Na-apia smiles and sticks out her tongue. She has never heard of the others crossing over to this world.

But as they carry it back to the village, the turtle does not retreat into its shell. Instead it snakes its head out and looks Na-apia straight in the eye. Then it bobs its head, first right, then left. Na-apia's eyes stray to the scar on its back flipper.

She claps her hand to her mouth in horror. "Four Aunts?"

No amount of pleading sways the others. Her mother shakes her head and leaves; her father brushes her cheek and says, "You are home, now."

She is desperately trying to lift Four Aunts out of the deep, black basin of fired clay at the center of the Sun Hut, straining her back as Four Aunts' fins scrabble to find purchase on the steep, slippery sides of the tub. When Manakhuria finds her, she is pleading with Four Aunts to take off her shell, but Four Aunts simply stares at her.

"Manakhuria! Come help me!"

But Manakhuria, her own Manakhuria, who taught her the soft spots of a man and how to make rice cakes without burning them, simply stands at the edge of the Sun Hut and crosses his arms. The Sun Hut has no walls. The oppressive sunshine of the dry season creeps in to the edges of the basin, haloing Manakhuria in light.

"Na-apia," he says softly and for a moment she luxuriates in the sound of her own name. "Turtle is swallowing up the River. If there is no ceremony to-morrow, how will the Sun return once Baboon has placated her? Her ship will not be able to pass. We will have no water and we will die."

"Help me get Four Aunts out and I'll find a snapper."

"Maia went back to the Lake. For you. There are no more turtles."

"Manakhuria, please. She helped me carry Swift Cousin to safety. We've hunted together. Her son carried me on his shell. She's family."

Manakhuria hangs his head. "Then you cannot be mine."

The next thing she knows, five other men grab her—men she has hunted and cooked with, men she has laughed with, men she has cried with—and she is carried to her parents' hut like a naked child, kicking and screaming her tantrums to the sky.

They tie the mats down tightly and take away her knife, leaving her standing in the middle of her parents' hut, her hands balled to fists and rage in her belly.

She waits until night-time, letting the rage roil and grow, and then she speaks:

The Turtle on the Lily-pad

"Mats of my home, loose your ties—I need to plant my feet and rise.
Mats of my home, your knots unbind—I need to leave you all behind.
Mats of my home, I set you free—I need to save my family."

The magic blows out between her teeth like a breeze, tiny, nimble fingers tugging at the ties binding the mats to the poles, the poles to each other. She walks to the edge of the hut and sidesteps out as it collapses behind her—her mother's patterned pots, the baskets in which she had kept her stones and the other flotsam of childhood, her father's loom—all of it is buried beneath the tangle of poles and reed mats.

She runs, leaving noise and confusion behind her, slipping in the slick mud of the swamp, stumbling over the hard roots of the trees and throwing herself on her knees at the edge of the Lake, the scale grasped between her hands.

"Grandmother," she whispers, but the magic in the scale merely twitches, like a dreaming kitten.

No. What had Grandmother said? That names change. And in that place, they do. Four Aunts was born Sweet Niece. Shy Husband was once Eighth Grandson. Other Wife is now Guarding Wife. She is Grandmother because she is the only Grandmother in a village where everybody else has a two-part name, but the man Maia killed was Second Grandfather, and if there was a Second Grandfather then there was a First Grandfather before him, and he would have been married to First Grandmother, and before she could become First Grandmother then she must have been—

"First Mother," Na-apia whispers, and the magic trickles out and disappears into the Lake.

She rises from the water like an enraged hippopotamus, waterfalls streaming from her shell, bending the persea sapling on her back as she heaves herself on shore. "Bored already?"

"They have Four Aunts," Na-apia tells her. "She will be cut

and eaten to prepare the return of the River, to bring back the Sun from the south."

Grandmother clicks her tongue. "What idiocy is this?"

"The Sun is caught in the South. They say a giant turtle is drinking up all the waters of the River, here on earth and up there in the sky. If a turtle is killed on Sun Day with the proper words, Turtle will release the waters and the Sun will return."

"Idiocy," Grandmother repeats.

But Na-apia looks up at her. "I know an old turtle who kept all the magic to herself. Maybe this one is your brother."

Grandmother laughs. "So, what, you forget everything I taught you?"

Na-apia shakes her head. "There are too many. I had to make a new spell to get away." She thinks with a pinch in her heart of the jumble of poles that was once her home.

"Pffffft." Then Grandmother sighs. "You're still mine. And Four Aunts is mine. And unless they want to supply me with an endless string of wives and nephews and cousins, we shall put a stop to this."

The village is teeming like a kicked anthill. Grandmother ignores them, ignores the stares of the lost-looking children hovering like dragonflies at the edge of the chaos, the men emerging sleep-numbed from their huts, the women shushing babies.

She heads straight to the Sun Hut, as though she has always known where it is, her long flippers beating against the hard, stamped earth in the village, spilling mortars and hearthstones on either side.

Three hunters stand in her way, spears raised, but Na-apia grabs two spears from the nearest hut and holds them to their chest. Grandmother pushes on, knocking them over.

Grandmother is too large to fit between the poles holding up the roof. There is a commotion; men and women come running with spears and harpoons in their hands. Grandmother shakes her head.

"Let me get comfortable," she says. Four Aunts may not be able to take off her shell in this world, but Grandmother can. As she hands her shell to Na-apia, the persea sapling swaying, she sees a glint of gold underneath the moss. The villagers gasp, step back. A moment, and Grandmother stands old and naked in front of them, gold on her limbs and around her throat and on her shaved head.

She steps to the edge of the basin and peers in.

"You always did attract trouble," she tells Four Aunts.

One of the huntsmen steps towards Grandmother, but it is one thing to grab Na-apia, whom he has known since she could first hold a spear, and another to grab a fragile-looking, naked old lady.

Na-apia puts down Grandmother's shell and takes hold of Four Aunts. Grandmother grasps her other side and they heave.

"What do you think you are doing?" The voice comes from behind them. Na-apia recognizes it. It belongs to the chief.

Grandmother snorts. "What does it look like I am doing? I am taking my daughter's son's daughter's daughter out of this prison you are keeping her in."

"We cannot let you."

Na-apia turns around and by the light of flickering lamps, she sees that they have surrounded the Sun Hut. They are all armed, even the weavers, even the flint-knappers, even the potters, with cudgels, with spears, with the poles from her mother's house. Even Maia.

Grandmother turns to face them, her eyes narrowing. Na-apia feels the magic gathering in Grandmother's belly and it is an ugly, roiling thing of black coils and fangs and anger. And Na-apia looks into the faces of those she grew up with, her very own First Mothers and Blue Cousins and Little Uncles, her parents, and Manakhuria, and Maia, little Maia, standing tall and defiant, her spear held straight.

And she finds herself saying, "The Guardians bleed."

Grandmother frowns and snaps, "Of course they bleed. Once you say the words, they are alive."

"Then you can sacrifice them?"

The magic within Grandmother stills, wary, curious. "What are you saying?"

"I am saying," Na-apia turns to the others, "that maybe you don't need Four Aunts. Maybe we can make you a Guardian, and you can sacrifice it instead."

Unexpectedly, Grandmother laughs. The laughter bursts out of her like an overripe fig, and it doesn't stop. She laughs and laughs and laughs until she is kneeling on the floor, wheezing. "You always surprise me, girl."

And she unclasps a golden collar and levers out a stone, a pinkish amethyst the size of New Aunt's closed fist. "Bring me some carving tools."

No-one moves. They don't understand. Even though Na-apia has told them story after story of Turtle Village; none of them had been listening.

"Never mind." Grandmother levers out another amethyst and uses it to shape the first one, sharp blades of magic whistling out from her pursed lips.

While the air stills, then bursts with birdsong, while the pink tinge of dawn laps the mats and poles, Grandmother carves. While Four Aunts knocks impatiently against the basin, while the hunters shift and sit on their haunches, while babies cry and children tumble and cuddle up to their parents, Grandmother carves. While the chief and Manakhuria and the other First Spouses watch her with suspicion in their eyes, Grandmother carves.

The light has turned the soft gold of true morning when she hands them a little figure of a turtle, snout and flippers and all. "Listen well; I'm only saying this once. When you are ready, place it in the basin and say these words:

The Turtle on the Lily-pad

"Spirit of the village, come and wake today,
Spirit of the village, come out of your shell today,
Spirit of the village, come and swim today,
Spirit of the village, come and die today."
Let it swim at least once around before you butcher it, or it will not understand being a turtle. And now, I am taking my daughter's son's daughter's daughter, and I am taking my Guarding Wife, and if you kill another one of mine again there will be a reckoning."

The villagers are unsure of what has happened. They shift, they look to the elders, but the elders have no answers. Finally, they shuffle aside to let her leave.

Grandmother looks sideways at Na-apia. "I kept First Grandfather's shell, you know."

Na-apia gasps at the enormity of what she is saying. She looks around at this village, so achingly hers. Her own village where no-one believed her, where no-one stepped up to help her friend.

She looks Maia in the eyes, drinks in the sight of her.

"Yes," says Guarding Wife.

Maia wades through the shallow lake until she sees it, tiny and pink against the emerald tones of the lily-pad. She reaches out and takes the turtle. Nearby, one of the many floating islands shifts, and another turtle meets her eyes before diving down, deep into the lake. Around its neck, rows of beads glint wetly in all the colors of missing years.

These Moonlit Tears
Toni Mobley

Toni Mobley
These Moonlit Tears

'When the world says, "Give up."
Hope whispers, "Try it one more time."'
– Author Unknown

Left to crumble beneath the sands of time, broken and forgotten, my kind blinked out of existence. They used to visit me, long ago, before I was cursed to this existence of nothingness. A small price to pay for love, or so I thought. I was the last of my kind, and the person responsible for my imprisonment was but a pile of bones beneath a crypt. I wondered if he thought of me as he lay dying, surrounded by his loved ones.

Some would not have called it a curse, after all, my wish was granted. In a way. I was finally a part of their world. I could see them dancing and walking and jumping. I could see them strolling through the streets with the sun on their backs, out of the water, content in the warm sand beneath their feet.

I have stood for centuries, the sun hot on my skin, the salty air stinging in my eyes, on display for all the world to see. But they don't see me, they never do. Because these tears I shed stream over flesh encased in stone, the rock on the ocean that I sit in is the only contact with the outside world I receive. Like a flower in a vase, I was beautiful to look at, but nothing else.

Like the fish that swam at my feet, I can hear the humans, see them, but I cannot speak to them, laugh with them, imagine the lives that they lead. It had been so long since I knew what it was like to feel, to taste, to touch. What I would give to experience that world again, to feel the warmth, to taste the salty sea, to live.

Maybe tomorrow, or the next, or the day after that. I still held hope because that's all I could do.

It was her again, the lady with the hair that shimmered like the inky depths of a raging sea, forever held back by a ribbon of blood. Like clockwork, she arrived in the dead of the night, her appearance heralded by the clacking of heels on the sidewalk. I looked forward to her arrival. Like the rising and lowering of the tides, it was soothing.

She paused by the railing, distracted by the spray that coated the rocks. She took solace in its mechanism, much like I did. Fiddling with the strap on her purse, she produced a single rose from within, bringing it to her lips.

I never understood why she did this, only that the ritual seemed to put her at ease. Content that we were alone, her piercing turquoise eyes coated in thick, black ashes rose to meet mine. Her face was passive, the same it always was when she viewed me. At least, at first.

Glancing nervously at the darkness that surrounded us, she skirted around the railing, making her way down to the rocks at the shoreline. If I had a heartbeat, this would be where it would resonate within my chest like the pounding of a war drum. Many tourists had taken this route before, and this mystery woman had done the same, but these rocks were treacherous. I'd seen the fury of nature, felt it, lived through it. One wrong placement of her foot and she would plunge into the icy waters. I always prayed it would never happen.

"For you," she whispered, voice thick with the tears she always held back.

I don't know why she was on the edge of despair, what life she must have lived, and it pained me to see her bring herself to the brink every night.

She brought the rose to her lips once more, standing on the tips of her toes to place it in my lap.

"Good night."

Good night, I screamed into the abyss.

She never heard me, no matter how loud I shouted. Stone was stone, after all. It never stopped me from trying to say it back. For years she was the light in my otherwise dark existence, neither the sun nor the moon nor the stars could shine as brightly as she did for me.

Careful to avoid the thick seaweed that swayed in the surf, she picked her way back up the shoreline, disappearing into the night. The petals glimmered in the moonlight, already coated in the sea. By the morning, it would be gone, stolen by the sea. I enjoyed it while I could.

Daylight arrived, the sun bright and unyielding in the sky above. Like always, the rose was long gone, a meal for a passing fish or duck in the surf. The crowds appeared, carrying umbrellas, and dressed snuggly in jackets with scarves and hats. Children screamed in delight, puffs of smoke curling out from their mouths like little dragons. I never noticed the passing of the seasons, the coming of storms. There was no point, they never bothered me.

Today was different, though. A darkness sat on the horizon, brooding and merciless. Wind snapped the branches of nearby trees, and trash littered the waves that crashed on the shore. A storm was approaching, nature was angry. The crowds were scattering, aware of the storm that rolled closer and closer, announced by a bone-biting blanket of rain in its stead.

It happened more often nowadays; the planet was infected, raging against a plague it could not control. Humanity. Once upon a time, I would have agreed with her. But as the day crawled to a close, and the moon chased the sun from the sky, and the familiar sound of heels clacking against stone met my ears, I couldn't help but think that not all of humanity was a blight in this world. At least, not her. My mystery visitor.

Right on time.

She leaned against the railing, her eyes crinkling against the cold and stinging breeze. The waves were vicious; the swell battered the rocks as thunder boomed high above. They anchored no boats in the waters, no people loitered on the streets, everyone had taken shelter. Everyone but her.

A frightening wind had picked up, howling across the bay with an intensity I hadn't seen for a very long time. My kind had names for these gales that brought with them the rage of a slighted god, but I had forgotten all of them. The names of the storms, my people, and the gods. Nameless, faceless entities whose presence was simply felt, never seen.

The woman leaned over the railing, but her eyes were not on the choppy waters. They rose to the icy wind, to the darkened sky. It was an endless abyss, swallowing the moon and casting a hungering shadow upon the world. The sea lashed out, soaking her arms as she recoiled to cradle it to her chest like it had scalded her.

Run. I wanted to scream.

She didn't listen because she didn't hear. Pulling away from the railing, she followed the promenade to the rocks, carefully picking her way across them. The wind lashed out, unravelling the crimson ribbon that held back her inky locks away into the darkness.

Run. I tried to scream.

She paid no heed, shrugging off every warning she was being given. Her hand fumbled with the clasp on her purse, her shaking hand grasping the stem of a fresh rose. It was a stark contrast to the darkness that surrounded us, like a beacon in an otherwise grim world.

Her hair whipped around her face as she took a step forward, and her foot plunged into the water. She flinched, nearly slipping on the rocks as she fought to keep her balance. When she tucked her hair behind her ears, it was to see that the storm had taken something else of hers. Her crimson coated toenails were as vibrant as the rose petals, bare to the elements.

For a moment, I hoped she would turn around, realizing her efforts were for nothing. I was a statue; I was nothing. She would not be deterred though; stubbornness was alive in those bright eyes. *Stupid human.*

Warning her was pointless, and yet I still tried. I had no power, no voice; resigned to be a mere set piece in a world that grew around me. Of all the humans I had met over the years, however, she was the only one who showed any emotion, any sign that I was more than a stone effigy.

The wind had picked up in record time, whipping the canopies of the trees into a frenzy. The water level seemed to rise instantly, and the rocks she once relied on now submerged. There was no way to reach me without succumbing to wet feet, and she knew it.

Exhaling, she bent over to wrench her other shoe from her foot, hurtling it into the bay. It sank to the depths, hopefully one day reuniting with its partner. Thunder rolled across the bay as lightning flashed overhead, exposing the promenade in a hot flash.

She yelped, losing her balance as her bare feet fought for traction on the slippery rocks. Everything within me lashed out, my voice screaming through my head as something shattered within me.

"RUN!"

Her head whipped up, baby blue eyes wide as can be, her mouth agape, as she stared at me with a mix of horror and fascination. She had heard me. For the first time since I had lost my flesh, they had heard my voice. It was too late though, as a wave rolled into the shore, coating the rocks she stood on in a thick sheen.

She watched in a daze, as if the world churned in slow motion, in the single beat of a heart. The water clutched at her, digging its talons in deep, wrenching her into the murky depths. She cried out as her head disappeared, hair streaming behind her like seaweed.

I raged against my bonds, against the ineptitude of my being. Countless had died over the centuries, and I felt nothing, because I could do nothing. I wouldn't let her die though, cursed to the abyss, alone and frightened.

My chest rose and fell, stone cracking as it fell into the raging sea. I had a heart, and a beat, and blood coursing through my veins once more. Warmth spread throughout me as I screamed over and over, parts of me broke apart, like the ice that coalesced across the shore in winter. Those fractals of shattered ice drifted out into the bay, sinking beneath the waves. I, too, found myself floating endlessly in the gloom.

The water rushed to greet me as I screeched into the void, searching for her. Time was running out. The frailty of humanity was not lost on me, and if I didn't find her soon, she would drift eternally. Fish shimmered into view, disappearing as soon as I caught sight of them. I knew these currents, these waters, every nook and cranny of the bay, and yet I knew finding her would be hopeless.

That's when I saw it, the glint of crimson gently descending to the seafloor. The water yielded to me, almost welcoming. The crimson came closer and closer, and I reached my hand out, my fingers brushing through it. It was her ribbon, floating like a feather in the depths.

"No!" I shrieked, searching the gloom.

There was no giving up. I would find her and I would save her. No one was there for me, to save me, and I wouldn't let her suffer the same way. I had to find her. The world rushed by, silent as the grave. The further I went from the shore, the darker my world became.

Until somewhere nearby, I felt something. A strange pulsating, rhythmic sensation rippled through the waters. It wasn't the waves, or the fish, or the wind, it belonged to something larger, something different. Something that shouldn't be here. Piercing the darkness like a bullet carving through flesh, I saw the glint of pale deep below. Diving into the depths, my body lurched as I realized what it was. I had found her. There was no time left as I plucked her from the angry sea, following the current to the surface.

We broke the surface not a minute later, emerging atop a flat rock poking out of the sea.

"Stupid human," I breathed, my chest heaving as the world raged around us.

I cradled her in my arms; the waters closing in around us. I could feel her flesh against my own, the slickness of her ebony hair splayed against my exposed chest, her pantyhose legs against my shimmering scales.

Something was wrong. She was cold, clammy, her lips a pale blue instead of a rosy red. My heart seized as I realized she was dying. The very mortality I admired was ending.

Her eyelids flitted open, the once sharp turquoise a pale grey. "Ariel."

I froze. That name, I knew that name. Once upon a time, it was mine. For years I had lost it, unspoken on the tongues of the humans who came to visit me. I was The Little Mermaid, nothing more. It wasn't the humans' fault. Time steals everything, even identities.

"Shh, you are far too weak." I brushed the hair from her face, watching the light slowly fade.

She wouldn't survive this, I knew that, and the look on her face told me she knew that. A sensation burned within my chest, an aching that seemed to tear a hole within me. I knew this feeling well; it had gotten me in trouble so long ago, cursing me to an existence of stone. I hadn't cared about anyone in so long. Not a fish, not a cat, and especially not a human.

"What is your name?"

I knew she needed to preserve her strength if she had any hope of fighting against the call of the deeps, but I had to know the name of the woman who would risk her life if only to give me a simple flower every night for years.

She coughed, a weak noise that crushed my very soul. "Eline."

"Eline," I whispered, my hand cupping her face.

Tears streamed across her cheeks, mirroring my own. Moonlight trickled through a break in the storm, bathing us in an ethereal glow. The end was close now, crowding around us like a thick fog.

"I-I can't do this; I can't let you die." The words were thick on my tongue. I knew what I had to do. Was it wrong of me to be selfish, knowing love might once again curse me?

I didn't care. I'd suffer another thousand years encased in stone, if only to give me one more moment with her. Gathering Eline in my arms, I sunk us beneath the waves. The moment her head was under water, she struggled, her eyes wide. It left a primeval terror alight in what little spark there was left within her.

My lips brushed hers as her struggling slowed, her eyes simmering in death. I pressed my lips against hers with all my might as the waters coursed around us. Time stood still, the world eerily silent. My crimson hair streamed out before me, intertwining with hers as her body went limp in my grasp.

"Eline?" I drew back from her, bubbles streaming past my face.

She was still and quiet, a serenity I had never seen upon her face. Like she was sleeping, a princess taking a well-deserved slumber after a hard day's work. But deep down I knew it was not sleep that was taking her, but death.

"Eline!" I shouted into the depths.

Water churned around me, producing a foam that swallowed us whole. My grip tightened, knowing that if I relented even a fraction, I would lose her. Her body floated of its own accord as the foam caressed us; it seeped into the pores of her skin like a sponge. I was mesmerized, entranced, as Eline's body disappeared in a haze of ivory froth. It increased in intensity, the ivory a blinding light that rivalled the sun. Until it wasn't. The foam becoming paler and paler.

Eline stirred beneath the milkiness, thick hair swimming out before her as the foam retreated, revealing a sight I had never thought I'd lay eyes on again. It worked. I had only heard stories, and I could never have been certain, but it had worked. Her eyes shot open as she gazed about us in wonder, first over me, and then herself. Where her legs had been, emerged a tail with scales of a shimmering turquoise, matching the intensity of her eyes. She stared in wonder, her mouth forming words she couldn't quite speak.

"It takes time to get used to."

This calmed her, as she reached out a hand to cup my face, the unspoken words clear as daylight, no—*moonlight*, across her face. My hand rose on its own, drawing strength from the warmth of her body against mine, our tails swishing in the water.

"Every day, for years, you came to see me. A tarnished statue by the shore. Unlike the others you didn't stop for a picture and then leave, you came to me to leave me a flower. Sometimes you'd tell me tales, speak of things that made little sense. I remember thinking it didn't matter that I didn't understand your words, all that mattered was that you cared enough to share them with me," I said, the sea wiping away my tears.

A smile lit her face as she swallowed, warming up muscles she had never had before.

"I remember when I was young, my mother told me a story of a girl who lived in the sea with hair the colour of fire, and scales that shined like a million emeralds." Fish darted past us, just dashes of silver in the dark.

Eline took a deep breath, as if readying herself for what was to come. "She longed to escape the confines of the sea, to be amongst those who walked upon the surface. Sneaking away glances at the world above, and one day fell in love with a boy, and the world he came from."

A prince.

"But her father disapproved, forbidding her of ever returning to the surface. She sat in her castle under the sea, desperate to see her lover again." Thunder boomed overhead, but she wasn't startled this time. "And I thought, that's ridiculous. Why can't she be what she wants to be, who she wants to be? She fell in love, and love was her curse. I felt that in such a way, it resonated through my being." Her eyes wandered across the bay, watching the lightning in the distance. "In my family, you could not be who you wanted to be, who you were destined to be. There was only one way, their way."

My heart ached, her story reignited the pain I had hidden for so long, reminding me of memories that I had thought vanished along with my mortality. Here was someone who believed in me, who knew that freedom was worth the price you had to pay for it. She had suffered, as I had suffered, and now we could suffer together.

My people were gone, but with Eline at my side, our story can live on. When the city awoke to their precious mermaid gone missing, the story will spread across the globe.

"Ariel?"

She grasped my hands in hers, a smile on her face as she stared into my eyes.

"Eline."

She held the same giddiness and crimson blush that I had felt long ago, before the stone was the only world I knew.

Our lips locked together as our bodies pressed against one another, the light of the moon spreading around us. When we finally pulled back, it was to a sea of calm, a sea that had never known that a storm had just passed.

"Let's go." I was eager to be gone of the bay I had called home. There was a wide world out there, larger and filled with more secrets than even I had known.

"Go where?" she asked.

With her hand in mine, I faced us towards the brightest star in the heavens.

"North."

She seemed fearful, and I couldn't blame her. "What's north?"

"The ocean."

Hand in hand, we swam past the towns and cities, the boats and ships. We swam towards a future where we could be happy, where we could be together, and where we could have each other. The opinions of anyone else didn't matter here in the vast expanse of the ocean blue.

"I love you," she said.

"I love you, too," I replied.

Love had imprisoned me, and now, love had set me free. All this time I had yearned for a prince, but perhaps a princess was what I needed.

The Tender Strokes of Music
Helen De Cruz

The castle of Ulmea lay bleak in the light before dawn, the thick layer of snow on its buttresses not softening its appearance. Hobb Aleindlib gazed with a mix of relief and trepidation at the building, after a long, exhausting climb up the snowy mountain, stiff fingers clutching the handle of his lute case.

He had begun to regret his life choices.

"You are the music-healer?" the old guardsman's voice sounded flat in the frosty morning air.

Hobb nodded.

"Duke Aleksander is gravely ill; there is no time to lose," the guard said. He preceded Hobb through broad drafty halls, up winding staircases, into a large room where the Duke lay in a massive ebony four-poster bed. The patient looked serene and pale.

Hobb glanced around, trying to locate his adversary. If the patient looked like this, Death was never far away. As he expected, the cloaked, faceless figure of Death skulked in a far corner of the room, melting in and out of the finely-woven Lowland tapestries, easily mistakable for the play of shadows cast by the dancing flames of the hearth upon the wall. At the direct gaze of a human being, Death slunk away. A good sign. The lack of boldness in Death's demeanor meant the Duke still had some time left.

A young woman with light blond hair tied in a severe knot sat at the side of the bed. Hobb assumed she must be the Duke's daughter, Salla, who had sent for him. Her face, worn with worry, almost broke into relief as she saw him.

"You must be the music-healer. Please, sit." Salla got up and gestured at the carved chair next to the bed.

Hobb pulled the chair a little closer to the bed, took his lute out of the case and began to tune its fifteen strings by ear. The instrument had suffered from severe temperature shock. One of the gut frets had loosened and every string was out of tune. Sensing the impatience of the Duke's daughter, he mumbled, "It must be tuned correctly."

The next few hours were crucial. The daughter might decide they did not need a music-healer after all, and then it would be a miserable climb back down the hill, through the snow in his stiff, still-wet clothes, and no payment for the effort. Thus, Hobb had to pick the piece to begin his treatment of the Duke with great care, for favorable first impressions as well as long-term success. He chose a Passacaglia. It began with a slow descending minor scale, setting a mood of sorrow and lament. Upon this simple theme, he embroidered increasingly complex diminutions.

All the while, he shot glances at his patient. Duke Aleksander had a great mass of white-blond hair that looked ill-matched to the rest of him—whatever was left of him. His face might once have been handsome but was now ravaged by illness. It could still go either way.

"He is mine," a cold familiar voice said. Death had approached the Duke's bedside now, wrapped in his rippling cloak, casting shifting shadows that made it impossible to discern him clearly.

"That remains to be seen," Hobb said, as he strummed through a series of chords in style brisée. "You and I will have a fair struggle over this."

"Duke Aleksander's life force is spent. Your efforts are useless," Death's voice intoned.

Hobb was well acquainted with Death's psychological warfare tactics. This was just the beginning. As the final chord ended and Death melted back into his hiding place, Hobb suddenly felt very tired. He smiled at Salla who had come in again. She cast one long look at her father and could not discern any difference.

Duke Aleksander's ailment had at first presented no cause for concern. He was the resolute ruler of a realm forever at war with its neighbors. Tall and broad-shouldered, he commanded instant respect whenever he entered a room. The older servants said he used to smile more when the Duchess was still alive, but even his daughter could not remember such a time.

One summer day, Aleksander woke up with a slight cough. The mild illness refused to go away. Two months in, the Duke experienced splitting headaches, nausea, and dizziness. In spite of extreme fatigue, he managed no more than a few hours of fitful sleep every night.

In the third month of his illness, the panic attacks began. They always started with a deep, uncanny sense of déjà-vu, followed by rapid and overwhelming waves of terror. The Duke appointed his daughter to rule in his stead. With no further improvement, and worn down by the continued physical assaults of his ailment, he lapsed into a state of lethargy, confined to his bed all day. Salla sent for sober doctors in black hats and cloaks, who brought ornate boxes with blood leeches, pills, and ointments, and made complicated diagnoses with grand-sounding names. To no avail.

As she began to fear for her father's life and the servants' whispers in the quiet hallways grew less circumspect, eventually bursting into open speculation about his succession, Salla inquired into the practice of music-healing. It was said that the people of the Southern Islands—where this practice was common—were near-immortal. They could charm snakes, they could run 100-mile foot races. She did not doubt these were wild exaggerations, yet at this point, she was willing to try anything.

Every day, Salla watched the young musician, as he played delicate tunes upon his rosewood lute. All the while, she was oblivious to Hobb's continued battles against Death, which went on unseen and unheard.

Just three years ago, Hobb had decided to leave the Southern Islands. He recalled how the captain of the vessel said to him, as he stared at the receding purple hills topped by golden domes, "You bought a one-way ticket. I don't understand how anyone can leave these Islands. Life is such a struggle on the mainland."

He had replied that he valued the craft of music-healing and its practice more than he valued living in comfort. But can anyone know what they will value more, several years hence? He thought about his tradeoff, often, while residing in that clammy, lonely castle. How wonderful is music-healing, anyway, as a profession? Is it worth all this misery, the cold and damp, no friendly or familiar face, but only the furtive glances of the servants.

"You know, they despise you," Death said one day. "They look down upon your Southern looks and manners. Why would you work so hard to please them? They don't even pay you well. Are you that desperate for dalers?"

"I don't understand," Hobb remarked, "Why not just let Duke Aleksander live a little while longer? You will get him, eventually. You will get us all. Why the rush?"

"It is his time," said Death.

The music-healer and Death stood face to face now, in Aleksander's bedroom.

"You know what will happen when he dies, don't you? Death asked quietly. "They will throw you in a dungeon and throw away the key. They are itching to blame someone, and you are a foreigner—the perfect scapegoat.

"They wouldn't do that!" Hobb said, put on the defensive,

though he had no reason to presume any loyalty of his reticent employers.

Death's words had planted a sense of despair within Hobb. Outside, an icy desert lay stretched out. Within, the marble black, moist castle walls offered little solace against that incessant cold that seemed to have taken permanent abode in his bones. Hobb felt a tremendous sense of homesickness. Vivid random memories of his home town plagued him: the smell of flatbread in an oven, the shouts of stall holders on the market square, a friendly stray cat in an alley, arching its back.

He had silent meals with the other serving personnel at a long wooden table. Upon his arrival, their questions had been the predictable ones, the ones people asked wherever he went.

Three years ago, he mistook those questions for genuine interest.

"Where are you from? The Southern Islands, you say? I already thought you look like *one of them*. Are you truly immortal? Can you fly? Do you keep a snake as a pet?"

He obliged them with an honest reply, though his interlocutors never seemed to listen: "No, we aren't immortal, but music healing is so common on the islands people rarely get ill, so we get old. I can no more fly than any other human being. I am afraid of snakes, but some people keep them. The venom is useful, in some instances." Lately, he sometimes lied, telling tall tales just to see what their reactions were and how far he could push before they would disbelieve him. He had not yet reached that limit, it seemed. And in any case, their enthusiasm dissipated quickly and he became the ignored outsider again.

One day, as the personnel consumed their bland barley porridge, Salla strode into the room.

She said, "I come to inform you that tomorrow I am making a journey to sign a peace treaty in my father's name that will bring the Duchy of Ulmea and the Kingdom of Venjä closer together. Esle, you will take guardianship of the castle in my stead."

The oldest man-in-waiting, Esle, smiled in acknowledgment.

"Now music-healer," she said to Hobb, "Please take good care of my father. And send word *immediately* if his condition deteriorates or otherwise changes."

With that, Salla left, and Esle was put in charge.

Hobb was aware of the elderly Esle's dislike for him. The man-in-waiting seemed to have a keen interest to see him fail that rose above mere skepticism. Struggling with hopelessness and homesickness, he argued with Death daily, trying to ignore Esle's eyerolls and sighs.

One bleak day, as snow fell even more thickly than usual, and the Duke was as gaunt and motionless as ever, he stared into the faceless blackness of Death's hood.

"Are you finally giving up?" Death asked.

"It is not over yet," Hobb countered without enthusiasm.

"Now, with the Duke's daughter gone, you ought to leave quietly, while you still can. Tomorrow's weather will be mild, and the snow is still fresh. It will be easy to travel. You can just slip away."

Death had in his boldness made a fatal mistake. In his attempts to discourage Hobb, he had revealed that Hobb was gaining ground.

Hobb tried to hide his triumphant smile, and said "You blundered. You told me that Duke Aleksander will live if I persist."

As he finished playing the Fantasia in the Second Tone, ending on a broad, major chord, Hobb met the gaze of Esle.

"You're looking mighty pleased with yourself," the man-in-waiting remarked coolly.

"The Duke will live," Hobb declared.

The Tender Strokes of Music

Duke Aleksander could not pinpoint the exact moment his illness began to wane. There was no clear turning point. At first, all he could do was lie still and drink thin gruel, only faintly aware of the lute music in the background. Then followed a period in which he experienced a strange sort of lucidity. It seemed he observed everything, including himself, from behind thick glass, or an opaque veil, that gradually wore thinner with each day.

His daughter informed him on matters of statecraft, but Aleksander's mind had become prone to wandering. He had to make supreme efforts to keep focused. As Salla told him about a free trade agreement with Venjä and her initial talks with Småll's stadtholders, his gaze moved to the strip of bright cerulean blue sky he could just make out through the window, to a spider spinning her web on the wall close to his bed, to the fine, blood-red coral beads on his daughter's necklace, to Hobb's eyes which were so dark you could not see the pupils, except when the early spring sun fell directly into them, and they shone a bright reddish brown.

The lute music flowed into his mind and into his heart without effort. The musician sat by his bedside, playing dazzling pieces that expressed hopeful, wistful, and joyful moods. One day, Aleksander lay quietly, entranced and enraptured by the music. A Toccata started with a slow, undulating, melody that expanded into a solemn polyphony. At the sweetness of that piece, Aleksander felt all the dread and sorrow of his past illness coalesce. Tears sprang into his eyes. He wept without restraint. He saw that Hobb looked both moved and pleased.

"I loved this piece. Never leave, Hobb," Aleksander sighed, "Never leave."

Hobb smiled, but the smile was melancholy and sad.

When Aleksander felt he had turned the corner, and might expect a full recovery, he paid Hobb (who had not received any payment yet) 500 dalers, a very handsome sum for six months' work, exceeding what the prime violinist made at the Royal Court of Venjä in an entire year. The Duke continued his convalescence, as he was moved from his bed to a heavy armchair. Then his daughter and Esle took turns walking with him about the room. In that period, watching and listening to Hobb was the high point of his day. He felt a strange lump in his throat whenever he saw the young foreigner play so earnestly. Aleksander wondered if that sentiment was love, then felt a tinge of disloyalty toward the long-dead Duchess.

The waning illness had left Aleksander a profoundly altered man. He still felt no interest in politics, and besides, why should he take over from Salla? In his name, she travelled to far-away lands to forge alliances, alliances he had believed to be beyond Ulmea's grasp.

The Duke's new-found delight in music became known in neighboring countries. He received a gift from Prince Aku of Venjä: a large contraption made of a modified harpsichord, wax cylinders, and carillon bells, that produced music without tiring. The Musicking Machine charmed everyone at court. Its polyphony was more complex than anything Hobb could coax out of the eight pairs of strings of his lute.

Meanwhile, Hobb's homesickness remained, but it was further compounded by a sense of uselessness and loneliness. Except for Aleksander, he was still friendless. Much as Hobb loved Aleksander, he could never adapt to that miserable climate. The spring, even as it rolled into summer, was still much too chilly. The stay at Ulmea had been cold but profitable. With no compelling reason to remain, Hobb handed in his notice and quietly left one early morning. Dreading the prospect of Aleksander trying to stop him from leaving, he did not inform Salla or her father, only Esle, who was exceedingly helpful in arranging a sleigh to pack his few belongings in and to find a ship that would bring him back to the beautiful Southern Islands that he missed so keenly.

The Tender Strokes of Music

After Hobb's sudden departure, Aleksander's mood grew somber, and he relapsed into illness. Servants hauled the Musicking Machine into his bedroom where it played its superb and soulless tunes, but they did not cheer him.

One morning Aleksander found he could scarcely breathe. A heavy weight lay on his chest. He could not see Death sitting on him, he could not hear Death's quiet, mocking laughter.

"I need music!" the Duke cried out, delirious. "I want music!" The men-in-waiting turned on the Musicking machine, but all it made was an ominous creaking sound. The moist and cold had gotten to its internal mechanism.

Salla told Esle to send for the music-healer.

"The one we had last year?" Esle asked, disingenuously as there had not been a music-healer before or since within the castle walls, "He has returned to the Southern Islands. He'll be hard to find."

But Salla insisted, and Hobb was summoned.

Staring into the Duke's face with great, hollow eyes, Death had inched up to the foot of the bed. The gentle tones of a lute stopped Death in his tracks. It was a Passamezzo, played in slow, solemn measures.

"You again," Death stated. "You won't be able to save him now. See how close I am."

"I won't give up on Aleksander," Hobb said.

Then Death said with a somewhat milder voice, "I grant your music is pleasing. I feel moved by your playing. But as for the Duke, everyone is better off with him dead."

"It is unseemly to speak about ill people in this manner," Hobb said.

"To the contrary," Death said, gusts of cold emanating from the faceless cloak. "There are many people we are better off without. While the Duke ruled, Ulmea knew nothing but devastating war and a starving population. But under his daughter Salla, Ulmea thrives and peace reigns. You do realize that she's making all these decisions about peace agreements entirely on her own?"

"I am skeptical," Hobb said, "that your decisions about who lives and dies would be informed with concern for what is good for a country. Your actions seem indifferent to how well or how ill a man rules."

"Perhaps," Death conceded. "However, I am willing to stall his demise once more on the following condition: you need to give me a song."

"I am not a great singer," Hobb said.

"That is my final offer," Death said.

Hobb switched the lute for an 'oud and adapted an old song from the Southern Islands. He sang of spring, which came lush and early on the Islands but brief and late in Ulmea. He sang of a delicate, single rosebud in June, of cups drunk in fellowship. How can we live in dread and in regret, if life flits away like a little songbird? How can we regret, if the elder flowers bloom in the sweet air, and dew glistens on grass?

For just one instance, Death could sense the tragedy and beauty that lies in the brevity of human life. Without thanking the singer, he silently departed through the opened window, into the cool, white mist.

The Duke was moved too. Suddenly alert and sitting up he cried, "Hobb—you are back! You have come back to me! Please, never leave again."

Hobb said, carefully, "I can stay with you. But I have a condition. I cannot stay in this dreadful castle. I do not feel at home in Ulmea, and I'm no longer at home on the Southern Islands either, it turns out, so it must be elsewhere."

The Duke replied, "I've come to realize that Salla is far

better at statecraft than I am. So, I have decided already a while ago that I should abdicate, and take along sufficient means to live quietly. I will go wherever you wish to go, if you want me, that is."

Hobb said, "Let's try to find a place that suits us both."

That morning, the servants came in to look in on their ailing ruler, expecting him dead. But he sat up in bed, his face rosy and healthy, his grey eyes sparkling with the sense of adventure, Hobb sitting beside him with a broad smile. The Duke said, in something of his former, booming voice, "Good morning!"

The Princess from the Caves
Jennifer Jeanne McArdle

"How do I know you're a prince?" King Girato of the Tanoo goblin clan asked Hendry. "Where are your jewels and servants?"

Girato's large ears had been pierced multiple times, bejeweled bracelets covered his forearms, and copper-colored embroidery shimmered on his loose purple robe. Gold chains and silk wrapped around some of the stalagmites sticking up from the ground in front of his throne.

Hendry shoved his hands into his pockets and prayed he hadn't left the letter with his father's seal back in his car. If only he could have brought his servant, Gustavo, with him. Gustavo was always reading about things and could have told him goblins valued ostentatious displays of wealth. Thank gods! Hendry pulled the letter from his pocket along with some lint.

"This letter is from my father, King Rothan of Dendron."

A goblin servant took the letter from him. Hendry noticed a couple of new goblins in robes nearly as resplendent as Girato's, one in red and gold and the other in blue and silver, enter the room from an entrance behind the throne. Girato examined the letter.

"Dendron is a human nation that still honors their king's authority and bloodline." Girato scratched the white fur on his chin. "Many of the other human nations have devolved into democracies."

Hendry bowed. "Your majesty, I've heard that a rare purple mushroom grows here that can be used for a medicine to treat my mother's paralysis. Due to a horseback riding accident, the queen of Dendron is paralyzed from the waist down. I have been searching for the last six months for something to help her. I hope to take some mushrooms from your caves."

Girato sat back in his throne. "While I can appreciate the nobility of your request—our own kingdom has suffered without queen for a few years now—I cannot allow you to take some of those mushrooms without getting something in return."

"My father will pay you heavily in gold for your kindness." Water dripped on Hendry's head from a stalactite above. The guard goblins were still gripping their spears tightly. Hendry had a small pistol in a holster around his ankle. How quickly and how many of them could he shoot?

"Does it look like I lack for gold?" Girato shook his head.

"Father," the goblin wearing blue and silver standing in the back spoke up.

"Yes, Niaa?" Girato turned.

"Isn't Dendron known to have rare flowers found nowhere else in the world? Think of all the nectar and honey they could send us if they owed us a favor."

"Hm." Girato tapped his claws.

"One favor is nice, Father," now the goblin in red and gold was speaking. "But what if Dendron were our ally? They'd send us nectar and honey every year."

Girato laughed, exposing sharp teeth and a long tongue. "I hardly think one favor will make Dendron indebted to us."

"What if he does the Charart Ceremony with Niaa?" Now the goblin in red was standing next to her father while Niaa blinked her large, black eyes.

"You can't be serious, Baata!" Niaa's fists clenched.

"He is a prince. You are a princess. It's been done with humans in the past, when our numbers were greater. Prince Hendry is the third son, not the heir. His parents won't have to worry about a non-human queen." Now Baata had her hand on Girato's shoulder.

"It hasn't been done with a human in a long time."

"It's not permanent." Baata shrugged and then turned to Niaa. "Niaa, you're the one who wants out of the caves."

"I never said that, exactly—"

"We shall not argue about this." Girato slammed his fist. "The Charart does not work on unwilling participants. Niaa must decide. Niaa?"

Niaa stared at the ground, her ears and nose twitching.

"Niaa?" Baata asked.

Between the bad air in the caves, his horrible hangover, and the throbbing bruises he'd acquired in his brawl the night before, Hendry felt like he was going to pass out. What were they going on about? He could hardly think. Where was Gustavo?

"Fine. If the human agrees," Niaa answered finally.

"Prince Hendry, do you agree to take part in the Charart Ceremony with Princess Niaa?

"What?" Hendry nearly forgot himself. Goblin or not, he was still a prince talking to a king. He adjusted his hat. "I apologize, but what does that require of me?"

"Do humans not—? We can do it now, here. You will take Niaa's hands and it will be done quickly."

"Of course I know that ceremony." Hendry hated looking stupid. It sounded simple enough, though; her hands might be slimy or covered in mold. But he couldn't go home with nothing for his mother. He'd always been less impressive than his brothers.

"Yes," he spoke louder than he meant to. "I will do the ceremony." Niaa walked towards him, staring past him and not at him. Girato stood from his throne. He whispered something to Niaa. A wizard goblin in a silver robe walked over to the king and bowed.

"Please give me your hands," the goblin in silver asked them, and Hendry obliged, praying he hadn't made a big mistake. Niaa stepped towards Hendry and the wizard goblin. The wizard took their left hands.

"Hold each other's hands," he whispered. Niaa placed her hand lightly into Hendry's. Its fur reminded him of a dog's, but her hand was shaped like a human's, except the nails looked longer and sharper. The wizard held their wrists. The room felt like it was spinning, and Hendry again cursed his bad habits. But, perhaps, it was the magic. The wizard spoke some words and their bodies glowed.

"It's done. May you find love this year and treat each other with patience and kindness."

"I will," Niaa said. She looked back at him; no one was moving.

Someone coughed.

"Oh, uh," Hendry realized this ceremony was much more serious than he'd thought. "I will?"

The wizard let go of their wrists and stepped back. Niaa turned to her father and bowed.

"Follow me," She whispered to Hendry. "Bow," Niaa insisted again, and Hendry finally dropped to his knees.

"Arise," Girato commanded Niaa and Hendry.

"Prince Hendry and Princess Niaa, I wish you luck on the year ahead. May your union become permanent, so you bring happiness to both our kingdoms."

Our union? Hendry thought. Suddenly, he could hear his own heartbeat.

"Charka, bring the Prince his gyapa mushrooms. Normally, we would offer the new couple a feast before their journey, but you must want to get back to your mother as soon as possible. Please give Niaa time to pack her things, though. This will be her first long trip away from the caves. I have put great trust in you,

Hendry, because of the reputation of your kingdom."

King Girato gestured widely and continued: "Although the binding of the ceremony only lasts a year, if you return to us after two, still together, we will have a wedding ceremony and send you back with great riches for your family from the goblin mines."

"A wedding?" Hendry spit out.

"Do the people of Dendron not celebrate new marriages?" Girato tilted his head.

"Why…yes! I am just shocked by the generosity. Goblins are truly noble creatures." Hendry's throat tightened. "But…we are not married yet?"

"No. Your magic bond will force you to know one another, but it is up to you and Niaa to make your relationship work. You are lucky. Princess Niaa is known as a great beauty among our people."

"Ah, yes." He glanced briefly at Niaa, whose head was down and hands clasped in front of her. Goblins were monstrous things that slunk around in the dark, eating moss, hissing in the night, stealing from farmers or travelers. He could see some veins in Niaa's wide ears. How could he kiss that mouth full of sharp teeth? He swallowed to keep from gagging.

Hendry waited in a room near the exit of the cave. After a few hours, Niaa emerged wearing a brown robe with a hood over her ears, dark sunglasses, a cloth mask covering her face and neck, and gloves. Her servants carried several suitcases.

"Where are your servants?"

"Only one man is traveling with me. He's back in town."

"Oh. The male goblin usually provides his promised with new servants. But I guess you were not prepared for this."

Hendry wanted to interrogate her, but he was nervous to do so near the goblin kingdom.

"I am sorry, Princess. I hope you can forgive me." He bowed. She said nothing, and they walked in silence through the woods to Hendry's green and silver sports car, a scratched up machine with a long nose impractical for uneven roads. The servants stuffed some of her things into the tiny trunk and tied the remaining bags to the roof of the vehicle. When they were finished with their work, Niaa hugged each of them.

When the servants finally departed, Hendry turned to Niaa.

"So, uh, I guess you can come along with me. I have to go pick up Gustavo from jail."

"Who?"

"My servant. He had to spend the day in jail."

"Why did he go to jail? What is that chemical I smell on you?"

"He went to jail because I got drunk last night and got in a fight with some guys. He's serving my sentence." Hendry shrugged. "You live in a cave and eat dirt. Don't lecture me about smells."

"Oh? Do I actually smell?"

"Well, yeah," Hendry lied and leaned his throbbing forehead on his car. "Now, can you explain to me what the hell just happened?"

"I thought you were confused back in the cave, but no one would be stupid enough to agree to a ceremony without understanding—"

"No, I don't understand. Excuse me for not knowing details of goblin culture. Not like you're from an important magical race."

"You are so arrogant, even for a human. The Charart Ceremony binds two people to each other for a year. It is impossible for the bound people to go more than three miles from each other, and they must touch each other every three days, or they will suffer great pain. If a couple survives the year bound, and a second year free, and is still together, then they will be married."

"How can a goblin and a human be married?"

"It used to happen a lot, especially in this country. But the human population continues to grow and ours shrinks. After one year, the spell is lifted and we can head our separate ways, if we want. But we will not be married. My father will not send your kingdom any of our treasures. I assume your kingdom will not send Tanoo goblins nectar and honey."

"But he won't try to have me killed?"

"No? Sometimes engagements fail." Niaa sighed and looked up towards the sky. "The sun is so bright today, I shall remain covered. Goblin skin can be a little sensitive in the sun."

She stopped speaking when she heard a click. She looked down. Hendry was pointing a pistol at her.

"What if I killed you? Would that break the spell?"

"What? I haven't done anything to you—"

"Answer my question." He took a step towards her, pistol still raised.

"You would kill me?" Niaa put her hands up.

"Answer me."

"You still wouldn't be able to go more than three miles from my corpse." The pitch of Niaa's voice raised to a squeak: "And you'd have to touch it every few days."

"Look. Maybe you've dreamed of marrying a handsome human prince—"

"Hardly!" She lowered her hands for a second and then raised them again. "You think we like pink, hairless creatures—"

"Whatever! The point is, we can make this easy. I won't kill you if you just do what I say. You keep this outfit on and don't tell anyone what you are. Once the year is done, you can do whatever you like."

"Fine. Just put down the gun. I just want to help my people get access to Dendron honey and nectar. But what is the worst that would happen if I revealed myself?"

"Our honey? We can talk about it once I've helped my mother." Hendry spat but lowered his pistol. "I would be laughed out of society—"

"You make your species sound so charming." Niaa grabbed the door on the passenger side, pulled it open, and sat down. He wanted to kill her! Here she'd been thinking that being bound to a soft human prince and getting to see the world would be better than rotting in the caves with her petty siblings. She wanted to weep, but she wouldn't let Hendry see her upset.

Hendry opened his door and got in the car. "I am sorry. But that's just what it is. You're in human country now. I don't wanna have to hurt you."

After about two hours in the car, engine starting to putter and grumble at the strain of climbing dirt roads, they pulled up next to a sheriff's office on the main street of a dusty little town. The late afternoon sun reflected from the chrome bits of Hendry's car.

"You should stay here," Hendry commanded as he got out of the car. She stopped. He still had a pistol, and she didn't know enough about human society yet. Hendry slumped up the steps, but adjusted his posture before entering the building. Perhaps, Niaa wondered, a hooded figure with her skin completely covered was more suspicious than a goblin.

She just had to survive one year with Hendry, she reminded herself, and then she'd be free to go anywhere she wanted. Maybe she'd go to the Federation of Republics. Every few months, her father set up a film projector to watch movies made in the Republics, and they'd drink flavored honey and marvel at the quick-footed-dancing, fast-talking humans that sparkled in black and white, fell in love, and pined for each other while dancing on shiny city streets. Baata used to make fun of Niaa because she loved watching the human romance movies.

Hendry stepped out of the office first, and behind him followed a second man. They shared a cigarette for a few moments. Hendry was lanky, with red-blonde hair and long features, and dressed in a pin-stripe gray and lavender suit. The second man was shorter and stockier, his black hair a little long with a slight wave, while a pencil mustache and well-groomed goatee decorated his face. His cream button-up shirt was unbuttoned enough to reveal hair on his chest.

Niaa hadn't known humans could be hairy. The hairy human smiled, revealing large teeth and causing his eyes to crinkle in a way that was oddly cute. She'd never thought of the word "cute" when looking at a human before. Niaa looked away from the two men to the flagpole on the top of the building. The green and white flag of Tabasdan waved in the wind. Most humans in Tabasdan, the nation that surrounded her Tanoo Caves, were poor farmers hardly able to grow crops in the dusty soil. Dendron, to the north, was wealthier.

The men finished their cigarette and approached the car, Hendry on the driver's side and Gustavo on the passenger side.

"Miss Niaa?" Gustavo said to her, his voice low and smooth. "Prince Hendry asked me to take you in my car. He says you'll be more comfortable there." She glanced at Hendry, who nodded.

"Right."

"Follow me, Miss," she followed him to a parking area and to a large black car. He opened one of the backseat doors for her. She slid into the backseat. Gustavo got into the driver's seat.

"I hope you don't mind being alone with me. Sorry you can't take off your mask."

"Huh?"

"Hendry said you are a follower of the prophet, Adersan. You can't expose your face or hair to men you aren't related to?"

"Oh. I'm used to it." It would have been nice and smart of Hendry to tell her beforehand what he was going to tell people to excuse her strange outfit, but it was clear that the Prince was neither of those things. Her outfit also wasn't quite the style of an Adersanian woman's, but she supposed it was a good enough excuse.

"Your father asked Hendry to accompany you to Rattesberg University. What do you plan on studying there?" Gustavo adjusted his mirror, so Niaa could see the reflection of his calm grey eyes in the glass.

"I haven't decided yet."

Gustavo turned the car's engine on. Niaa felt the vibration in her whole body, but it was much less jarring than in Hendry's car.

"Might I ask which noble house of Tabasdan you're from? My family used to do a lot of business with Tabasdan."

"The Klepper House," Niaa answered after a few moments, remembering the name and hoping they weren't a house Gustavo knew well. "Sorry, it's been a long day. I'm tired."

"Of course, Miss! Sorry, it's just I love meeting people from all over the world."

"No, no. You did nothing wrong Mr.—"

"Just call me Gustavo." Niaa heard the loud engine of Hendry's car and watched him pull quickly out onto the road. He remembered the three-mile rule, she hoped. Gustavo carefully exited the parking lot and followed Hendry.

The young woman, Niaa, had fallen asleep within a few minutes, although the road was bumpy. Hendry had slowed down significantly, and his car was struggling. At this rate, they wouldn't make it to the next city before dark. Her story seemed terribly suspicious. When had Hendry had time to meet her or her family *and* get the mushrooms yesterday?

But Gustavo couldn't hold that against Miss Niaa. There was a strange quality to her voice, too—maybe the accent? But it was more than that. There was an undertone, a vibration that made him think of the fast-beating wings of bumble bees and hummingbirds, of summer days, drinking lemonade and playing amid the flowers of his great-uncle's garden when he was a kid.

When the sun was nearly down, Hendry's car finally puttered to a full stop. Gustavo stopped his car.

"What's happened?" Niaa asked from the back.

"Looks like Hendry's car has died." Gustavo got out to help Hendry.

"Prince," Gustavo said after twenty minutes, "I don't have the know-how to fix this car. We'll have to get a real mechanic. It's too late now, though. There's a bit of a clearing down there in the woods. We could set up a tent and rest here for the night."

A couple hours later, Niaa was sitting around a campfire. Gustavo had set everything up himself. Her servants had packed her a tent, too, thank the gods, so she had some privacy. She had wanted to help poor Gustavo—of course she could make a fire and cook! But Hendry gave her a stern look. Gustavo offered her some bread and boiled beans from a can. They were strange foods for Niaa, but she was hungry enough not to care. She ate in her tent and went back out when she finished.

"I'm going to sleep," Hendry told the others before he went to his tent. She felt better now, at night. She breathed in the smell of the tall pine trees around them and looked up to the twinkling stars. Perhaps it would not be such a bad year after all. Most goblins were anxious to spend too much time outside, far from the caves.

Gustavo was smiling, watching the stars himself.

"Thank you," she said to him after it was clear Hendry was fast asleep. "For all the hard work you did today."

"Oh, no worries. If you don't mind me asking, why didn't your father send anyone to help you? He trusted a stranger to take you to Dendron?"

"Well…it's just our tradition."

"What do you mean?"

"Uh." Niaa pulled her knees into her chest and wrapped her arms around them. "To be honest, I think my dad is ashamed… about my converting to a foreign religion."

"What? That doesn't seem right."

"Sometimes fathers make stupid decisions." Niaa wished she could pull down her mask and hood and feel the night air on her face and her ears. "Why did you agree to go to jail for Hendry?" she asked after a few moments.

Gustavo laughed. "He promised me a big bonus for my time. Hendry's always trying to get out of things; he has the money and fame, but none of the responsibilities of his eldest brother."

Niaa rolled her eyes. "It's not just. One man can't serve another man's punishment."

"Can I speak honestly, Miss?" Gustavo scratched his head. "That is just how Dendron is—it'll never be a democracy, like the Republics. Hendry is a prince. I'm from a lesser-house with a failing reputation." He scooted just a bit closer to where she was sitting. "The smoke was bothering me. Anyway, people in Dendron are too comfortable with the little scraps the nobles throw at them and too loyal to their little towns among the valleys and mountains to organize a country-wide revolution."

"I can understand. In my kingdom—I mean, in my reading—I was reading once about a people that had become divided over a whole continent. Each small kingdom sat a great distance from the others, all of them trying to survive in a world that didn't want them. So, because of that fear, the people clung to their royalty. Even if that royalty could be devious." Niaa hugged her knees even tighter. Gustavo moved a little closer, waving smoke from his face.

"I read about a princess once," Niaa continued softly, "who was forgotten by her older brother and sister. Everyone thought she was weird because she always wanted to stay outside too long and never wanted to go to court. Her brother and sister were happy to ignore her for years. Until, when she got older, people noticed she was beautiful and suddenly wanted her. She became afraid because she knew no matter what she did, her siblings would see her as a threat. So, when she got the chance to leave—she took it."

Gustavo turned his head, trying to find Niaa's eyes. He bit his lower lip. "Niaa, that sounds like quite the story. Maybe when you get to the university, you will decide to study politics or history." He placed a hand on her shoulder. Niaa nearly jumped. "And you will already have a friend in the city." He laughed and his eyes crinkled again. He really was very cute—for a human. "Shall we both go to sleep, now?"

Late that night, Gustavo woke up. He looked through the tiny window of his tent. In the trees, he saw something glisten. It was a figure, standing on a thick branch, arms outstretched. The bright moonlight danced on what looked like wings, maybe— they were such a deep blue, like the middle of the ocean. A blue you could fall into and that would wrap you tightly and keep you safe. He rubbed his eyes. When he looked out the window again, he could no longer see the figure.

At dawn, he woke up before Hendry and Niaa and walked around the perimeter of the camping area. In the grass, he found two blue scales that shimmered in the sunlight. He pocketed both quickly.

When they all woke up, Gustavo suggested he take Niaa with him to the city so they could get her set up in a nice hotel while he looked for a mechanic and Hendry waited with the cars.

"You think I would trust you alone with her at a hotel?" Hendry scolded.

Gustavo tried not to be too offended by Hendry's disrespect and wondered what they were hiding from him. Hand in his pocket, he squeezed the blue scales for comfort and distraction.

The Princess from the Caves

They managed to get Hendry's car fixed, and they all arrived in the nearby city shortly after sundown. Fog hung around the city's many abandoned buildings. Ten years ago, this had been a booming factory town, but now people were leaving, or wandering, begging in the streets. They drove past the poverty and into the downtown area, which still had shining, tall buildings and flashing lights. Hendry picked the hotel, the tallest one in the city, procuring three separate rooms. The hotel wasn't well lit, but the carpets were a plush, deep red, and gold paint covered the molding and the light fixtures.

Alone in her room, Niaa looked out onto the sprawling city, feeling dizzy at the sheer number of humans she saw. Finally, Niaa could let her skin breathe. She drew herself a hot bath in the ivory tub, drenching herself in some oils and soaps from back home, letting the scents relax and distract her from the smells of tobacco smoke and other chemicals staining the hotel. She supposed she was spoiled, like Hendry, in some ways.

As she scrubbed the dirt from her body, she looked at her own hands. How much stronger human hands looked, especially Gustavo's. How pleasant her journey might have been if he had been the human man she was stuck with!

She stood up and looked towards the huge mirror on the other side of the wall. Was she ugly to most humans? She lifted her arms. Even she felt a little entranced by the deep blue scales that covered the flaps of skin that stretched between her upper arms and thighs. She stared at her eyes. There was a famous Elven poet who had written about goblin eyes, but she couldn't remember his exact words.

She heard a knock at the door.

"Miss Niaa?" It was Gustavo.

"Just a minute!" She rushed to put on her clothes and sunglasses. Finally, she pulled the door open.

"Oh! There you are! I wanted to ask if you wanted to go down to the casinos with me."

"That would be lovely."

"I'll bet everyone will be jealous if you're with me." He offered his arm. Niaa took it, noticing how strong it felt under his shirt, and a small shiver went up her spine.

"Why is that?"

"They will think, 'That man's wife is so beautiful, he has to cover her up so no one tries to steal her away!'"

"Wife?"

"I'm just kidding, my dear." He shrugged. "Sorry—"

"You should be so lucky," she giggled.

The staff and male guests donned tuxedos while the female guests wore sparkly dresses, feathers, and jewelry, painted their lips bright red, and donned shoes that clicked as they walked on the shining black and red tiled floors. Were there any goblins here? She saw a couple of elves and one orc bodyguard.

Gustavo didn't seem embarrassed walking with a strangely dressed woman. Niaa's ears filled with the ringing of each machine, the shouts of excitement from the tables. Even with her glasses on, the flashing lights were overwhelming.

"What's that?" Niaa motioned towards a table with tiles with symbols on them.

"Oh, Turn Tiles? It's a bit complicated."

"I'd like to learn," she told him and walked towards the table. The faces of concentration on the players and the light clacking of the tiles were so appealing. They approached a table, and one of the casino employees offered to teach her. Gustavo sat with her as the worker explained the game.

"Go ahead." Gustavo told her after learning the rules. "You've got the knack of it, but I'm not smart enough for this type of game."

Niaa lost her first two hands, but she won the next two, ending the game.

Where had Gustavo gone? She scanned the room, but didn't see him. Finally, at the bar in the back, she saw Gustavo talking to a tall human woman in a short red dress that ended in fringe around her knees. Gustavo said something, flashed a smile, and she leaned towards him. Niaa made her way towards the bar. Who was this woman? Did Gustavo think she was pretty? She was a terrible judge of human beauty. As she got closer to the bar, a sound distracted her.

"I wasn't cheating!" She heard a goblin's voice. Niaa whipped around to the source of the sound, and saw a red-orange goblin in a blue tuxedo. In order for that tuxedo to fit, the goblin must have removed the webbed skin goblins had between their arms and thighs. Two large men were dragging him out of the casino.

"Let's not make things worse. We know how your kind gets about money."

"Does the dealer have any proof? Or you just don't like my face?" Niaa froze in place. Should she help him? What if he had been cheating?

"Niaa!" She turned to see Gustavo standing behind her. "Oh boy, looks rough. Having a goblin in a casino always makes people edgy."

"Why is that?" Niaa folded her arms over her chest.

"They always tend to be very lucky." He shrugged "So people think they're using some goblin magic."

"But goblins don't have magic that affects luck."

"Really? Can't say I know much about goblins."

"I want to make sure he's okay." Niaa took off in the direction of the bodyguards and the goblin. Just then the guards were walking away from an exit door. She pushed past them and threw the door open, the night air suddenly filling her lungs. The goblin was pulling himself up from the ground. His suit was now dirty and wet, having landed in a puddle in the alleyway.

"My brother, are you okay?" she asked the goblin in their language.

"Gods, who are you?" He stood up.

She stepped towards him. "I am Princess Niaa, of the Tanoo Cave Clan. Brother, I want to help—"

"I don't need help from someone like you."

"We are both goblins."

The orange goblin got close to her face. He poked her in the chest. "But you don't even want the humans to know you're a goblin. That's what this get-up is about, huh?" Niaa heard the door open behind them.

"Niaa! What are you doing?" Gustavo called.

"After the humans kidnapped me and stole my scales, King Girato banished me from Tanoo. Our scales are valuable on human black markets. I don't need help from Girato's daughter."

"Get out of her face! Come on, scram!" Gustavo was at Niaa's side.

"What's this?" the goblin backed up but continued speaking in their language. "Is he the one making you hide yourself? Pathetic." He put his hands up and looked at Gustavo. Speaking in the language Gustavo understood: "You don't really care for her if you can't accept her for who she is. I have better things to do than talk to the princess of a doomed kingdom." He turned and ran to the streets.

"Niaa? Are you okay?"

"Yeah." Niaa felt dizzy.

"Niaa, let's get back inside. But why did he call you a princess?"

Niaa turned to face Gustavo.

"Please, Gustavo. I am sorry, but now is not the time." Maybe Hendry was right about hiding her species.

"Okay, I understand." He ran his fingers through his hair. "Let's go back inside."

Niaa nodded and walked towards the door back into the hotel, Gustavo following behind her. She pulled the door open and entered inside.

"Ah, Niaa. Don't think me too crude, but you walk like you're floating. I could watch you move all day."

"Gustavo, you must be known as quite the charmer in Rattesberg." His comment helped her to not think of having her own scales removed, but young male goblins back home wouldn't dare talk to their princess like he'd just spoken to her.

He accompanied her back to her room in silence. She wanted to talk to him about what had happened, but then she'd have to tell him the truth.

"Niaa," he said right as they got to her door. "I don't understand what happened with that goblin. You should be careful, but…" He took her hand in his. "Having compassion is never easy, but don't let the world beat it out of you. Then what's left of you? I am not making sense."

"No…it's alright. Thank you." She looked down. He was still holding her hand.

"Oh! Well. Good night." He let go, and she shut the door, feeling her hearts thumping hard in her chest.

The next morning, they got Hendry out of his room. Gustavo chased away two young women who realized they'd just spent the night with a rich prince and were trying to hang around. It was midday by the time they got back on the road.

"Sometimes that boy doesn't know when to stop drinking," Gustavo mumbled.

"Hm?" Niaa asked.

"Hendry gets into too much trouble—being a prince won't save him one day."

"We don't have alcohol where I'm from," Niaa watched as they passed people still using horses and carriages.

"I thought Tabasdan was famous for its vodka."

"I mean—my family specifically. Doesn't drink." Niaa felt extra hot and wished she could remove her excess clothing. Would Gustavo call her disgusting or try to shoot her? Or try to steal her scales?

"You're better off not drinking. When I was younger, I used to party almost as much as the prince."

"Did you meet as many girls as Hendry?"

"Ha! More." Gustavo winked.

"Really? Do hu—women from your town—think you are handsome?" What was human dating like? She barely even knew what dating was like for goblins.

"Well." His cheeks looked a little redder than usual. "It's not so much my looks—though, I like to think those aren't bad—more the reputation of my, er, skills."

"Oh." Niaa sat back and wondered if human men had to have the same type of "skills" that goblins did. "And now?"

"I took a little break from all that." The expression on his face changed, and Niaa decided to drop the subject.

The next couple of days were pleasant, spent mostly in the car, driving. Gustavo was so well-read, he could go on for hours about various topics. Niaa told him about the card games she used to play back home with her servants, being careful not to say anything that implied she wasn't human. Gustavo not knowing she was a goblin or a princess was freeing, relaxing.

Late in the afternoon on the fourth day of their trip, they saw carnival lights blinking in the distance from a large field. Hendry stopped his car on the side of the road, so Gustavo pulled over.

"Let's go, shall we?"

The others had no choice but to follow him, although Niaa couldn't help but ask Gustavo, "I thought Hendry was in a hurry to get back to Dendron to make the medicine for his mother?"

Gustavo shrugged.

They passed by performers eating swords and playing with fire, stands selling jewelry and magical trinkets, women claiming they could predict the future with cards, and sickly, sweet-smelling food. Hendry downed a few homemade brews, his gait getting wider and his voice louder with each step.

"If only you could enjoy the carnival without your mask on," he spoke loudly to Niaa as they looked over trinkets. He put his arm around her shoulders. She ducked away, and then he burped right in her face.

"You're making a fool of yourself." Gustavo grabbed Hendry's shoulders and held him for a few seconds.

"Aw, Gus, don't be so serious." The red color leaked from his face. "I'm just having a bit of fun."

"Apologize to Niaa," Gustavo still didn't let go.

Hendry looked down for a few moments and then looked towards Niaa. "Sorry. I guess."

Niaa shook her head. Then she noticed a game nearby where you could throw darts at balloons.

"Oh, it's fine. But look, Hendry. Didn't you tell us you used to play darts?"

"Oh yeah! Look at that!" He skipped towards the game, leaving the other two behind.

"Are you ok, really?" Gustavo asked her, once Hendry was out of earshot.

"Yeah. It's fine."

"I've known Hendry my whole life. I know he's not evil, but he's got a lot of growing up to do. It's good your father didn't try to marry you off to him. I know how those lesser lords with single daughters get around princes."

Niaa forced a laugh. "Right." The crowds of humans around her stank of sweat. She'd never heard so many people talk at once and was developing a headache.

"What about you? Has your family tried to marry you and your 'skills' off to someone?"

"Sure." He laughed and dug into the ground with his foot. "My parents prefer I marry a noblewoman, but most don't want to join my family out in the boonies and flower plantations, and my great-uncle is pretty eccentric. But only my great-uncle's opinion really matters. He just wants me to marry someone who makes me happy." Gustavo looked at her for a few moments and then patted her shoulder. "I guess Adersanians can't date outside their religion, right?"

"Huh?" Niaa asked. Her head really was pounding now.

"Never mind. Let's not lose Hendry."

Hendry soon grew bored with the games. He saw a tent in the distance claiming to the home of "Freaks, Oddities, and Magical Musings".

"Shall we check it out, Gustavo?"

"Looks a bit tacky—"

"Aw, come on. Lead the way, chap!"

Gustavo shrugged and walked ahead.

Once in the tent, Niaa saw tiny humans, huge humans, bearded women (what was so odd about a woman having hair on her face?), and humans who hammered nails through their tongues. Towards the back were the bones of mermaids, the eggshells of griffins, and the skins of dragons.

"When we were kids, they used to have *live* magical creatures at these things." Hendry scoffed. "Where have they all gone?" He looked at Niaa.

"Can you blame them for hiding from a world that would call them freaks?" Gustavo interjected and put his hands on his hips. Niaa wanted to put her hands on those hips, too, and feel if they were as strong as his arms and hands. What an odd thought!

She wasn't too bothered by the remains of other magical creatures; it was sad, but it wasn't the same as if there had been goblins there. The goblin from a few nights ago had scared her more than this tent could.

"I was hoping I'd see some vivisected goblin bodies and learn more about them after meeting some in person," Hendry moved closer to Niaa.

"Perhaps they're too clever to be caught by the slow, shallow men who like these displays." She straightened her back.

Hendry stared back at her, and the air chilled instantly. She could carry a human corpse for a year.

"It is getting late!" Gustavo interrupted. "We should get going."

They exited the tent, Niaa still feeling like she was ready to tear Hendry into pieces. Gustavo took her hand as they moved through the crowd of people, and the anger inside her drained, mostly. Because Hendry wasn't in a condition to drive, Gustavo took them to a clearing some miles down the road and they set up tents again. This time, Niaa helped Gustavo as Hendry slept in the vehicle. Once they'd gotten a fire going, they sat together.

"I didn't tell you the whole story earlier." Gustavo said after they'd been sitting for a while. "I fell in love with a commoner. My parents were upset. My father is part of the Wizard's Guild and can't inherit a title. So, I am my great-uncle's heir. They wanted me to marry someone who could help the family's finances, and we argued. So, I started spending time with my great-uncle because I knew he could override my parents' decisions. I convinced my uncle that I could run the family and our finances and not make as many mistakes as he did. I don't need to marry a woman from a rich family. He told my parents to allow me to marry the woman I loved."

"And then?" Niaa felt a pit in her stomach.

"…she admitted she actually didn't love me. She just wanted to be a Baroness. But she felt too guilty and couldn't go through with it."

"Why wouldn't she want you?"

"You can't force love. I took the job as Hendry's servant shortly after my engagement ended. I wanted to get away from my gloating parents. I don't regret anything. The situation forced me to get to know my great-uncle, who loves me like a son. And my ex-fiancée taught me to be more open minded and conscious of how much I have that others don't. Now I know I can marry for love, too."

Niaa squeezed his forearm. "I'm sure you will find someone."

He smiled. "I wish I could see your face."

"We should go to bed, yeah?" Niaa turned her face away.

She couldn't risk it because of Hendry. And…what if Gustavo didn't like it?

"May I sit up front?" Niaa asked Gustavo the next morning before getting into the car. Hendry wanted to leave early the next morning to make up for the time they'd lost at the carnival. "It's easier to talk if we sit closer together."

"Oh, Miss Niaa, if you want to be close, then let me oblige," he flipped his hair.

She gulped.

"I'm just kidding!" He opened the passenger side door for her as Hendry revved his car's engine.

She got into the car. She wanted to talk more but couldn't think of what to say. Each moment felt heavy, pregnant with lost potential. She could smell Gustavo's soft leather gloves and fresh aftershave.

His fingers brushed her gloved hand, as he shifted gears, but she moved her hand to her thigh. He flashed a small smile. "Do you know what your black sunglasses remind me of? You know the Elven poet from a few hundred years ago. Marcolaides."

"Yes. I've heard of his poetry but we never had a copy of his work in our libraries." Goblins were in the business of surviving, not collecting books.

"Really? We had to memorize some of his work in school. The poem goes:

a message to those
who doubt the divinity
of all creation

look, to the black, black
eyes of the lowly goblin,
where galaxies swim"

Niaa's head flooded with a hundred feelings. Gustavo's right hand reached up towards her face, but she turned away.

"Sorry, I'm not allowed," she breathed out. Before she could say more, Hendry revved his engine and zoomed ahead.

"I'm not dealing with another breakdown." Gustavo turned back to the road.

"We should hurry up." Niaa insisted, fearing the consequences of the spell.

"Nah, I'm done chasing him."

Niaa bit her lower lip. "We can't let him get so far ahead."

"If he breaks down, he'll have to wait for us." Gustavo shrugged.

Niaa's fingers twitched. A sound-wave, like that of hitting a sheet of metal, but extra-loud, washed over them, and Niaa doubled over as though she were punched in the gut.

"Niaa! What was that? Are you ok?"

"Keep driving," Niaa gasped, the magic pulling at her skin. Gustavo sped up quickly. The magic finally released her, causing her to gasp. They saw Hendry's car up ahead, smoke rising from the hood.

"Ah, shit." Gustavo pulled over. "Are you okay?"

"Yeah. Go check on Hendry."

Hendry and Gustavo decided they had to leave Hendry's car behind. Gustavo moved most of the stuff out of his trunk to Gustavo's car, and Hendry slid into the backseat.

"We have some of the best wizards in the world in Rattesberg." Hendry told her as Gustavo packed. "We'll figure out a way to break the spell."

"That's fine with me." She lied as she still had to figure out how she could use this situation to help her people. But she feared Hendry would make things harder if he knew how much she cared about that. She touched her finger to his knee.

"What are you doing?" He jumped back.

"We have to have some physical contact every once in a while, or we will be in pain."

"Primitive magic."

"That primitive magic broke your car." She turned her head back around when Gustavo approached the driver's seat.

After crossing into Dendron, the landscape grew more hilly. Niaa's eyes widened at the fields of tulips in the distance.

"Maybe after we drop you off, Hendry, Gustavo and I could go sight-seeing to some nearby places." Niaa tested her luck.

"I don't know if that's a good idea," Hendry sounded thoughtful but not angry.

"There's a wonderful cafe nearby the university where you can borrow books." Gustavo's shoulders seemed to relax. Maybe she could convince Hendry to tell Gustavo the truth—

"If you follow that road a few hours you get to Gustavo's great-uncle's farm. If Gustavo hadn't gotten out of there to Rattesberg he'd probably be married to one of his hillbilly cousins—or no, wait—didn't you try to marry some peasant built like an ox?" Hendry laughed.

"There's quite a bit of cousin marriage in the royal family tree." Gustavo responded without taking his eyes from the road.

"True, but if it were up to me, I'd marry some exotic princess from a far-off land—bring in new blood."

"You'd have to stop sleeping with hookers for that to happen." Gustavo sighed.

"Ha! What do you think, Niaa? Do you think it's about time I settle down?"

She leaned her head against the window. "I don't care whom you marry."

"That's a bit harsh. I *did* rescue you from your cave." Hendry forced a smile.

"Huh, what cave?" Gustavo interrupted.

"Ah, Gustavo. I've always been terrible at secrets, and these long drives make me so bored."

Niaa shivered. What game was Hendry playing? They came upon a large billboard on the side of the road with a picture of a long-limbed creature with large ears and sharp fangs, slime dripping from his mouth, and green boils on its skin.

"*This Year's Election: Send the Goblin Back to His Cave!*" the sign read in bright red letters.

"What is that?" Niaa asked.

"Oh, boy," Hendry laughed loudly, the sound piercing Niaa's ears.

"It's not that funny, Hendry." Gustavo shrugged. "Some local positions are decided by election. The tax collector of this part of Dendron is nicknamed 'The Goblin.'"

"Why?" Niaa felt sick.

"He's famously greedy and corrupt." Gustavo answered.

"Goblins are greedy, disgusting creatures that live in caves and eat slime. Duh!" Hendry shouted.

"Oi, Hendry. You don't have to shout."

The ugly drawing had burned the back of Niaa's eyes. She glanced at Gustavo. His expression was neutral. How stupid had she been! Why did it feel like someone had kicked her in the chest, repeatedly? They finally arrived at the gates of the Rattesberg Palace. Niaa thought it was a gaudy thing, with peaked towers, white and gold paint, and plenty of fountains with naked humans.

"Niaa's staying at the palace." Hendry told Gustavo. "I'll handle the rest. You've earned a few days off."

The newspapers praised Hendry for bringing back the gyapa mushrooms to help the queen. The palace wizards were busy brewing medicine for her spine, and Hendry was to be honored at a ceremony.

A couple of days later, Gustavo was invited by Hendry to go golfing. Gustavo didn't play golf; he was there to make sure Hendry's rich friends didn't mock him too much, but Gustavo didn't mind. He wanted this chance to ask about Niaa. He hadn't seen her since dropping her off at the palace. Why hadn't they dropped her off at the university?

He figured Hendry had been lying about her identity. The goblin at the casino had called her a princess. So few countries still had royalty, so that narrowed things, but he couldn't figure it out. When got lost in his thoughts, he played with the blue scales in his pocket. Would he ever see the angel who'd dropped these scales again?

"You think you could do me a favor?" he asked one of the palace servants while Hendry was distracted. "I've got a book I'd like to give to the woman who arrived with Hendry. But I don't want Hendry to know about it." Gustavo produced a small red book from his bag.

"I'll see what I can do. I feel a bit bad for her—they don't seem to want her to leave the palace. Do you know who she is? Some people say she's not actually human. Still, the maids say she has great manners."

Gustavo had been so dense! She wasn't human, which explained the costume and the lie about her religion to explain that costume. What was she?

"Niaa, it's Hendry," he spoke more softly than usual. "I'm alone." He unlocked and opened the door.

Niaa was seated at the end of her bed, her head exposed. Her large ears twitched as he entered the room, but she was staring out the window, where she could see a very tall and old tree, its branches nearly clasping the windowsill.

"Sorry about the rough few days, Niaa. I know it must feel a bit stifling locked in here. But you know how terrible people would act if everyone knew you're a goblin. I'm protecting you." Hendry took a deep breath and then sat on the other side of the bed. "Niaa, I have a solution for our problem that would benefit both of us."

Niaa turned to Hendry now; she wiggled her diamond nose. Hendry stopped himself from recoiling.

"The Grand Master Warlock can't break our bond, but he has a spell that could turn you human. Then we could have a proper engagement. We are both the youngest royal children in our families. We could help each other."

"What if I don't want to be human?" Niaa asked, thinking of losing her blue scales, her ears and nose shrinking.

"But you would be a beautiful, rich princess. You wouldn't have to hide in a cave. I know I haven't been kind to you. But I'm ready to settle down. You're intelligent. You understand royal life." He paused. "Your father has wealth he'd give me."

"You're asking me to change myself, totally, for you."

"What kind of life will you have out of the goblin caves looking like…how you look?" He forced himself to try to put his hand on her shoulder, but she slid away. He snatched his hand back. "I don't know of any noblemen in Dendron who will trade honey or flowers with goblins, especially without royal permission," he hissed. Hendry stood up and smoothed his shirt. She'd probably change her mind, soon enough, Hendry thought to himself before exiting.

Niaa spent most of the day wondering about what Hendry had asked her to do. After the moon rose that night, Niaa put her gloves, mask, robe, and glasses in a bag she carried over her shoulder. A soft breeze rustled the trees outside. Centuries ago, goblins had lived in trees and mountains, not in caves. That scaled pretty skin that stretched from their upper arms to their upper thighs facilitated gliding. And the long claws on her hands and prehensile feet helped climb trees. In the caves, most goblins didn't climb or glide; they only got a chance during the few hours of the night when they harvested nectar. Near her window was a tree perfect for climbing down. She hopped onto the windowsill.

She leapt from the sill to the tree trunk, gripping hard, feeling her claws sink. She shuffled down the tree to the ground, then snuck through the small patch of woods to the edge of Rattesberg proper. Once there, she dressed herself in the clothes that would hide her appearance. She wasn't brave enough to walk around without them.

She had learned that there was a large casino called the Rial not too far from the palace. She made her way there, past closed shops and a few apartment buildings. The city smells of smog and garbage filled her nose. As she got closer to the casino, she smelled fried food, and the streets became more crowded with humans of all different nationalities.

The Rial was known for its Turn Tiles tables. She entered through large golden doors, the attendants giving her a slight bow as she passed. They didn't seem to react to her strange dress. The casino accepted her Tabasdan money so she could buy into a Turn Tiles game. She won four rounds in a row and attracted a small crowd that kept buying her drinks.

The alcohol gave her a different feeling than eating the hallucinogenic tena moss back in the goblin caves. She felt so relaxed, the multi-colored lights reflecting off the shining silver décor of the casino seemed extra bright but also blurry. Everyone's smile looked so warm and nice. She took her winnings, and walked to the bar. She leaned against the counter, which was a deep shiny blue, reminding her of her own scales.

"Have you ever played poker, Niaa? Let's try a game. You're clever enough to win big," one of her new friends asked.

The other players at the table let her practice a few hands, a balding man with a thick mustache and a cigar was especially encouraging.

"Now look, Miss," said Cigar Man. He took a deep drag before speaking again, "I heard that you're from some strict religion, and you can't show your face, but if you are going to play poker, most players get a bit uncomfortable if there's someone playing with their whole face covered. You can see our expressions to guess when we might be bluffing, but we can't see yours."

Niaa gave a quick glance to the security team near the door, two men and a large orc, the small horns on his forehead looked extra sharp. Would it really hurt for them to know what she was? She thought of the goblin at the other casino and of the signs about the politician. But she wasn't a cheater or covered in boils. The liquid courage in her stomach bubbled through her veins. If they wanted her to play poker unmasked, then fine. She would.

"Hold on." Niaa brought her hands to her face, removed her glasses, her eyes squinting at the sudden rush of light into her pupils. She pulled the mask off, and as she did, her hood fell off her head to her shoulders, her ears popping free with a satisfying spring.

"I knew there was something fishy. You're a goddamned goblin." The cigar had dropped from the man's mouth.

"Sorry, we don't let goblins play at the tables. Just the slots," the dealer said as he swept the cards into his hand.

"Why can't I just play? I won't do anything. I'm no wizard. I've no magic. I'm just—"

"We don't need you stinking up the table." Cigar Man's breath reeked as he spoke.

"What is wrong with you? You didn't think I smelled two minutes ago—" Her fist slammed on the table.

"You better get moving," Cigar Man poked his finger into her chest.

"Don't you dare touch me," she shrieked and swatted his hand away, jumping backwards and knocking over her chair. The crowd was parting, and security was moving towards her. She untangled her feet from the chair and she dashed towards the opposite door. The crowd moved slightly for her. Her head still felt like mush, her senses a bit fuzzy from the alcohol, but she thought she heard some people booing.

"Don't listen to them. You're a cute little monster," someone cackled.

Once outside, she ran down the street, grabbing the pipe on the side of a building and climbing upward to the roof. She dashed from one building to the next till she got to the forest. Her head spinning, somehow she made it through the trees, over the fence around the palace grounds, and back up through the window to her room. Once there, she collapsed on her bed, her lungs sucking in air so deeply, her chest felt like it would burst.

Hours later, she soaked in her bath, watching the dirt leave her body in swirls. Hendry was right. She'd never have a normal life outside the caves as a goblin. And what if she returned home to her brother and sister, who just wanted to be rid of her?

She pulled dirt and other bits from under her claws. She could do worse than Hendry, right? She'd be a wealthy woman in a wealthy kingdom, and all these humans would be her servants, catering to her whims. So what if Hendry was a drunk? Unwanted goblin princesses weren't meant to find love or happiness. Her species just needed to survive.

She heard a soft knock on her bedroom door, and heard it click open.

"Miss Niaa?" came a woman's voice. The door to the bath swung open, and a stout servant woman entered.

"Oh, my! I heard you were a magic creature, but I didn't know you'd be…"

Niaa stood up from the bath and pulled a towel from next to the tub, wrapping it around herself, for comfort more than modesty. She wouldn't be a goblin much longer, anyway.

"We all thought you were a magical creature—not one of us guessed you were a goblin, though! I mean, you still look enough like goblin drawings I've seen before, but in person you're prettier than I imagined a real goblin to be. Sorry. Actually, I have something to give you without Hendry here."

"Ah, thanks." Niaa dried her hands and the woman moved back towards the door, her eyes on Niaa's scales.

"Forgive me, Miss Niaa, but you give me hope. If a goblin, of all things, could get asked by Prince Hendry to stay at the palace, maybe the rest of us homely peasant girls have hope, too." She cackled and left the room. Niaa picked up the book.

POEMS BY MARCOLAIDES

She opened the cover. Inside was a small handwritten note.

"Niaa,

We had so much fun during our road trip. You made dealing with Hendry tolerable. I'm sorry if I said something wrong. I hope you're okay. My room is just above the garage where the royal family keeps all the cars. You should stop by sometime.

-Gustavo"

She hugged the book close to her chest. Perhaps she'd stay a goblin just one more day. She wanted Gustavo, her first human friend, to see her, just once, how she really was. Then she'd know what to do.

Late that night, she snuck out of her room. She made her way towards the garage where the cars were kept. She could see the light in Gustavo's room was on. There was a fire escape ladder that led to a balcony outside his window. She climbed it, and peaked inside Gustavo's room. The sting of his comments about goblins from just a few days ago still hurt, but maybe he didn't know any better.

He sat at his desk, the low light of a lamp illuminating the soft features of his face as he leaned over a book. He looked so peaceful. Why should a monster interrupt his solitude?

You are no monster, she told herself.

She breathed in deeply and knocked on the window. Gustavo jumped at the noise and then turned.

"What? Niaa?" She heard him say. He walked to the window and twisted the lock, then pushed the pane open. "What are you doing here so late?"

"I've been locked in my room," she told him. "I managed to get out by climbing a tree next to my window."

"How did you? I'll have to speak to Hendry—why would they do something—"

"Gustavo, calm down, please." She placed her hands on his shoulders and squeezed. He gulped. She was wearing her hood, but not her mask or glasses. He turned to look at her glove-less hands. His breath caused the small hairs of his mustache to move.

"Niaa, What have you been keeping from me?"

She removed her hands from his shoulders and pulled her hood down. His eyes widened. She unhooked the buttons of her loose robe, and letting it slide off her body and pool to the floor. His eyes wandered from her ears, her black eyes, her mouth, down her slender, strong body, the glistening blue scales, to the tips of the sharp claws on her feet.

"I am a goblin princess, Gustavo. My father wanted to ally with Dendron, so he had his wizard magically bind me to Hendry for a year. He hopes that we will come back after two years to marry and to solidify the alliance and set up a trade deal where we get access to the flowers and nectar from Dendron. My people struggle to survive, hiding in the caves, taking what little nectar we can get."

Gustavo put his hand in his right pocket. He removed two blue scales and presented them to her. "You were the angel I saw that night."

"I am a goblin. No angel."

He raised his hand to her face and turned it back to him.

"Whatever you are, I think you are beautiful," he whispered.

Panic rose inside Niaa. This had to be a human trick, right? Did he want to steal her scales? She had to get out of here. She backed away from him.

"Tomorrow, we will complete a spell that will turn me human. Then Hendry and I will get married. He wants my father to reward him with my goblin kingdom's wealth. And with a Prince of Dendron as an ally to the goblins, perhaps I can help my people."

"Oh, Niaa. You will marry Hendry? That's no life for someone like you. You are smart and have a good heart." He tried to grab her hands in his, but she put them behind her.

"Who cares what Hendry is like? Humans hate me. And I have a duty to help my people."

"I could help you escape. We could get you back to your family."

"I have a duty to my people. You remember the way the goblin was treated at the casino. They…am I really so disgusting to you?" Nia lowered her head. She felt Gustavo's hands on her waist. He pulled her down, and they both sat at the edge of the bed. Gustavo touched her cheek gently.

"I am sorry. I could never think you are disgusting." He pulled her head to his chest. Niaa realized that the gramophone in the corner was playing a song, something sweet and bouncy, the jazz instrumentals dancing into her ears, massaging her mind. Gustavo leaned back, and she lay against his chest. He started to hum lowly, along with the tune, his deep voice vibrating his chest and giving her goosebumps that raised her fur.

He ran his fingers over her scales, finding the sensitive skin between them. Her toes and fingers curled. Niaa wasn't sure how much time passed like that, but eventually his humming stopped, and he began lightly snoring instead. She sat up. He was kind, but she'd seen what humans thought of her people. Humans and goblins had mated in the past—she couldn't think like that. Hendry would never let her. She couldn't incur Hendry's wrath on Gustavo.

She stood up to leave, but turned back one last time. She quietly moved around the bed and knelt next to his face. His full, pink lips looked so sweet, attractive as the center of a pink daisy in full bloom. She moved her face close to his and touched her own lips to his, breathing in as he breathed out, the smell of him making her want to run her fingers over his body and explore how different or similar it was to her own.

She heard a noise outside and straightened in surprise. It was just an owl, she realized.

She yearned to stay longer, but if she stayed, she'd lose her conviction to do what she had to. Goblins were lucky at cards but not in all other things, like humans. She exited through the open window, a few stray tears leaking from the corners of her eyes.

Gustavo woke up a half an hour later and realized that Niaa had left. He was still in shock. He paced around his room. He felt like such a moron, thinking of what he'd said about goblins. Of course she wouldn't trust him! Niaa was nothing like he'd have imagined a goblin to be, both in appearance and character. She was so fascinating. He couldn't stop thinking about her or worrying about her future with Hendry.

As soon as the sun rose, he made his way to the library, picking through books about goblins. How much time did he have before Niaa and Hendry did the spell? He couldn't let her throw her life away.

But was Hendry really that bad? And maybe it was best for her people, he thought as he read about how few goblins there were left in the world. *No.* She deserved someone who would care about her. What human would care about a goblin? He looked down at his book with its inaccurate, gross drawing of a goblin and thought of seeing Niaa in his bedroom: the feeling of her head on his chest, the intensity of her gaze, the beautiful colors of her body, the softness of her skin and fur, the magic of her voice, and the curves of her very human-like hips. Who cares if she wasn't human? He wanted to make her happy. He wanted to feel her against him again.

He went back to his room. There, he grabbed the phone from his desk and dialed for the operator and asked to be connected to his great-uncle's farm.

"Do you want to sell more flowers than ever? I have a new business opportunity for our family," he told his uncle.

"Gustavo!" shouted one of the servant boys from the stairs. "Hendry has taken the red convertible coupe. He said they were driving up to Mara's Hill."

Gustavo jumped to his feet. Mara's Hill was the nearest celestial spot to Rattesberg. It was a place for complex spells. He had no time to waste. Gustavo put on his leather jacket and driving gloves and goggles.

"Get my Silver Bullet ready," he commanded. "I'm going for a ride."

He charged down the stairs and hopped onto the bike, revved the engine a couple of times, and sped out onto the road, dust clouds kicking up behind him.

Around fifteen minutes later, he was pushing against gravity, climbing to the peak of Mara's Hill, its long, yellow-green grass waved in the wind blowing against him. In the distance were three figures that he could barely see through his now dust covered goggles: Hendry, the Grand Master, who was busy kneeling on the ground and drawing in the dirt, and the hooded, robed, Niaa. He stopped his bike and got off it, kicking the stand out, pulling the goggles up from his eyes, and then walking towards the others.

"Oi! Gustavo? What are you doing here?" Hendry called out.

"I'm here to speak with Niaa," he shouted back and kept approaching. The Grand Master looked up from his work.

"You know, she's my fiancée, Gustavo. This is highly inappropriate."

"Gustavo?" Niaa shouted.

"I'm here, Niaa. I'm here! Don't do it!" He returned, his voice echoing loudly through the hills.

She started running towards him, the hood of her robe flying from off her head, revealing her ears and her goblin face. Gustavo opened his arms, and she ran into him, wrapping him in her embrace. She smelled refreshing, like rain during spring-time.

Gustavo looked up to see Hendry charging towards them. He grabbed Niaa's arm and pulled her back. "We have a spell to cast. You're going to be my fiancée. You can't just go around hugging male servants." He turned to Gustavo, nostrils flaring. "What do you think you're doing?"

"I came here to stop Niaa from agreeing to the spell. And to apologize. I said a lot of stupid things to you, Niaa, when I didn't know what you were. But I shouldn't have said them to begin with. I am an ignorant human. I know I don't know you well, but I care about you, Niaa. You don't have to marry Hendry."

"It's none of your business! Her father agreed to the arrangement. She agreed to turn human for me."

"She will never be happy with you, Hendry. You are a cowardly drunk. Maybe Niaa will turn into a beautiful human princess, and her father will send you riches. But you won't magically fall in love with her or change your ways just because she changes form."

"How would you know?" Hendry spat.

"Unlike you, I don't want her to change. I want her, just as she is."

"What?" Niaa gasped.

"What a bunch of bullshit." Hendry pulled his pistol from his pocket and pointed it at Gustavo. "Go home, old chap."

Niaa leapt at Hendry from the side, knocking him from his feet and onto his back, sending the pistol flying from his hand. She pinned him down and opened her wide mouth, revealing sharp teeth and a long, thin tongue. She quickly slashed the claws on her right hand across his right cheek, leaving a thin cut, then she stood. Gustavo ran over to the pistol and picked it up.

"What the hell!" Hendry rolled to his side.

"Whoa!" The Grand Master Warlock stepped in the middle of them. "Let's all calm down. There is, perhaps, another solution to Hendry and Niaa's predicament. Unfortunately, I cannot break the bond that binds Hendry and Niaa, but I can move that bond to another, willing participant. Gustavo, I could move the bond to you and Niaa. But the rules and length of the spell would remain the same."

"Niaa," Gustavo turned to her. "I would be willing to be bonded to you, for the year. I spoke to my great-uncle this morning. Uncle William owns one of the biggest flower farms in the whole country. He is more than willing to begin selling nectar, honey, and flowers to the goblins. We could both live with Uncle William for the year—he doesn't care you're a goblin. Humans in that part of the country are more used to magical creatures—we can try to make them accept you, too. It won't come without its challenges, but I'm willing to try."

"More hogwash." Hendry held his bleeding cheek. "I'm the one who found Niaa. Where is my goblin gold?"

Gustavo turned to the prince. "We would need royal permission to begin trading with the goblin kingdom. And whoever in the palace helps arrange that permission would get a cut of the revenue, Hendry. You know you'd get bored of being married to Niaa within a week. You aren't heartless."

"Fine. I always imagined I'd marry a mermaid, anyway. Sorry for that business with the gun…and for trying to force you to change your species. Just take this damn curse off me."

"Niaa? What do you say?"

Niaa squeezed Gustavo's hand. "Let's do it."

The Grand Master arranged all three of their left hands, then he mumbled some words. When the spell was finished, Hendry and the Grand Master stepped back. Gustavo pulled Niaa into a tight embrace, breathing her in and feeling two strong heartbeats against his chest.

"Wait, you have two hearts? What other secrets are you hiding?"

"You have much to learn." She stuck out her long tongue, touching the tip to his cute little human nose.

Eli and the Golden Caves
Cliff Jones Jr.

There are some truths that can't help but ring false, some revelations so unsettling that the only thing to do is laugh them off and just go about your business. People, once they reach a certain age, aren't half so open-minded as they imagine themselves to be. This is why so many fairy stories involve children.`

I was still a child when my understanding of the world and humanity's place in it was shattered beyond all hope of reconstruction. I accepted this new truth at the time, but the older I get, the more I doubt myself. It would certainly be easier if I could forget the whole thing or make myself believe it was only a dream. But I know it wasn't.

It started with me running through the woods. I had no idea where I was headed, just far away from my school. I couldn't go back there. I wasn't even sure I could go home again, not after the mess I'd made.

Corporal punishment was still a thing back then, and I'd taken my share of beatings for my smart mouth. But today I'd picked up the paddle first and smacked the principal with it right across his fat face. There was an initial moment of shock when neither of us fully believed what had just happened. But Mr. Ortiz's expression soon changed to righteous indignation, and then pure malevolent fury. I could tell that he was about to really let me have it, so I grabbed the first thing off his desk I could use as a weapon, and I struck first. It was some kind of an award, a big bronze globe atop a black pyramidal base. I'll never forget the feeling of that thing colliding with the side of Mr. Ortiz's head. The dull, wet sound it made. I didn't expect it to give way so easily, to *collapse* like that. Compared to metal, a skull isn't much, I guess.

So I ran. And I kept running, long after I probably could have stopped to catch my breath. I felt like there was nothing left for me back home. It was honestly a relief to get away from my parents, my brother, my sisters…I'd always fantasized about running away, and here I was finally doing it.

Eventually, I came to a creek and decided to rest there awhile. The water was flowing at a nice pace, and it looked relatively clean, so I took a drink. No immediate diarrhea, so I figured I'd be all right there for a few days. Finding food was harder. It wasn't the right season for blackberries, and I didn't know much else about foraging. I spent one hungry night in the dirt using dried leaves as a blanket, and in the morning, I took a chance on some mushrooms. They *smelled* fine, at least. For mushrooms. They didn't taste like much, but I survived to tell the tale, so I guess I chose well.

After dark, I found a hollow spot on the creek bank and settled in there for the night. I still had no clue what I was going to do next, how I was going to go on with my life. The weight of this finally hit me, and I started sobbing like a little baby. I felt like I was probably going to die out there and there was nothing I could do about it. I doubted I could find my way back to the school even if I tried.

Sometime in the night, I had a creeping sensation that I was being watched. I stopped crying and scanned the darkness all around me for something to confirm my suspicion. After a while, I ventured an unsteady "Hello?"

Then all at once I saw them: two little people—a man

and a woman—with pale baby faces and no hair on their disproportionately swollen heads. Their eyes were the strangest part. They were so large and dark that they didn't seem *human*. I just sat there in silence for a few minutes, paralyzed at the sight of them, until the man spoke up: "Don't be afraid. Follow me."

That was all the little man said, but it was enough for me. I walked behind the two of them as they led me into a cave I'd never noticed before. Trying to recall this now, I must have been in some kind of a trance. None of it felt real. I couldn't say how long we walked, but the deeper we went into the cave, the brighter everything got. There was this golden light that seemed to come from the air itself. No shadows anywhere. Eventually, the cave opened up into a cavern so vast that clouds covered its ceiling, looking almost like an open sky. Countryside spread out before me, lush and green as anything on the surface.

Finally, I made the connection to where I'd seen creatures like these two before. "Are you…*aliens*?" I asked.

The woman, who'd been silent so far, answered in a foreign language. But somehow I understood her: "No more than you, child. This planet is our home, and we've been here far longer than your kind. We simply avoid the surface because the conditions are harsh and corrupting. If you stay down here with us, you'll see: Death is unnecessary."

We walked until the countryside became a city of stone, metal, and plastic. It was called "Alnoven," if I remember right, just one city of thousands buried beneath mountains and bedrock in a global system of Golden Caves. At the center of the city stood a sprawling palace. I felt no fatigue even though I'd barely eaten in days. Something about the air down there sustained me. Or maybe it was that golden light. My elfin guides brought me to the ruler of Alnoven, whose name was something like "Bregan."

Up to this point, I can tell the story clearly because it didn't depart *too* drastically from my understanding of the world. Those little gray aliens I grew up hearing about weren't actually aliens, and they lived underground. I could sort of handle that. But meeting Bregan was a bridge too far. He wasn't human, not even close like the little people were. But he wasn't an animal either. He made *me* feel like an animal. Seeing his powerful reptilian features towering over me, I understood the overwhelming dread that all the old stories of dragons were trying to communicate. But it wasn't only that. I was actually *embarrassed* to stand there where Bregan could see me. I'd never be anything more than an ape, no matter what I learned or achieved in my life. I was pitiful. Ridiculous. I still feel that way, all these years later.

At first, Bregan was furious at my guides for bringing me there, but then his son Mav spoke up: "Let me keep him, Dad! Please?"

So I wound up staying with Mav as something between his personal servant and a family pet. My memory of life there in the Golden Caves is kind of hazy, but I do recall a few things, like fragments rescued from a dream. I'll fill in the gaps with guesses and let you decide what rings true and what doesn't.

Mav taught me what happened to the dinosaurs the same way you might hear about European colonizers setting sail in the fifteenth century. Apparently, a global climate shift made the surface pretty much uninhabitable for their kind. But even way back then—millions of years before humans, or primates of any kind—some of the dinosaurs were advanced enough to move underground and survive there, adapting to their situation. And that's what they've been doing ever since: adapting and evolving and genetically engineering themselves into something as far beyond humanity as we are beyond cattle.

As for the little gray people—the ones you already know about with their flying saucers and crop circles and all that— they were bred as companions for the reptilians, the same way we breed dogs. They started millions of years ago from early amphibious cetaceans. So they're kind of related to dolphins, but only like humans are related to lemurs. I learned all of this from Mav, since I couldn't make sense of the writing they used down there and nobody but Mav ever really spoke to me, except to give me short commands or to call me to the dining hall for mealtime.

Mav also taught me to fetch. We played a variety of games together, but I always got the impression he was simplifying the rules for me. I mean, you can teach a dog to catch a tennis ball in its mouth and bring it back to you, but you can't expect that dog to pick up a racket and compete in a tournament. The game we played most often involved a golden sphere that floated in the air and moved around on its own depending on how you looked at it and gestured with your hands. I saw others moving similar spheres around through a series of rings set up in the palace garden, but all Mav and I ever did was send the one sphere back and forth with little variation.

After a few weeks of living in the palace, my initial terror of Bregan and his people began to fade. True, they were still much bigger than me and had way too many teeth, but they no longer seemed so monstrous. I guess you can get used to anything given enough time. Or maybe there was some kind of reptilian mind control going on; I really couldn't tell you. Whatever the reason, I gradually started to feel like one of them, like I actually belonged in Alnoven.

When I finally got up the courage, I asked Mav, "Do you think I might be able to go back and visit the surface world for a little while, just to let my parents know I'm okay?"

"I don't think my dad would like that," Mav answered. "So let's not tell him." His throat let out a series of rapid clicks, which served the same purpose as a smile.

Mav arranged for one of the little gray residents of Alnoven to accompany me, and we set out that night. This time, the tunnel opened up in the woods just down the road from my house. I still have no idea how they knew where I lived. It's probably best not to dwell on that.

When I got to my front door, I could tell something was wrong right away. It was too dark to see the yard very well, but everything seemed overgrown and faded. When my mom answered the door, that impression was only strengthened. She had gray hair and lines on her face like she'd aged twenty or thirty years.

When she first saw me, I knew she recognized me, but then her face hardened, and she pretended not to know me at all. "Can I…help you?" she asked.

"Mom? It's—It's me," I stammered. "It's Eli!"

"That's not funny." Her stern expression deepened into cold rage. "How dare you? You should be ashamed of yourself! My son is dead!"

"*I'm* your son, Mom. Me! Where's Dad?"

"My husband passed away last year. So you're hassling an old widow who's lost everyone she ever cared about. I hope you're proud of yourself."

She tried to shut the door, but I held it open long enough to say, "I'll prove it to you! I'll be back—I'll come back with—with something to prove I'm telling the truth!"

And that was that. My own mother didn't want anything to do with me. I'd been gone much longer than I thought, apparently. And I'm sure it didn't help that my principal probably died from that head wound I gave him. So I was a murderer, my dad was dead, and I still looked like a kid, so nobody would believe I was who I said I was. Unless I brought back something to show everybody Alnoven was real. That might do it. I knew that none of the little people or the reptilians would ever show themselves just to help me out. We didn't have that kind of relationship.

So the next night, I grabbed one of the golden spheres and went back on the same path to my house. I made it all the way through the tunnel before I started to hear footsteps behind me. I was so close I figured I could just make a run for it. I didn't even look back. I ran as hard as I could until I was back on the front porch of my childhood home. I knocked, but before anyone could answer, I felt a burning shock in my veins, and I collapsed in a heap, letting the sphere I was carrying drop with me. I watched helplessly as it rolled to the edge of the porch and fell off the side.

When someone finally answered, it wasn't my mom.

"Oh my gosh, are you okay?" It was some blonde lady I'd never seen before answering the door of my parents' house, of *my* house. "Are you hurt? What's the matter, sweetie?" She nudged me around trying to position me better, but I was paralyzed and unable to speak for a good half hour.

And that's really the end of my story. I tried to find my way back to Alnoven, of course, but the cave entrance just wasn't there. It wasn't anywhere along the river I could find. And believe me, I looked. I'd been caught trying to steal from my master Bregan, and he had no tolerance for that. I was like a dog that had bitten somebody or dug too many holes in the yard, and they'd just let me "go free" in the country.

I can understand how being a free man is better in a sense. But honestly, if you believe what I've told you, you can see how none of us are free, right? It's better to be allowed into the house than left outdoors to fend for yourself. I won't make it another century on the surface, while Bregan, Mav, and the rest go on and on. Call me selfish. Call me a coward. I don't really care what humans think. I just want to go back to the Golden Caves, to find my place in Alnoven among the little people and the reptilian lords of Earth.

If you're listening, Bregan, take me back! I beg you. I'm sorry. I'm so sorry.

Insomnia Ate My Soul
Lucy Zhang

Impale my hand on a stop signpost for all I care, she told Seb. Melatonin didn't work; she'd take anything at this rate. She sat in front of the spinning wheel, setting the tension of the threads and running the leader gently through the orifice. Then she spun. As the wheel turned, she placed her finger on the spindle, watched red bloom across her whorled finger. Seb said this was the fastest way to fall asleep. Of course, shortcuts had consequences and she might not wake, he cautioned. She waved her hand, droplets of blood flying from her wound like Lysol spray. Seb shrugged, *your choice.*

Seb was here to monitor her sleep, listen to her heart and breath rate, tape electrodes to her forehead scrubbed with acetone, watch the brain wave machine pens scribbling and graph paper unfurling. *And after this, you'll eat my soul?* She confirmed again. But of course, that was how deals were made: give and take, sleep for dreams, dreams for sleep. Seb had insisted she understood what she'd be giving up—no more tea parties or chance encounters with fairy godmothers. *Aren't you my fairy godmother?* They both laughed. *And you'll watch out for anyone?* She continued. Otherwise, the prince might climb through her window if she suddenly stopped responding to his calls.

The best choice was what the king and queen referred to the prince as. The best choice, she thought to herself each night, under an open window so the cold could seep through, her nipples hardening like stale peas, slipping down her dress to prevent her spine from sinking into the mattress. She'd press her fingers between her legs, rub in circles to the tick of an imaginary metronome, repeating *the best choice the best choice* until her fingers grew numb, and the white canopy draped above her bed became the only sky she could fathom. *Of course,* Seb said. He was reliable, probably a result of getting hurled down to earth from La-la land, sense and expediency hard-knocked into his head, not at all like the fairies who kept gifting her things without price tags. *When will I fall asleep?* she asked, eyes shut, head lolled to one side. *Soon,* he said. *Don't wake me up,* she reminded him. As her breathing slowed, Seb placed another blanket over her body and locked the window.

Vasilisa and the Night Witches
Laurel Beckley

"Are you here of your own free will, or by compulsion, Vasilisa Ivanova?"

Vasya stared deep into the eyes of her questioner.

Major Vera Yaba, regimental commander of the 588th, crossed her arms and started tapping her foot. Her too-thin leg bounced with each pulse of her boot-tip. Behind her, mechanics darted about the snow and mud-covered airfield, rushing to replace their precious Polikarpov U-2 biplanes' wheels before the night's bombing run against the fascists.

"Largely by my own free will," Vasya replied.

Yaba's eyes narrowed, her large nose twitching as if detecting the lie.

"And twice as much by compulsion!" Vasya added hastily.

Yaba snorted. She seemed to fill the entire space of the mobile pop-up hangar. "Very well," she said, although her eyes narrowed further. "And you were sent to report on the extreme efficiency of the 588th?"

The German Army had been pushed back, back, back since the fall of Stalingrad the previous winter. Their powerful tanks and vicious airplanes were no match for Soviet determination. Their wolf soldiers were nothing against the selfless bravery of the Red Army.

At least, that was the party line.

Vasya knew better.

The Red Army was fighting hard, but their resources were running low. Every effort was made to increase efficiency and economy—which was why the all-women 588th Night Bomber Regiment's nightly wheel replacement was so alarming. The 588th was achieving remarkable results, but the Stavka could no longer ignore the wastefulness. The three commissars sent one by one by one to investigate had mysteriously vanished, and for some reason the Stavka had sent an injured junior sergeant sniper to complete the investigation. Vasya had experienced enough of the brutality of the Soviet machine towards its own people to know when someone was being set up.

"Yes, ma'am."

"And you have three days to conduct your report?"

Vasya nodded, not trusting her voice. She'd lost so much—family, comrades, her career as a sniper—but there was so much more to lose. She didn't dare disobey the Stavka, not even when the fall person was her.

Yaba turned towards the blonde officer standing beside her. "Junior Lieutenant Azizovna will let you get familiar with the regiment and our operations. We have much work to do to prepare for our sorties, so no idle hands, yes?"

Azizovna saluted. Yaba stalked off, bellowing orders.

The junior lieutenant studied Vasya for a long moment. The sun peeked through the clouds, casting dark shadows under her eyes and leeching the color from her hair until it was as grey as the snow surrounding them. "You may call me Anya," she offered.

Vasya blinked at the informality. "Vasya," she replied, giving a tentative smile. The other girl seemed about her own age.

Anya smiled back. It didn't reach her eyes. "Let me show you around."

It was the middle of the day, so the regiment's planes—Anya called them "princesses"—were grounded. Her reluctance vanished as she gave Vasya the tour, waxing poetic on each princess' pilot, navigator, mechanical quirk and maintenance cycle, and pointing out how the 588th managed to double and triple their sorties by grouping mechanics by function instead of assigning them to individual aircraft.

"It's against the order of operations, but very efficient," Anya explained, ignoring Vasya's limp and her struggle to keep up.

"Is that why the wheels need replacing each night?" Vasya asked.

Anya frowned. "I just remembered that Major Yaba wanted you to have a seated job, inside the hangar, to rest that leg."

Before Vasya could protest, she was hustled inside and confronted with a mound of bolts, screws, pins, nuts, and other metallic objects she couldn't name. The entire mess was surrounded by empty bins that looked like they had been recently up-ended to create the organizational disaster. Several pins were still rolling about the metal floor.

"Major Yaba said to organize this," Anya said, and left before Vasya could protest or ask more questions.

Vasya stared in dismay. In a regiment that prided itself on order, efficiency, and operational success, this chaos was worthy of a firing squad.

But the task presented more important problems.

Vasya might be under orders to investigate the 588th, but she had no authority to trump the command of a junior lieutenant. If she disobeyed Anya, she could be shot—but if she failed in her mission, she'd be killed by a firing squad, if she was lucky. Vanished to Siberia and the rumored super-soldier labs, if not. She did not think she would be lucky.

"How will I ever organize all of this by tonight?" she murmured, but sat down to begin sorting.

She finished as the red night lamps flickered on, throwing the hangar into hazy light, revealing odd rib-like vertical studs. She squinted. Those looked like bones. She focused harder on the interesting architecture. The beginnings of a headache throbbed between her eyebrows, and in a pulse similar to a dying heartbeat, the struts running parallel to the floor shuddered from femurs into plain aluminum and steel.

She rubbed her forehead, smearing lubricant across her skin. The hangar was just a normal mobile hangar, built for expedient maneuver in a rapidly changing battlefield. Exhaustion was making her delirious.

"I see you finished the task," Yaba said from behind her.

Vasya jumped and turned, heart pounding.

The regimental commander loomed, shadow stretching crimson across the hangar's floor. Anya stood beside her. "Here," Yaba offered, holding out a flask. "For your pain, and for finishing so quickly. Truly you are a daughter of the Soviet Union."

Vasya took the flask and drank, nearly coughing up the stiff vodka. It burned down her throat, but the pain in her leg dulled.

She took another sip.

The pain weakened further.

She took a third.

Her head spun deliciously as Yaba handed her a pirozhki. Vasya gobbled down the pastry, her half-starved stomach and alcohol-addled brain screaming with joy as she washed everything down with a reinvigorating fourth gulp.

She felt like she could conquer the fascist army all by herself.

Yaba smiled, but Anya just bit her lip and wrung her hands.

"Good. Now you can watch the might of the women of the 588th in action," Yaba declared and led the way out of the hangar.

Vasya followed, squinting into the darkness.

Women darted about each plane, loading bombs and fuel to ready their princesses for the night's duties. Anya stepped away, headed to her own princess for the night's sorties.

Vasya's head spun, exhaustion hitting like the slug from a German Kar98k. The pain returned, the memory of the wolf soldier's teeth sinking into her thigh, ripping away flesh and life. Her leg buckled and she put a hand against the hangar for balance.

Yaba patted her on the shoulder, gently pushing until Vasya was seated on the ground with her back leaning against the hangar's outer wall.

The exhaustion she'd been fighting caught up with her. The supports poked her through her thick sniper jacket, feeling more and more like bones as her eyes drifted shut to the lullaby of the U-2s' engines.

She dreamt the engines were pestles grinding in mortars, and that she rode in a hangar with chicken legs instead of tracks and human bones in place of metal walls.

Vasya woke to a blinding headache and a boot kicking her in the side.

Yaba and Anya stood above her, the former scowling, the latter worrying her lip.

"Have you found your answers, Vasilisa Ivanova?" Yaba asked.

"I don't dare to speak," Vasya croaked. She felt like vomiting.

Yaba's lips curled into a smile. "No laze-abouts," she declared. The morning light made her teeth sharp and pointed. "Today you help replace all of the princesses' wheels."

Replacing the wheels of a Polikarpov U-2 was a relatively simple process. Unlike the multi-engine or jet-propelled fighters and heavy bombers, the U-2 was an ancient biplane. Its parts could be easily replaced or jury-rigged.

But not wheels that were completely destroyed. Each princess sported tires that weren't just balding or flat—they all had fist-sized chunks punched through the thick rubber. They had to be completely replaced, the spares taken from swiftly dwindling stocks.

As grease from the plane worked its way deep into her

knuckles, staining them black and brown, and the cold spring air turned her cheeks red, Vasya's mind churned frantically.

Rubber was in short supply ever since the Japanese seized the rubber plantations in Southeast Asia, and synthetic rubber productions had been diverted to the high-priority infantry and logistics trains. The 588th—important though it was to the war—was putting a significant dent in the Soviet Union's stockpile. Significant enough the Stavka had sent people to investigate for possible fraudulent misuse of materials.

Her initial theory of bad piloting being the cause was unfounded. The princesses themselves were just fine. Their chassis and frames were undamaged, as they would not be in a hard landing. Only the wheels needed fixing. And from what she could see, there was nothing amiss on the makeshift runway.

Something very strange was afoot with the 588th Night Bomber Regiment.

Whatever was going on, Vasya only had two more days to figure it out—and Yaba clearly planned on keeping her so occupied or muddy-headed that she couldn't finish the task that had already vanished three commissars. This was an impossible assignment, and all she had was the clothing on her back, her sewing kit, and the scope of her old sniper's rifle.

Vasya swallowed a lump that was not entirely due to her hangover and thought hard.

By the time they finished the wheels of the fourth princess, Vasya had a plan.

As they moved to the fifth aircraft, she doubled over, clutching her stomach and moaning for the latrines. The mechanic pointed, and Vasya stumbled dramatically to the privies. Ducking inside, she ripped off her sniper's jacket and dropped to the ground, using her back to lock the door.

When she had first been issued her sniper's equipment, her

jacket had been a standard issue brown winter coat. Over the harsh winters, it had gained a white lining made from undershirts, transforming the clothing into reversible camouflage. But she needed something that would hide her legs in the snow too, since she no longer had her snow pants.

With the light streaming between the wooden slats to guide her, she tugged off her white undershirt and began sewing. She'd finished her make-shift sniper's suit right as someone banged noisily on the door. She shrugged her jacket on, stuffing the addition into her pants so it wouldn't fall out, and reported back to the mechanic.

Yaba offered Vasya the flask as the sun sank behind the horizon and the hangar's red lamps switched on. "For your good work replacing the wheels."

Vasya smiled and brought the rim to her lips, but closed her mouth, letting the liquid dribble down her chin and onto her jacket and hoping that both the darkness and the dark material would prevent Yaba from noticing. She took another sip. Then a third.

Yaba gave her a pirozhki. The smell—warm, delicious, nourishing—was torture to Vasya's starved body. She took a huge bite and wobbled. Her leg buckled and she stumbled into Anya, using the motion to tuck the rest of the pirozhki into her jacket.

Anya half-carried her to the hangar. "Here, let me help you sit against the wall." She cast a frantic glance back to the major.

Yaba nodded, slightly.

Vasya fell heavily against the hangar, drunkenly patting Anya's cheek as the other woman leaned forward to straighten her out. "You're a good friend," Vasya slurred, and dropped her head back against the wall, eyes closed. After a minute, she let out a good snore for good measure.

Anya coughed. "Ugh, she *reeks* of vodka."

"Then she should stay asleep for the entire night," Yaba said. "Come, Anya Azizovna, we have fascist dogs to kill in Sevastopol."

Vasya cracked an eye open once the crunch of their bootsteps faded. Mechanics and pilots bustled about, preparing the princesses for their flights. No one was watching the drunken sniper sleeping against the corrugated wall. She waited.

Darkness settled and Vasya reversed her jacket, releasing its long white bottom half.

Then she pushed herself upright and ran as quickly as her bad leg could manage towards the makeshift airfield, flopping onto the icy ground where snow met mud, and pulled her scope from her pocket. There were no shouts of alarm over the familiar sewing-machine rattle of the U-2s' engines.

Slowly the planes took off.

Vasya pressed her scope to her eye. It was a moonless night, and she could see little.

What she saw confused her.

As they rose into the sky, the Polikarpov U-2s seemed to *transform* from stocky biplanes into stockier bowls and sticks— like mortars and pestles. Their engine noise changed too, moving from sewing-machine rattles to the low grinding of stone on stone the higher they climbed into the sky.

The noise of something scraping behind her pulled Vasya's attention from her failing vision. She rolled over, jaw dropping as the hangar rose from the ground.

Unlike the other mobile hangars, with their wheeled tracks and engines that gave the Red Army extreme mobility, the 588th's hangar had *legs*.

Two legs.

Chicken legs.

They sprouted from underneath the hangar like an unnatural extension of the building, flesh and scales and talons instead of metal tracks. The hanger itself seemed to have changed too, turned from metal to a cobbled together contraption of bones. Human bones. Animal bones. Gleaming a faded red from the red lanterns and starlight.

A whimper escaped Vasya's mouth.

The legs lurched forward into a steady, ambling walk east, the bone-hangar shifted and rolling with each step. The refueling trucks rumbled behind the hangar, creating the strangest convoy ever seen. They would not stop until they reached their next airfield outside Sevastopol.

If she didn't hurry, she'd be left behind.

The horror before her was nothing compared to the reality of Order No. 227. Not one step back. No deserters. No traitors. Forward momentum only.

She ran.

Her bad leg trembled beneath her, but she pushed harder, running past the slowly-moving trucks and to the hangar. The legs were short enough that she was able to catch the edge of the doorway and haul herself up and in, rolling to a stop against a wall.

The movement caught the attention of the mechanics riding inside. Vasya froze, pretending to be asleep as one of the women came over.

"Snoring like a lamb," she announced.

The mechanics chuckled and returned to their card game. Their laughter and unity only underscored the fact that Vasya was alone with this ever-mounting mystery. They were complicit. She was the outsider.

She was riding in an aircraft hangar with chicken legs instead of tracked wheels.

It was impossible.

Yet here she was.

Panic brewed in her chest. She'd thought she'd left these horrors behind in Stalingrad. That only the fascists tapped into the dark arts. Her lungs contracted as she fought to take tiny, delicate sips of air. She knew what was going on in Siberia. She knew, and pretended not to know. It was the only way to stay sane. The exhale came in a pained wheeze. Gasping would only alert the mechanics.

She had one more day to solve the mystery, and she could not do it exhausted and half-starved. She was a good Soviet soldier. She would do her duty. She had no choice. She ate the pirozhki and fell asleep.

The third day dawned cloudy, mirroring Vasya's spirits as Yaba once again kicked her awake and set her to work replacing the princesses' wheels.

The mechanics were no help. Their eyes shifted and their mouths twisted with each sideways question Vasya asked. Their only responses to more direct questioning were guttural grunts or subtle shakes of the head.

Anya was worse. She nervously scuttled behind one of the princesses' double wings each time Vasya looked her way.

When Yaba came to check Vasya' progress, she looked smug.

She seemed to have grown overnight, her legs more implausibly thin and long against her broad torso. Her eyes snapped with cunning and victory, and she smelled like gasoline and the charred remains of her enemies.

"Have you found your answers, Vasilisa Ivanova?" she asked.

"I don't dare to speak," Vasya replied. She was no closer to solving the mystery than she had been when she arrived. If anything, she had more questions than ever.

"Then since you have finished your first tasks so quickly, you can organize the nuts and bolts again." The major paused. "They seem to have fallen out of their boxes during last night's move."

Vasya's shoulders slumped, but she headed back into the

hangar. She was greeted with a pile double to the one from the first day.

Her shoulders slumped further. Her leg ached, and her fingers were frozen claws from the cold. It would take her hours to finish this task and give her no time to prepare for her final chance at discovering the mystery of the 588th.

She was halfway through when Anya joined her. The other girl sat on a crate and watched but did not help. Her blond hair really was shot with gray, the shadows under her eyes unending. Finally, she said, "Please don't drink the vodka tonight, Vasilisa Ivanova."

Vasya paused, a screw clutched in her grease-stained fingers. "Why not?"

Anya's gaze darted about the hangar. They were alone, but she kept her voice to a whisper. "The commissars didn't last to the third morning. Drink nothing."

Before Vasya could question her more, a mechanic walked into the hangar. Anya stood, pretended to survey Vasya's work with a critical eye, then gave a curt nod and walked out.

Vasya's stomach churned with anxiety and hunger.

Tonight was her last chance.

She swallowed down her fear.

She refused to fail.

She would die fighting or not at all.

When no one was looking, she stole a bit of rope, gloves, a helmet and a pair of goggles and hid them in her jacket.

Night fell.

The red lamps turned on.

When Yaba came, Vasya pretended to drink the vodka and eat the pirozhki. Anya's eyes narrowed, but she said nothing, not even when Vasya reenacted her fall from the previous night.

"Drunken fool," Yaba muttered as Anya pulled Vasya to her

feet. Vasya swayed as if she were in a drunken stupor. "Lean her against the hangar."

Anya obeyed, and Vasya was left alone.

She waited until everyone was gathered about the twelve princesses before she stood and reversed her jacket. Then she snuck over to the first plane, lying down in the mud and ice beside it. As Anya and Yaba settled themselves into their seats, Vasya used their noises to mask the sound of her pulling on her stolen helmet and goggles.

As the mechanics swarmed, loading the plane with its payload, Vasya looped her rope about the tail of the plane.

This was the tricky part.

The Polikarpov U-2's body was thin, and she wasn't certain she'd be able to lay down on the tail without crushing it. She'd also be facing the machine gun positioned at the rear of the plane.

She climbed aboard the tail as the last of the bombs was loaded behind the plane. She lay flat against the tail, lashed her rope tightly about her waist and tried to avoid trapping any steering wires.

"Did you feel that?" Anya asked as one of the mechanics spun the propeller and the engine caught. Vasya was so close that if the other girl turned, they'd be face to face. If they engaged in any aerial attack, she'd be discovered.

"No," Yaba called back.

The plane taxied down the runway, picking up speed until it lifted roughly into the air, tail dragging.

The wheels bumped back onto the ground.

Finally, sluggishly, it lifted into the sky.

"We seem really heavy tonight," Anya said into her speaking tube. Vasya couldn't hear Yaba's response.

The plane shuddered, the sewing machine rattle changing into grinding thunder. Vasya clutched the tail of the aircraft as it transformed from wood and canvas, elongating into rough stone.

Wind buffeted her cheeks and jacket. It tugged and pulled

at her wildly, threatening to pull her right off even as her mind struggled to reconcile this wild magic. She began to slip down the column and frantically tightened her rope until she was firmly wrapped against this strange surface, fighting to stay on.

And they still climbed into the air.

She couldn't turn her head to move her cheek from the stone to see what became of Anya and Yaba, although she felt the column shift every so often and saw dark objects fall through the air and explode into vicious red flames on armored tanks, clumps of huddled men and trucks.

Yaba crowed with delight at each successful hit, her laughter a cackle that stretched all the way to the moon.

No searchlights caught them with their blinding beams, and no German aircraft took to the sky. The other princesses and their crews also hit their targets, and smoke and flames joined the night clouds. Their outlines were strange and dark and not plane-like at all against the navy clouds.

The concussive blasts of the bombs drowned the howls of pain and anger from the monsters below, and Yaba's laughter swallowed the world.

A part of Vasya cheered with Yaba at the destruction of the fascist army, watching their military might shrivel beneath well-placed bombs.

But the rest of her was terrified for morning. Her deadline was hours away, and she had little to show for it. Tomorrow, she would have to face Major Yaba.

It was still twilight when they turned back to the hangar, the princess changing partway into the return journey, turning from stone to plane in a grinding, rattling shimmy.

Vasya cut her rope and jumped off the plane as soon as they hit ground.

As she leapt, Anya yelped. "Something grabbed my hair!"

Vasya dropped flat to the ground, pressing herself flat against mud and snow. Her leg ached.

"You're just paranoid." Yaba's voice echoed across the airfield. "It probably got caught on your seat. You wear it too long anyway."

Vasya ran as fast as she could until she reached the hangar—it had settled into its resting place for the day, its long legs gracefully hidden—and dove onto the floor. There was no time to waste reversing her jacket.

She had just arranged herself into something resembling a drunken sleep when she heard footsteps enter the hangar.

"Something was on our plane! I *know* it," Anya said. "We were very heavy coming back."

"Nonsense," Yaba replied airily.

A boot connected with Vasya's ribs and she groaned, rolling onto her back and blinking her eyes open.

"Your deadline has arrived," Yaba announced.

Vasya staggered to her feet. She could barely put any weight on her bad leg. It felt frozen solid.

Yaba's smile grew. Her nose was larger than it had the day before, and she seemed precariously balanced on stilt-legs. "Have you found your answers, Vasilisa Ivanova?"

"I don't dare to speak," Vasya replied.

Her mind raced.

She didn't know the full mystery.

She had more questions than answers.

But it was either be shot for impertinence by Yaba or sent to Siberia by the Stavka.

She knew which fate she feared most.

Her voice shook as she added, "But if you don't mind, I'd like to ask you some questions."

Yaba's smile widened. Her teeth were pointed and long. "You may ask me what you want, but remember that not every question has a good answer."

"I only have three questions," Vasya said. "The questions

the Stavka asked me to discover."

"The more one knows, the sooner one grows old," Yaba replied.

"If you only touch down once every night instead of the multiple sorties you claim to make, why are the wheels so damaged?" Vasya asked.

Anya moaned.

A gleeful fire lit in Yaba's eyes.

"The rubber is synthetic and does not take to the transformation," Yaba answered. "It is a price the Motherland can afford to pay."

A twinge of pain rippled through Vasya's hands. She looked down in horror. They were wrinkled and aged beyond her nineteen years. She looked back up, meeting Yaba's gaze. Two more questions.

"What happened to the three missing commissars?"

Anya moaned again and covered her face.

"They were men and could not handle the truth," Yaba answered. "It is a price the Motherland can afford to pay."

Another twinge, this time to her face. Vasya touched her cheeks with her aged hands, feeling deep lines on skin that was once smooth. Her heart hammered against her chest, but she straightened her back. She would finish her investigation. She was a good soldier.

"My last question: who are you?" Vasya asked. She knew this answer already, but she wanted confirmation.

Anya wept, her shoulders heaving with each sob as she shrunk toward the ground.

Yaba grew until she blocked out the predawn sky.

"I am what will save Russia," Yaba answered. "It is a price the Motherland can afford to pay."

A final twinge, at her scalp. Vasya tugged on her braid. Her hair was as white as her jacket.

"Now I have a question for you," Yaba said. "What are you willing to pay for the safety of the Motherland?"

Vasya stared deep into the major's flaming eyes.

She had already paid for the price of knowledge with her youth. The only thing left to give for her country and her family was her life, and she had long since pledged that away in a fateful room with mustached men in green uniforms and gilded epaulettes.

There were things more terrible than men, though, and fates more fulfilling than simple victory. The monster before her proved that.

The fear that had been roiling inside her vanished, leaving her with a calm resolve.

Vasya took a deep breath. "Everything."

Anya lifted her head, hope shining behind the tears.

Yaba's smile eclipsed the sun. She extended her hand instead of a flask. "Welcome to the Night Witches, Vasilisa Ivanova. We have work to do."

The Price of Victory
David Costa

Red lightning fell from the dark sky, its thunder roaring like the demons that roamed the land.

Atop his perfect horse, Lord Diogo Lopes patrolled his realm, protecting the fertile fields from Belziraz's destructive touch. His faith had protected him from the demon-mother's taint, but only steel would drive her minions away.

As he reached the border, the line that separated the lush greenery from the corrupted barren fields, Diogo pulled the reins. His soldiers stopped their stunted and misshapen steeds beside him.

"It's getting worse," Diogo said to the captain, a bulky man that desperately tried to conceal the effects of Belziraz's curse. He managed to hide his growing tail and most of his fur under his armor, but it was clear to everyone that his face was slowly turning into a snout.

"Every day's a struggle, my lord." It was hard to tell if he was talking about the rampant corruption or his own condition.

"It is," Diogo agreed, eyeing the withering trees and the spreading decay. "We need strong men or the taint will reach the castle in a matter of months."

"I can lead another expedition." The captain used his good hand to scratch his furry face. Despite his bestial appearance, the captain's humanity and courage remained untouched, serving as an inspiration to every soldier. May Meireor bless him! "Maybe we can find survivors outside the border."

"Too much risk for an unlikely reward. We can't afford to lose anyone, especially you." Diogo heeled his horse. "When the darkness comes to swallow our home, we'll fight back with what we have. I pray to Meireor that our steel stays sharp and our hearts won't falter when the demon-mother brings her horde."

They rode for hours, assessing the destruction caused by the bloody lightning and the demonic raids, occasionally helping villagers reinforce their homes. When heading back to Castle Lourel, Diogo saw a woman singing under a tree.

Her sweet voice sang of the green fields with such passion that she might be seeing them for the first time. Beautiful, like her voice, her face showed no imperfections, and there were no bald spots on her head. Although much was covered by her snowy dress, she appeared to be untouched by the demon-mother's taint. Someone like her would give him the heir he deserved, a man strong enough to face Belziraz.

"Fair lady," he said from atop his horse. "I've never seen anyone as graceful as you. My heart, my castle, and my lands are yours."

She looked at him, unimpressed. "Such things will never win my favor."

Diogo nodded. "Then I shall find something that will."

Atop his loyal steed, Diogo kept his gauntleted hand close to the sword's hilt. This deep into the Deadlands, demons were everywhere. Imps peeked from behind piles of bones. Marrow-suckers impatiently gripped their spears. Something kept them away. Diogo hoped it was his prayers.

When he got to his destination, the once-green forest of Adaya, his jaw clenched. In his youth, this forest was teeming with life. Now a deafening silence hung over the dead trees, their lifeless trunks and branches tangled in what appeared to be dark vines.

But those were no vines. Diogo was old enough to remember the day the forest fell and the monster that ravaged it. The Demon with Matted Hair.

Like spider webs, the massive strands of dark hair became denser, and Diogo was forced to dismount. Unsheathing his sword, he advanced cautiously; the insatiable demon had devoured every battalion sent to Adaya.

"Where are you going?" The cavernous voice echoed. "You'll make a fine meal…"

"Show yourself, fiend!"

From the trees came an enormous mass of tangled hair, with a giant beak and ivory tusks as big as a man. Standing on four sharp talons, the demon was as tall as the dead trees. When it got closer, Diogo could see old bones stuck to the demon's hair.

After a brief prayer, Diogo charged. He swung with all his fury, but his sword became entangled in its dark hair. The demon laughed.

Roaring, Diogo punched it, but his gauntlet became stuck as well. The dark mass moved upwards and Diogo was pulled in the air.

"Give up," the demon said.

Diogo punched it with his left hand but it got tangled. Keeping his calm, he kicked it, but both legs got stuck.

The beaked head came down, and the demon's bloody eyes focused on Diogo. "Why are you not afraid?"

"I am armed with more than steel. Meireor will protect me."

"Your brethren also prayed before they died." The demon let out a blood-curdling cry. "Where was your god when I ate them!?"

The massive beak opened.

"Meireor! Save me from our common foe! Hear my plea!"

The beak closed around Diogo's neck.

A sickening crunch.

To Diogo's surprise, the beak shattered. The Demon with Matted Hair squirmed, howling in sheer pain. Diogo was released from the tangling hair and pulled his sword free. With a mighty swing that cut through its tusks, he silenced the demon.

Diogo found the lady under the same tree, singing. Her divine voice caressed his ears and stirred his heart. Although she wasn't dressed like royalty, she had a lady's bearing, and barely glanced at him when Diogo approached her.

"My lady," he said with a courteous bow. "Lands could not win your heart, but I bring you something that might." He produced an ivory tiara with floral carvings. "A gift, made from the tusk of the Demon with Matted Hair."

She looked away immediately. "Throw that hideous thing away!"

Confused, Diogo did so. "Does this trophy offend you?"

"Yes!" Her face was still twisted with disgust when she looked back at him. "Very much!"

Diogo fell to his knees. "Tell me, how can I win your love?"

She sighed with annoyance. "Never say your god's name again, and I shall love you forever."

"You have my word."

"Would you abandon your faith for me?" The indifference in her face was quickly replaced by incredulity. "Would it be that easy?"

"Nearly impossible. But I would do it for you."

Although shy at first, Andreia, the lady under the tree, grew more talkative as months went by. Any time that was not spent fighting the demon-mother's minions Diogo gladly spent with her.

Andreia was caring, more so than any woman Diogo had ever met and, although they never shared a bed, every night she'd come over just to thank him for his love.

Diogo was surprised when one night she came to his room, wearing nothing but a long nightgown. Andreia stood at the edge of his bed and invited him with a gesture. "I heard gossip about the sort of thing a woman and a man do in their private chambers." She smiled shyly. "I would like to try it."

Andreia had never been this forward, but Diogo couldn't say he didn't like it. He approached her and gently pulled the straps of her gown. The nightdress fell to her feet and Diogo gaped. Her skin was immaculate, her form magnificent. She truly was perfect.

She lay down and Diogo caressed her naked legs. By the sound of it, Andreia was enjoying the moment as much as he. But when his hands got to the nightgown resting at her feet, Andreia screamed: "Stop!"

But it was too late. He had already uncovered her feet. Her hoofed, goat-like feet.

"Cover them," Andreia said on the verge of tears. "Pretend you never saw them and keep loving me."

"No need to pretend." Diogo caressed a hoofed foot. "This does not tarnish your beauty."

Andreia embraced him with all her strength. "Belziraz cursed me," she said in tears. "I prayed for years, begging to get my feet back, but your god always ignored my pleas."

"It makes no difference. Hooves or not, I will always love you."

Clutching Diogo's hand, Andreia screamed in pain. The bed was bloody like a village after a demonic raid, but instead of feeling devastated, he felt hopeful.

"Push, Andreia. Push!"

After Andreia's deafening scream, the midwife presented

Diogo with a bloody baby. No hooves. No signs of Belziraz's taint. A perfect baby boy. An heir.

Glowing with pride, Diogo showed her the immaculate baby.

"No hooves," she said, half surprised, half thankful. "Let me hold the fruit of our love." When the baby was safely in her caring arms, she asked: "What shall we name him?"

"Afonso."

On his throne, with Andreia by his side, Diogo discussed last night's attack with his generals. As usual, Andreia looked disgusted when anyone spoke about demons.

"We do not have enough men to reinforce the borders." Diogo scratched his chin. "The militias no longer——"

The throne room's door burst open.

There he was, the pride of his life, the future of the realm. Although still in his youth, Afonso walked with the commanding presence of a lord. His eyes had the resolve of a demon slayer and—why was his shirt stained with blood?

"By Meireor! What happened to you?"

"I was training when——"

Andreia started yelling. Flames engulfed her as she rose in the air.

Diogo shot up from the throne. "NO!"

"Why!?" She cried in pain while her skin burned. "You promised!"

In silence, Diogo watched Andreia. Like a burning shirt, her body turned to ash, slowly revealing a demonic form.

"You said you would love me forever!" There was no longer pain in her voice, but sadness. Angst.

The guardsmen unsheathed their swords when they recognized Belziraz, but Diogo ordered them to lower their weapons. With tears in his eyes he stared deeply into hers. "And I always will."

Gilded Goose Feathers
Betsie Flynn

Where do I begin? This morning seems as good a time as any, since it's finally Midsummer and you've returned. Make the most of the light you seem to have brought with you, that's my advice. Perhaps together you'll have enough fervour to press the gloomy tendrils of night back and back again.

My lady—my queen, of course, to have it right—would have slept as late as ever today, but the giggles of maids like me skidded across the early morning air, clattering like a smashed cup on a hard stone floor. We all picked wildflowers yesterday evening and slipped them beneath our pillows, ready to print the face of true love in our dreams. I don't remember what I dreamed of; isn't that silly? But flowers are never wasted. Waking up to their fragrance was a delight. Walking together, holding hands, we'd gathered oxlips and thyme, violets, and musk-roses. Woodbine and eglantine, too. We found ourselves dancing guilelessly in the sleepy breeze.

To tell you the truth, whispers as gentle as that breeze had been gathering for some time. Soft gossip that our queen might have grown less bright than she had been at her wedding, less full of joy. As gentle, yes, but also as persistent were these rumours that murmured about her feelings. Winter is so stark and cruel here, as you have reason to know. It stretches long. Long enough that even a queen could find her eyes growing weary and her cheeks turning cold. We'd all noticed how her once exuberant gowns had grown increasingly bland. The mischievous touch of Spring had done little to add colour to her wardrobe. Offering her verdant greens or cosy pinks soon became something we had to prepare ourselves to do, like breaking the ice on the washing barrel and dipping our hands deftly in.

This morning, it was my turn. To be honest, it seemed that my turn came oftener and oftener. That was to be expected, I suppose. We'd spent our girlhoods together, after all, paddling in the waves of the balmy shoreline which girdled the land. "Won't you let me braid flowers into your hair, sweet Queen? A crown of petals and blossoms would bring out the light in your eyes," I said.

"I wish Falada were here." Her tone was flat, as if she'd given up hope of joy already, so early in the day.

"Alas, alas, if your mother knew, her loving heart would break in two." I made my eyes large and woeful and used the voice I'd always used when I'd donned our favourite sock puppet, Falada the magic horse. She could talk, you see, but she didn't really have a lot to say. It was all in the expression and the voice I used. We were very young when Falada was made, alright?

Really, she must have been feeling pretty woebegone if she brought up that old game. Falada had long since fallen out of use—over-loved, he'd become increasingly threadbare. I tip-toed to the top of a kitchen chair and nailed him to an archway downstairs so that he could offer me some comfort when the geese were being particularly haughty. Did you know the geese are my special job? Waterfowl remind me of home, and I'll put up with mud and honking as long as they bring gulls to my mind.

"What's on your mind, Your Majesty?" I took up her comb and got to brushing the sleep knots out of her stubborn hair. I started at the ends, gently working my way up towards the roots. She sighed.

"I didn't think it would be so lonely, being queen."

"Oh no? I thought being queen was all you'd ever wanted. Your mother would certainly be proud of the changes you've made here. Perhaps you should write her a letter?"

She flashed me a look that, if I were anybody else, would have meant I'd overstepped my role as maid. But then she sighed again. "I have written, obviously. But she's busy, I suppose, and ships are ruled by the tides. And anyway, one of us had to want it, right? If not you, why not me?"

I'd never wanted to be a queen, you see. A princess? Why not! Princesses get to embroider flowers on fine hems, on silken nightrobes, on well-stuffed cushions, patchwork blankets, and whatever other already beautiful thing they can lay their hands on. They make the little things more splendid by touching them, princesses do, and what's not to like about that?

Queens, though, are a different breed entirely. I knew a queen, once. She was so strong and wise that she bolstered carefully-drawn trade agreements through years of balls and celebrations. She kept her lighthouses manned, she listened to her advisors and the common people both, and she even trained teachers at the palace in the great royal library.

The queen's own daughter grew up as playmates with one teacher's child. The two girls were of an age, after all, and soon grew so close that they went as a pair to the princess's new kingdom when she was married at Midsummer. The two girls, together with their long-time toy-chaperone Falada, filled out each others' interests with grace. The teacher's daughter had learned the importance of relationships from watching her common-born mother interact with the queen. She had read at length, too, about the intricacies of statecraft—the human side to the geography of the known world. The princess, on the other hand, gloried in colours, scents, and shapes. For her, flowers and embroidery were as beloved as the gulls in the skies or the geese in lakes and ponds.

"Can I be candid, my liege? The queen is lonely. My company is not enough for her. Last Midsummer, when you married, she glowed. She gloried in your bright and loving gaze. But you have been gone for such a long time. As the nights lengthened, they dragged shadows beneath her eyes. She waited up for you by candlelight, jumping at the sound of every closing door as if it were the hooves of your horse in the courtyard.

"I know you have boroughs to visit, and winter is as good a time for hunting as can be had here, but can't you see the changes in her? Yes, yes, she's kept busy. She's reignited a zeal for education that hasn't been seen, apparently, since your grandfather's time. Or was it great-grandfather? I forget. What I do know is that both of our mothers—mine and hers—would be proud of her. I might have been born a princess, but your wife was born to be a queen and for that, she needs a king who's by her side in the dark of Midwinter as well as the light of Midsummer. If you'll excuse me, my King, I have geese to tend."

The king waved the young woman off, his wife's closest friend for all that she spent the bulk of her time among geese. How could he have been so short-sighted? These two had come together from a strong land with temperate seasons, one where a princess could afford to fritter her hours away playing horse-puppets and chasing after wild birds, longing to fly. Or, if not, to capture flight in her bold embroideries. Why, he was leaning on one such embroidered cushion now! One where they could afford to let young girls learn, if they wished. These girls had never known the bite of his dark autumns, the begrudging freshness of his frosted springs, or the depths of his winters. He'd thought his new wife would be safest and happiest staying in their castle for the first year of their marriage—doubting that she could stomach the pace of his progress throughout the land, where he brought hope to his subjects in the dark months.

Lost in thought as he was, the king didn't notice that his wife had entered the room. She was much changed, it was true, with her subdued clothing and prominent cheek bones. Had the turning of the year really so much power, even within the confines of the castle? "I have missed you, my wife." he said as welcome.

"And I you, my love. The light left when you did—" she began.

"Ah, but that's where you're wrong!" he smiled, "I left my light right here. I've been chasing shadows cross-country ever since."

The king stood with open arms and so quickly did the queen run to him that she almost stumbled. She would have, no doubt, had his hands not been there to catch her.

"Next year, you can come with me," he promised, "if that is what you wish?" The queen beamed with such joy that her cheeks felt fit to break.

"I would like that very much," she said, "there's so much more for me to learn than I ever found in my mother's books!" And with that deal brokered, the king kissed the top of his wife's head and listened to her list the new dresses she'd have her best friend—the most nimble needlewoman for all that she tracked feathers through the castle—make for their upcoming trip.

This Marble Tower
Toni Mobley

"Never stop dreaming."
-Unknown

"Rapunzel, Rapunzel, let down your hair."

A command I had heard echoed for years on the lips of strangers, with shadowed faces, concealing eyes that never saw me. It was a routine that was as old as time, or rather, has lasted for as long as I could remember. I liked to believe I couldn't trust the memories of a child, but every day was the same, and slowly despair twisted me into not caring.

Threading the locks that I had delicately braided through a system of pulleys at the window, they cascaded down the side of the tower, hitting the soft earth with a thud. I waited for the gentle pull that would tell me it was done. I didn't bother trying to sneak a peek at my visitors anymore; it wasn't worth the effort. If the supply of food and drink and books continued, I was content in my little world.

Although I'd be lying to myself if I didn't admit how much I yearned for the emerald forest that stretched just beyond my window, to the snowy peaks in the distance, and beyond that to the glittering ocean. I used to live there, in a castle of pale stone, unyielding to the expansive blue that hugged it from all sides.

I remembered the gardens of roses and daffodils, peonies, and chrysanthemums. The stables with the ivory horses that I would find any excuse to sneak down to. Or the kennels that housed the hounds who would keep my father up throughout the night.

There it was. A soft tug at the end of my hair. The wheel turned, my hair coiling into a heap at my feet as I brought the basket to the window. The dark cloak of my supplier disappeared into the distance, gone for another week. I liked to imagine it was my father coming to visit his estranged daughter out of guilt for what he had done. That the extra helping of roasted hazelnuts, slice of carrot cake, and loaf of bread was his way of showing affection, repentance. But I knew better. My cloaked purveyor of necessities was more likely a member of the palace guard, a hunter employed by my father, a lowly servant boy.

Sitting back on the couch smothered in cushions I had sewn by hand, I flipped the lid off the basket, inhaling the scents of honey and sweetened syrup as they entangled themselves with the salty brine of the bone broth I used to make my soups.

A flittering sounded at my window, and like my mystery visitor, it was right on time. Perched on the sill overlooking the window box of herbs was a crow. She folded her wings, cocking her head.

"Penny, so good to see you again," I said.

Sliding across the floor, I grabbed the cup I kept on the shelf just for her, staring at the wriggling contents. She squawked in excitement, hopping from foot to foot. I poured the creepy critters into the window box and Penny jumped after them. Penny was not your average crow, however. She sported a head of ebony and the wings to match on a body of white. Sometimes I liked to imagine she wore a vest.

When she had swallowed every creepy crawly I had gathered from around my humble abode, she flew into the room, settling herself into the makeshift bed I had made her. Calling it a bed was generous. It was a lumpy pillow made of scrap linen, but she loved it all the same. While she slept, I would knit, cook, or paint, or sing, or stare listlessly out the window. The same things I did all day, every day, for the last five thousand days. My eyes strayed to the bright yellow splotches painted across the ceiling. They represented stars, and yet each one of them was a tally for every day I had spent locked away.

"Well, I guess I should get started on lunch," I said to my only friend.

Penny cooed in response, tucking herself under the fabric. Gathering my hair to coil it into a thicker braid, I made to move to the couch whereon the coffee table sat an assortment of glittering hair bows and bejeweled pins. But I knew the moment both feet were on the ground that it wouldn't be so simple. My muscles tensed as pain shot through my legs, electricity tingling down into my toes. Swaying on my feet, I limped to the vanity, crying out in pain as I eased myself into the comfortable chair I had drowned in a sea of cushions. It was only getting worse, this ailment that had me cast from my family's side, locked in a tower to hide away the shame. My companion raised her head, calling to me.

"I'm okay," I whispered, knowing that it was a half-lie.

The raven made to snuggle back into her make-shift bed, but her gaze snapped to the window. She cocked her head, listening, waiting.

"What is it?" A moment later, I smelt it. Smoke.

Using the chair and walls as support, I hobbled back towards the window, peering out into the early morning gloom. But I realized the gloom wasn't the normal touch of a dawning day. In the distance, smoke curled high into the sky. It wouldn't be the first time an adventuring party had sought refuge in the forest around my tower. My father often entertained visitors from neighboring kingdoms.

Sighing, I grabbed my hairbrush where it lay on the couch under the window. There was little need for me to dwell on it, and I didn't, returning my attention to the brush in my hand, coated in that wonderful scent of roses. Idly brushing my hair, my eyes strayed to that smoke curling into the distance, and although I knew there was no reason to be alarmed, I couldn't help the lump that sat at the back of my throat, or the pit that formed in my belly.

The day passed in a blur. As much as I tried to distract myself from the growing plume of smoke that drifted closer and closer, my usual hobbies felt hollow. I took no joy in painting another star on the ceiling with the broom I had converted into a paintbrush or sipping on my chamomile tea while I read the new book that was tucked into the bottom of the basket under the food. Even the sweet honey and syrup coated bread and crunchy roasted nuts brought me no solace. Today was going to be a very different day, and part of me wished otherwise.

I didn't realize how right I was until after I met the halfway point of the story, when my eyes watered, and I couldn't hold back a cough. Looking up from the yellowed pages, I knew instantly something was wrong.

The forest came alive around me, but not the way I expected. It did not come alive with the sounds of twittering birds and the calls of frolicking deer; it came alive with crackling and spluttering of flames. The trees blazed with an intensity that had me frozen to the spot, unable to comprehend what had happened in those few short hours after I turned away from the window. No longer did it smell like the simple, comforting smoke of a warm fire. No, this beast was acrid. It heralded the scent of danger.

Leaning out of the window, I squinted into the distance, desperate to see where it came from and where it was going. The devouring flames consumed the woods, and yet the thicket and bramble that grew over the rocks that formed a protective wall around my humble abode kept them at bay. Another sound broke through the crackling of the flames, however, and I stilled, my heart hammering against my chest. This sound came not from burning trees or fleeing animals. I knew this sound very well. It drew closer and closer, the slashing and the clashing mingled with cries of anger and despair. These sounds belonged to men, and suddenly the fires made sense.

A war raged outside my tower in the woods, and somehow, I ended up smack dab in the middle of it with nowhere to go. Penny alighted on the windowsill, peering out.

"Maybe they won't notice us," I mumbled without an ounce of conviction. A stone-grey tower peeking out from the tops of an emerald green sea was quite conspicuous.

The only reason I never received visitors was because of my father's influence. These were the king's woods, and no one could traverse them without his permission. Apparently, that didn't matter anymore. My heart felt like someone had plunged their hand into my chest and gripped it. There could only be one reason that the king's wood was the epicenter of a fierce campaign. What could have happened to the king to allow this? My exile has saved me from countless strife over the years that plagued the city at the edge of the sea, but then it leads to this. Could he already be dead? The seat of that intricately carved throne of marble cold, waiting for the next tyrant to take it up?

Something moved far below me, where the wall of stone and bramble and thickets merged, hiding the only entrance to this small glade that shielded my tower from the outside world. Here and there, leading closer and closer, a bush shook, followed by the sound of something moving through it. An acrid taste sat at the back of my throat, and my hands shook as I gripped the edge of the windowsill. Something was coming.

Penny opened her wings, ready to fly, but I held my hand up, willing her to wait. She eyed me curiously, our gazes shifting from one another to the bramble as something emerged. The gasp that came out of my mouth alerted the man who stood at the edge of the bramble, his hand clutching his stomach, blood dripping from his brow. Our gazes met, and he held out a hand.

I could just catch his words on the pungent breeze, and my heart skipped a beat.

"H-help," he breathed, collapsing to the ground.

Penny danced from foot to foot, squawking madly.

"Not now," I chided her, throwing a cloak around my shoulders and pulling the hood over my face.

There was one way down from this tower, and I had never considered it before today. When I was first brought here, there used to be a staircase that twirled around the outside. Evidence of its existence could be seen in jagged stones that jutted out like weird thorns, just large enough—and firm enough—to hold the weight of a scrawny woman.

Easing myself out the window, caressed by a cooling breeze that smelt of death, I gripped the jutting stones, lowering myself from the tower. When suddenly it was not stone beneath my feet, but something soft, my heart soared.

I did it. *I actually did it.* I could feel the beat of my heart in the tips of my fingers and toes, and pain throbbed from my back down my legs, but I paid it no heed. For the first time in my life, not only did I leave the tower, but no one helped me. My father locked me in there knowing my injury would serve as a better deterrent than anything else, and today, I proved him wrong. But there was no time to dwell on this small victory. Laying on the ground several feet from the tower was my mysterious visitor.

The world was different down here, out of the confines and safety of my marble prison. Where the floor was made of white tiles, this one was made of emerald blades of grass that shimmered like waves. Where the walls, painted with my murals of a fantasy world that only existed in my head, paled compared to the giant boulders of solid stone draped in a blanket of ivy and thorns. Down here, the world was vibrant; it was alive. And that frightened me. Every flutter of a bird's wings, every chirp of a cheery insect, every crackle of wood from the fire burning on the other side, had me flinching.

A moan escaped the lips of the stranger, and I dashed to his side, kneeling beside him. My eyes swept over the cracked armor that wrapped around his body like a suit. Caked in mud and blood, with several gashes across his shoulders and back. It was clear he had been amid whatever conflict roared outside my doorstep.

Placing my hands on his shoulder and wincing at the chillness that spread beneath my palms, I rolled him onto his back. He cried out, clutching his stomach with both hands. Blood stained the cracks in his hands where gloves should have been.

Scooting back, my hands shot up in the air. "I'm sorry!"

Struggling to open his eyes, he squinted up at me. I became lost in those hazelnut orbs, amazed at how close he was, how close I was, to another human being.

"Y-you're…beautiful," he breathed, his eyes rolling back in his head as it hit the grass with a thud.

The shock dropped faster than I thought it would, and I found myself staring at the handsome stranger passed out on my lawn. There weren't many options left. I couldn't leave him here to fester as food for the howling scavengers that would roam the woods after the fires and roving marauders disappeared. But that left only one option.

Gathering the longest and straightest sticks I could find from the bramble and thickets hugging the stone walls around my glade, I piled them into a stack beside the passed-out man. Once I had a healthy collection, I organized them in rows upon rows, until I had what vaguely resembled a bed frame laying in the glade beside him. Unfurling my hair from the bulbous and intricate style I had draped over my back, I let the braids fall unburdened across my shoulders. What I was after were the pins and bows I had used to keep everything in place. Weaving the bows around the sticks, tying them together and securing them with the pins, I sat back and looked over my masterpiece.

I turned to my unconscious guest. "Well…this is the best I got."

Removing the heaviest of his armor, I discarded it across the glade, not knowing, or really caring, about the value it held. The blood that pooled around his abdomen coagulated, telling me he'd survive. But not if I left him down here. I rolled him onto the make-shift platform, laying him on his back with his arms and legs straight, giving little room for him to move. I just hoped he wouldn't wake up in the middle of what I was about to do and roll off the edge to his death.

Penny alighted on the platform beside him, cocking her head left and right.

"Watch him for me, okay?" she cooed, nestling into the comfy space his sleeve made between his arm and his chest.

Tugging on the individual braids in my hair, I formed knots around the platform, weaving my hair above and underneath the platform. I gave them one last tug and decided it was the most secure it could ever be. Dragging the platform to the bottom of the tower, I leaned back, my eyes trailed to the window box at the top of my tower. From down here, it looked much harder to climb up than it did climbing down. Now for the hardest part.

Sucking in a breath, and ignoring the stabbing pain in my back, I wrapped my hands around the protruding bricks and made for the top of the tower. My hands burned, my back ached, and fire seemed to burn through my extremities. But I made it to the top of the tower, collapsing onto the couch below the windowsill. Catching my breath, I sat up, wincing as white-hot agony coursed through my body. Time was running out.

Threading my braids through the pulleys, I heaved, once, twice, three times, and suddenly the wounded man was airborne. Every time I yanked on my hair, the platform crawled closer and closer to the window. The unbearably slow process was hampered by the increasing ferocity of what would normally be a gentle wind and the aching in my body. The platform rocked unsteadily in the breeze, thudding against the stone. Every noise it made, every time it moved, my heart would seize in my chest.

Electricity thrummed through the nerves of my legs,

increasing the pain in my back. No longer did it feel like the aching of someone who had exercised a tad too much. Now it stabbed, prodded. It felt like a rope about to snap, and I prayed it would hold. My hair cut into the palms of my hands, and after one last heave I saw the platform raise above the windowsill with my mysterious visitor laying peacefully atop it. If you could ignore the blood staining his clothes. Threading my excess braids around the metal hooks at the top of the window, I leaned over the couch, pulling the platform into the room. Tipping it towards the seat, I gently pulled the man onto the cushions. I fell backwards, exhaling. Pain exploded through my back, traveling up my spine and down my legs. I cried out, Penny hopping to my side as I hugged my knees to my chest, tears streaming across my face.

It took longer than I wanted for the pain to subside enough to unfurl myself and sit on the couch. My companion still slumbered, his chest rising and falling with each ragged breath. Pain wracked his body, and I understood some of what he felt. But whereas I was incapacitated now and then, he had a hole in his abdomen. Limping to my vanity, I gathered several strips of cloth and an amber bottle of antiseptic oil I made from crushed leaves and herbs I'd been given in previous baskets. Kneeling beside him, I peeled back the soaked linen shirt with a sickening plop. The man stirred, a moan escaping his lips. His eyes fluttered, those brilliant hazelnut orbs staring at me in confusion.

"You're not a dream," he whispered.

I frowned, pouring the oil onto a rag, the hand holding it suspended over the gash in his stomach. "Why would you think that?"

"I thought I was losing my mind."

Ignoring his comment and chalking it down to hysteria from his injury, I pressed the antiseptic soaked cloth into his wound. He groaned, throwing his head back.

"Stop squirming."

He glared at me, biting his lip. Wiping the cloth gently against the wound, I removed as much of the crusted blood as I could, until the wound itself was visible. Leaning back, I hobbled to the vanity, grabbing my thinnest threading needle and my finest twine, returning to his side.

"Lucky for you, the wound is clean. You'll survive."

He exhaled. "Thank you."

I nodded, threading the twine through the needle and poking it through his skin. He didn't squirm this time, giving no sign it hurt. When I finished, I washed my hands in the basin and took a seat at the vanity, not wanting to be closer than I needed to. I hummed a simple melody, one whose origin I couldn't quite place. There might have been words to it, and many more verses, but I hummed the same four lines, over and over. It was a mantra to me, something that calmed me when nothing else could. And right now, I really needed to calm down. Anxiety was snapping at my heels, reminding me of the pain that was increasing in my back and the overwhelming circumstances that had led to me climbing down from my home.

The mystery visitor cleared his throat, licking his lips.

"Oh, I'm sorry. Are you thirsty?"

He nodded.

Turning on the stove, I waited eagerly for the teapot to whistle, pouring a cup of chamomile tea for each of us. Handing him a cup, I took my seat back at the vanity and watched him. His gaze kept wandering to my hair strewn around the room, some still attached to the pulleys, and the make-shift platform hanging from the window. His eyes widened, like recognition dawned in his eyes.

"Wait—that's all hair! Real hair?" He exclaimed, eyes roving the braids, his hand reaching out to touch the nearest one.

I slapped his hand away. "Yes, and I'd ask you to keep your hands to yourself."

"I'm sorry, you're right…it's just, well—there's *so* much of it!"

"I suppose so." My father had a fondness for long, flowing

locks. I foolishly thought it would earn me his love, and how wrong I was.

He nursed a cup of tea, his gaze wandering over the murals on the wall, and the stars on the ceiling, before turning his gaze back on me.

"What's your name?"

I looked him up and down. "What's yours?"

He didn't hesitate. "Prince Wilhelm."

A snort escaped me, and I covered my mouth with my hand.

"What?" he glowered.

I waved at him dismissively. "A prince. Really?"

"Why is that so hard to believe?"

How ridiculous! A prince wandering without a chaperone in my father's personal woods?

"Because I am a princess. Last I heard I didn't have any siblings, and my father doesn't take kindly to strangers. Especially those who wander his woods without his permission."

His eyes widened. "It's true, then…"

"Pardon?"

He hesitated, confusion furrowing his brows, before something clicked. "No one told you, did they?"

"Told me what?" Placing my hands on my hips, I stared him down. I tired of him skirting around the issue, desperate to get a straight answer from him.

He sucked in a deep, nerve-wracking breath, running his hand through his thick hair.

"I can't believe I'm the one who has to tell you this." He fished inside a pocket in his vest, producing a withered scroll with a crimson wax seal. He placed it on my lap, observing me.

"Tell me what?"

With trembling fingers, not quite understanding why I reacted that way, I unfurled the letter, straightening it out on my lap. The intricate cursive lettering dragged across the parchment in ebony ink was chicken scratch to me, but as my eyes adjusted, they formed letters, and those letters formed words. And with each word, my heart grew heavier, and the pain that coursed through me disappeared, replaced by a white-hot rage. It consumed my very soul, like the raging fires that enveloped the forest outside. My entire life had been a *lie.*

"Have you read this?" The words were heavy on my tongue. My mouth struggled to say them out loud.

He nodded.

"Until his deathbed he insisted he had no daughter. That I had died young because he was afraid I was a curse sent to unravel everything he had worked so hard for. Do you know what he worked hard for?" He nodded.

My gaze drifted over the letter one more time. "Trying to conceive a new heir, and do you know what that got him? Nothing. His only heir, a cripple locked away in a tower. What sort of father does that?" I looked to the prince, the pity in his eyes sickening me. "But now, this letter tells me, he's dead, the throne vacated, and the kingdom in turmoil. So, I suppose I got the last laugh." I choked on the last word, my throat thick, my tongue suddenly too large for my mouth.

"There is no need to cry."

I crumpled the letter in my hand, tossing it across the room. The tears fell across my cheeks, unburdened, and I glared at him.

"Why not?"

His eyes came alive. "You're free."

The words rang hollow. Free? What did that even mean for someone like me? Freedom. A word I'd only read about it in the books that were delivered three or four times a year, in fantastical stories written about far-off magical worlds where women were idolized as innocent maidens that needed protection. The same world my father thought I belonged in. But instead of sending dragons or knights in shining armor to protect and save me, he built a prison of stone, destroyed my only attempt at escape, and left me to rot.

Stomping across the room, I grabbed the knife sitting by the stove and brought it to my throat.

The prince raised his hand, dashing towards me. "Wait! What are you doing?"

I scoffed, slicing the knife through the rest of my hair, listening to it fall to the ground with a satisfying thud. "My father liked my long hair. In fact, it was the only thing he liked about me." And now that he was gone, so too would my hair disappear.

He took his seat back on the couch, watching me. My father may be gone, but I still felt hollow inside.

"You said you were a prince, correct?"

He eyed me suspiciously. "Yes."

"Are you here for my father's throne?"

"I promise you I want nothing to do with it." He winced, clutching his stomach. "But what I want doesn't matter. Your kingdom is in turmoil, princess, and only you have the power to fix it."

"What are you saying?"

"Come with me. Return to the castle where it all began. Together we can make a united front, two kingdoms, one crown."

"You want me on the throne?"

Is that why he was here? Snooping around my father's personal woods chasing a legend he wasn't sure was even true… why would someone do that?

"Yes."

Silence filled the void where our voices had been, and as the sun set, it cast the sky ablaze to match the fiery ground. I watched the tops of the trees, spared from the fire's hungry grasp, sway in the evening breeze.

Could I do what Wilhelm thought I could? A young girl cast out and locked up, allowed to return and reclaim something that they had previously denied her. Is that a future I even wanted? But then I remembered, it wasn't about what I wanted; it was about what my father wanted. And he wouldn't have wanted me sitting on that throne. My resolve hardened.

"Rest, Prince Wilhelm. For tomorrow, we head home."

The faintest glint of dawn hugged the horizon, a glimmer of magenta and a shimmer of gold. I'd woken up long before the prince had, weaving the hair I had chopped up into a rope and securing it to my bedpost. The platform was still sturdy, and I knew he'd be in no position to walk from the tower, through the forest, and to the castle on the cliffs.

I don't even know if I can do it. I shook the negativity from my head. It'd be painful, but it was the only option. My kingdom needed me, and unlike before, I wouldn't sit by while others took up the mantle.

The prince yawned. "What are you doing?"

"Climb in." There was little time for explanation. The fires had died down, and if his kingdom already had its eyes set on the throne, we couldn't wait until the sun had fully risen.

Wincing, he climbed onto the platform, laying himself out flat.

"Now, whatever you do—don't move." He nodded.

A tiny black dot swooped down from the sky, alighting on the platform beside him.

"This is Penny, she'll watch over you."

He sheepishly waved at the bird, who cocked her head sideways in response. Without further ado, I pushed the platform out the window and lowered the coil of hair piled onto the couch until a holler from below told me he had made it safely. Casting one last longing glance around the only place I had known, I untangled my braids from the pulleys and tossed them out the window. Climbing down wasn't as painful as yesterday, but I was stiff, and I knew that this would be the easiest part. The worst was yet to come.

When I made it to the bottom, I gathered the braids and wrapped them around the platform, forming a sled. I'd seen a drawing of one in one of my books before, and I knew that although it hurt me to walk, he definitely couldn't. Once the certainty of the secureness of the hair could be established, I hooked two of the thickest braids around my shoulders like a harness.

"So, you're going to drag me to the castle?" I could see the pain in his eyes, the way he held himself so the wound in his stomach did not buckle.

"Yup."

I turned to survey the place I had called home. Funny. The view from down here didn't coincide with the view I had held in my mind. The marble that glinted like the arm of the Milky Way in the sunlight was intoxicatingly beautiful. But I never saw that from the inside. All I saw was a prison. Where even with all the windows open and the sun shining its brightest, the room of the tower was always shrouded in shadows. At night, the darkness smothered me like a mound of blankets, suffocating me. Down here, though, all I saw was my home.

"Not anymore," I breathed, striking out from the only home I'd ever truly known.

It was much harder than I thought: leaving the only place I'd ever known, dragging someone who easily weighed twice what I did behind me, the slick grass beneath my feet, and the unbearable knowledge that at any minute my back would say enough was enough and I'd tumble into the bramble and thickets of thorns. My feet were numb already, and I started dragging them. Tiny pinpricks of pain would explode from my back and down my legs, but I'd simply bite my lip and keep moving through it. *I can do this.* But my body rallied against me. The further we went, the more pain I found myself in. I could no longer see the brambles or the thickets or the stone wall or even the top of the tower. We'd left it all behind, that glade of emerald grass, for this world of blackened tree trunks and grey stained dirt.

Nothing changed for miles and miles. But distance meant little to me, and there was no way for me to gauge it except the increasing pain. It's all I could feel now, and it blinded me to the tiny stones and gnarled roots in my path. They tripped me, my legs buckling. Collapsing into the dirt, I screamed into the dead of the forest. Ash swirled around us, but nothing replied. Maybe I couldn't do this. Maybe this is where my story ends.

"It's okay, princess," he said, struggling to keep his eyes open. "I'll pull us the rest of the way—" But the moment he made to sit up, he recoiled in agony, clutching his stomach.

"It's fine," I breathed. I just needed to wait for the pain to subside…

Then I heard the oddest of sounds. A sound I had not heard in a very, very long time.

My eyes adjusted to the cloud of ash that I'd kicked up during our journey, revealing something on the path ahead of us. "Is that—"

"A horse." The excitement in his voice was palpable, and I couldn't help the smile spreading across my face.

Holding my hand outwards, I whispered. "Here, horsey."

The horse snorted, tossing its head.

"It's okay."

Its ears flicked forward and after a moment it put one hoof in front of the other and stopped before us, nudging me with its muzzle. Its long whiskers tickled my hand, and I planted a kiss on its forehead.

"Thank you," I whispered.

Removing the braids from my shoulders, I extended them, hooking them around the horse's chest, back, and shoulders. It undoubtedly looked awkward and incredibly stupid, but after encouraging the horse to walk forward a bit I realized—it worked. Coaxing the horse towards a row of stumps, and with great difficulty, I mounted the gorgeous ivory horse.

"Let's go seize our destiny," I said.

The horse tossed its head and walked onwards into the forest of ash.

I didn't know how far away the castle was, and if I had

to be honest with myself, doubt existed in whether we were headed in the right direction. Until suddenly, the forest parted, revealing a long marble promenade that was in stark contrast to the dead forest we had emerged from. The horse's hooves struck the cobblestone, and my heart soared. There, at the end of the promenade, decorated with spiraled columns and statues of dancing, barely clad women, was a castle. It wasn't just any castle; it was my castle. The place of my birth, and of my parents, and their parents before them. A crowd gathered along the promenade, soldiers at first, but as the horse plodded along, the crowd not only grew in size, but diversity. Women and children gathered, curiosity alive on their faces. They muttered amongst themselves, but even I could hear what they said.

"Who is that…" whispered one.

"I don't know," said another.

The crowd collapsed behind us, following in silence. One of the soldiers in the crowd called out, recognizing the man in the make-shift sled.

"Prince Wilhelm?"

The prince stirred, turning around.

"Who is that?" the soldier asked again.

"It's the princess."

The crowd erupted in murmurs. The same phrase repeated over and over: 'I thought she was dead.'

The horse made it to the wide double doors set into the castle, guarded by worried attendants. The soldier from the crowd rushed forward, whispering to the attendants. Their eyes widened, and they pushed the doors open. I ushered the horse forward, its hooves striking the rich stone of the hall. At the very end, on a dais, sat a marble throne.

"Wait," Wilhelm called.

I pulled the horse to a halt, turning back to stare at him. With great effort, he pulled himself to his feet, standing beside me.

He nodded at the crowd behind us before whispering, "You should walk the rest of the way."

He was right. Clutching the horse's mane in my hand, I threw one leg over and slid off its back. Wilhelm caught me, trying to disguise how much the effort hurt him. My knees buckled, and I made to move forward, but I couldn't keep myself standing. The pain shot through my legs, freezing me to the spot.

"I can't."

"Yes, you can." Bending down, he gathered me in his arms.

"Wilhelm!"

"Hush," he whispered, carrying me slowly towards the throne.

The crowd surged after us, waiting with bated breath. One of the attendants walked forward, wringing his hands. Penny flew from the platform, alighting on the back of the throne, calling to me.

"Princess Rapunzel?"

"Queen Rapunzel." Prince Wilhelm set me down on the marble throne, stepping aside so all those who had followed us from the bridge could see me.

"Rapunzel has returned. But not as a princess, as a queen."

The hall erupted in a cacophony of celebration. The smiles of the citizens were genuine, and I couldn't help but mirror their reactions.

"Are you ready to lead your people, my queen?" The prince asked with a smirk.

I nodded. "Yes."

Gravity
Claire Olivia Golden

A Retelling of "The Light Princess"

Despite what they might tell you, I wasn't born without feelings. The truth is, I felt too much, and so it was better to not feel anything at all. Feelings will destroy you if you let them. But I will not let myself be destroyed.

Stories have always been distorted when someone else tells them. They will make me out to be callous, unemotional, detached. I see how they would think that, looking at me. It's just not the truth. Only I know the truth.

This is how it starts.

A king, a queen. An expectation to have children. That expectation is now placed upon me so I know how it feels, and I wouldn't wish it upon anyone. That's how many stories start, and mine is no different. The queen, my mother, faced with the responsibility of creating the next generation, because somehow it was her responsibility and not my father's as well. I don't know what my mother would have done if she hadn't been placed under the weight of everyone's expectations. Maybe she would have done something entirely different with her life.

But what was a young woman, barely twenty years old, supposed to do when an entire kingdom looked at her and commanded her to have a child?

She had the child.

The child was me.

Only it wasn't quite that simple. It took years of trying. A decade of whispers and rumors of people wondering what was wrong with her. Not the king, never the king, only the queen. What was wrong with the queen? What sins had she committed for her body not to bring forth children? Would she doom the kingdom to a future without an heir?

My father, for his part, was as helpful as always, which is to say that he sat in his office and murmured to his advisors while pushing papers back and forth. I am sure that he felt productive by doing this, but all he accomplished was making a mess of his desk that his advisors had to clean up and offering no moral support whatsoever to my mother. But she was used to fending for herself in a world that had never looked out for her, and so she got by how she always did—through the force of her will.

And they wonder where I got it from. My tenacity, or pigheadedness, depending on who you ask.

When she finally became pregnant, the rumors still didn't shut down; now the people whispered of witchcraft and sorcery. If you think our land isn't accepting of magic now, it's nothing compared to how it used to be. There was truly no winning for her. I often wonder how many hidden magic users there are, secreted away for fear of being shunned or worse if their magic using comes to light. Malthea can't be the only one. And while I do not possess magic myself, I am a magical thing thanks to her interference. There must be others like me. But I may never know.

So there my mother was, pregnant, me on the way, and now the pressure was on to produce a male heir. For of course she couldn't catch a break. When I emerged an entire month early, sickly, scrawny, and covered in the caul, the kingdom took a step back and began to whisper. I have been surrounded by whispers since before the day I was born, and I will be surrounded by them long after the day I die.

Gravity

Aside from the fact that both my mother, and myself, almost died during my birth (and they wonder why women don't want to have children), I was a normal child. I did not get to experience normalcy for very long, however, because everything went wrong the day of my christening. This was a tradition in the royal family. The christening was a chance for the kingdom to celebrate the birth of a prince or princess and for the royal family to come together as one. Essentially, it was a family reunion with the entire kingdom watching, so no pressure. Family reunions are always bound to go south even when it isn't such a high-stakes event. And this one was no exception.

You see, my father had one responsibility: to put together the guest list. And he managed to omit the most important person he could possibly choose.

I can only wonder how that conversation went over, later. If my father tried to blame my mother for leaving him with too much responsibility. He often tried that, putting the blame on my mother for his incompetence, and it was never fair of him to do that, but especially in this case. She had nearly bled to death during childbirth and was still pale and shaky several weeks later when the planning for the christening was underway. There was no way she could be held responsible for planning the guest list. Yet if I know my father at all, he would claim it wasn't a man's job to do such a task, and if only my mother had done it we wouldn't be in the situation at all.

Perhaps he is right about that. But even if he's right, that doesn't mean it's fair.

He forgot his sister. Sibling relationships are always complicated, I have heard, making me glad that I don't have any siblings myself. There was no way my parents would risk having another child after the danger my mother had been in, and after what happened at my christening…well, I'm getting ahead of myself. However, their sibling relationship was more tumultuous than most because his sister, Malthea, was the oldest child. When she was fifteen years old my father was born, and on that day, she lost her claim to the throne—the throne she had been training to ascend to for her entire life. Fifteen years of training thrown away just because she was the wrong gender. Because of this, she harbored an immense amount of spite for my father. It wasn't his fault. But it wasn't her fault either. Pushed aside for a newborn baby boy, she watched him get all of the attention she had once received, and she watched her hard work be swept away overnight. Things were not peaceful between them.

During the years while my father was being trained to ascend to the throne, Malthea disappeared from the public eye, and no one knew what she got up to during those long years. It would only come to the surface later—the darkness to which she had descended. Still, I cannot say that I blame her. I did not deserve what was coming to me, but neither did she. My father remained oblivious to her feelings, just as he has remained to my own. I think it's just his character. But that is not an excuse for how he treated his sister.

And now that my father was a father, he had forgotten to invite Malthea to the christening.

I was four weeks old, still too small for my age, when my parents presented me to the kingdom. They named me Lillian Elizabeth Sage after my mother's favorite flower and both of my grandmothers. A long name for a small girl, and I would never grow much over the years. I suspect this was owing to the nature of my curse. And this was the day it would be placed upon me.

As the guests streamed into the chapel, which was adorned with silken banners and luxurious floral arrangements in the manner of a royal wedding, my parents stood to greet the guests.

Gravity

My father, clueless as he always was, greeted his sister without an inkling that he had forgotten to invite her. Perhaps if he had apologized when he saw her, the crisis could have been averted, although I do not think so. He greeted her like any other guest and an usher showed her to her seat.

Since she was part of the royal family, she sat near the front, by the silver bath in which I would be christened. While everyone took their seats, my mother recalls seeing Malthea slip to the front of the chapel and run her slender fingers through the cool water of the font. My mother was feeling too sickly to ask what she was doing, and I wouldn't have blamed her anyway for not wishing to interrupt a guest. Who wants to tussle with their sister-in-law?

I don't think it would have made a difference. She had already administered the magic, so when it came time to christen me, the spell took effect.

My nursemaid held me to her chest, swaddled in a pink lacy blanket that was a gift from some great-aunt. The master of ceremony poured water over my head and announced my name to the crowd. My nursemaid felt a flutter of anxiety as she suddenly couldn't feel me in her arms anymore. I was there, but there was no weight to me; I could have floated away if she didn't grip me more firmly. In fact, she squeezed me so hard that I squealed.

"Princess Lillian Elizabeth Sage Couronne," chanted the crowd.

My nursemaid tucked the blanket more firmly around me.

It didn't take long after that for the truth to come out. The newborn princess didn't have any gravity.

Malthea liked a play on words, and it turned out that not only was I lacking in physical gravity but in the emotional sort as well. I was a dream baby because I did not shed a tear. From that day forward, no matter how hungry or tired I got, I did not cry. This was wonderful at first, and it seemed to be the lesser of my problems, but in time it would grow to be more troublesome, at least for everyone around me. However, for the time being, the most pressing concern was the baby that floated away into the air.

I can only imagine the shouting that took place when my… *problem*…was first discovered. By then, all the guests would have left, and it would have been just my parents and the nursemaid. If they suspected Malthea right away, they wouldn't have said anything. But as they did research into my *condition* (they loved finding these ways to describe it to avoid using the word *curse*) they realized that this was magic at play.

And while magic wasn't forbidden—because whenever you try to outlaw something, it only comes back more dangerous than ever—it was certainly frowned upon.

It wouldn't do to have the crown princess disturbed by magic. Something had to be done.

And it didn't take long for the word to get out. The best way to tell everyone about something is to decide that something should be a secret. The moment my parents turned to each other and wondered if they should keep this under wraps was the moment the secret began to leak. I believe it was my nursemaid who told her friend who told someone else, and so it goes from there. It was never going to stay hidden, not when I had to make public appearances, not when hiding the princess away would be suspicious enough to get people investigating. It was one month after the curse befell me that the kingdom began to whisper. However, it turned out that was a good thing for my parents because it meant they could crowdsource. The more minds you have attuned to a problem, the more likely that you will find a solution.

So, the research began. Doctors and scientists from all over the kingdom came to the palace to poke at me and determine what was wrong. My childhood was filled with appointments, examinations, and procedures. I would study the history of our kingdom and go immediately to be hypnotized by someone my mother had found in a nearby village. After a meeting with advisers, it was time for my teeth to be inspected in case it was the enamel causing my disease. They were grasping at straws, yes, but a parent would do anything to cure their child.

I should note that I did not view it as a disease, not at first. It was just the way I was. You aren't born thinking there's something wrong with you. It's something you learn over time. What child wouldn't enjoy flying? Doesn't everyone dream of doing so?

After a few years, however, I began to dream of the opposite. I began to dream of walking.

We always want what we can't have.

But for the most part, I was content. Sure, there were times when I thought it might be convenient not to be tethered to my parents to prevent me from going up, up, up into the sky, but I liked the way I was. I didn't think there was any need to change me. I believe this is when the rumors about my lack of "emotional gravity" began to circulate. I wasn't taking my disorder seriously enough. I wasn't bothered by it. It's bad enough when someone is different...but when they don't show enough chagrin about it, that's when people really start to get nervous. Didn't I *want* to be normal? I wanted to be treated normally.

When I was ten years old, I had my first real argument with my parents about my *condition*. They had the local cobbler make a custom pair of shoes that were loaded with lead. The goal was to strap these to my feet so that I would be held down to the ground. I didn't like them because they were ugly and because I wanted to float around that particular day. This is the first time I can remember my mother yelling at me, though it would not be the last.

"We have sacrificed so much to help you be normal," is what she told me. "Why are you being so obstinate?"

It had not occurred to me that I was being obstinate. I was existing the only way I knew how. "I like being this way," I told her.

"It doesn't matter whether or not you like it. Princesses can't float."

That's the day I learned that being a princess meant my feelings didn't matter. From that day forward, I determined it would be best if I didn't show my feelings at all. I only wanted to please my parents. Doesn't everyone? If you accuse me of not having enough gravity just because I am not showing my emotions, then ask yourself who made me feel that I couldn't show them in the first place.

Everyone assumed that I didn't cry because I didn't feel emotion. But that couldn't be further from the truth. You can feel emotion without showing it. You think I want to cry in public just to prove something to people who will judge me no matter what? It's better to show emotion when you are alone and there's nobody to think things about you.

I wanted to be able to walk just so that people would leave me alone. More than that, though, I wanted a friend. I wanted someone who wouldn't care whether I was on the ground or in the sky, and who wouldn't judge me for showing too much or not enough emotion according to some arbitrary standard. The real curse was loneliness.

I withdrew further into myself, showing less and less emotion, until people believed me to be no more than a hollow princess. Until I believed myself to be hollow as well. I talked to no one outside of lessons. I couldn't go outside on my own anyway without someone walking alongside me holding a cord that was wrapped around my waist. I might as well have been wearing a leash for the amount of freedom it gave me. Perhaps I would have stayed this way forever, locked in my room talking to nobody and no more than a prisoner in my own home, if it weren't for two critical changes. The first happened the day after my eighteenth birthday and the second followed soon after that.

This is what happened.

After a particularly dreadful spat with my mother, all I could think about was getting out of the castle. I put on the awful lead-lined boots, updated throughout the years so they would continue to fit my growing feet, and hurtled out of the window as fast as I could. The lead boots pulled me down to the ground, and I slipped them on before marching off as quickly as I could. It was never easy to walk in these, because my body continually tugged upward like I was being pulled into the sky. All I wanted was to get away.

As I walked into the forest that surrounded our kingdom, I tried not to dwell on my argument with my mother, but of course it was the only thing I could think about. Didn't she understand that I was trying my best? She made me out to be some sort of rebellious monster who wanted to be different. I thought back to the phrase she had been repeating all these years: "Don't you want to be normal?" Again, I wondered why I had to change in order to be treated normally. That was all I wanted. I hadn't asked for any of this.

Didn't I want to be normal? "It sounds like the problem is you wanting a normal daughter!" I had screamed back. "Maybe it's your fault that I am this way in the first place. Did you ever think of that?"

It was like I had slapped her. And in the moment, I didn't care. All I had to do was get away as fast as I could. So here I was, trudging through the forest, looking for something—anything—to take me outside of myself. Stupid lead boots weighing me down, I strode as fast as I could until something made me stop in my tracks.

A lake. One I had never seen before. But I had never been this far away from the palace before. How many other things were out there that I just hadn't discovered because I hadn't ventured far enough? I had never been submerged in water before aside from my daily baths, where I always had attendants to help clean my body and hair. I imagined the water swirling around me and a deep sense of longing pooled in my veins.

The lake was roughly the size of a jousting field. The depth I couldn't ascertain, and although I did not know how to swim,

I knew I had to get in immediately. At the side of the lake, I sat down and removed my shoes, clutching a nearby boulder to keep myself grounded. The shoes I set on the grass. Then I slipped my bare feet into the water and a chill ran through my entire both—not just because the water was cold, but because it felt like coming home.

Without stopping to remove my clothes, I slid the rest of the way into the lake and experienced instant relief like I had never felt before. The water wrapped around me like a silken blanket, embracing me gently. I let go of the shore and allowed my body to sink, holding my breath, ducking my head under. It was then that I realized the true miracle of the water—here, I had gravity.

I was not floating away. The water was holding me just like the ground held everybody else. I did not need a cord, an assistant, or lead shoes to keep me tethered; the lake was allowing me to stay within its grasp.

So I stayed. All the king's men could not have dragged me from within its depths. Although I had never learned to swim, my body took to it instinctively, like I had been born to do this. Eventually I loosened the ties of my dress and set it next to my lead shoes to dry in the sunlight. I swam for hours until the sun sank low in the sky, and I became aware of time again. I would not have left but for the emptiness in my stomach that told me it had been hours since my last meal. It would not do to have a search party come looking for me and take away the only peace I had felt in years.

I dragged myself out of the lake reluctantly and immediately my feet came up from the ground and started to float away. I grabbed my lead shoes to fit them onto my feet and keep me rooted. My petticoats dripped lake water down my body as I trudged back to the castle. But I wasn't going home. I had already found my new home.

Gravity

As if this wasn't a miraculous enough discovery—a lake that could counteract my curse—it was less than a week later that I met Rhi.

Of course, my parents learned of the lake when I showed up at the drawbridge dripping wet. But when they learned of its mystical curative effect, they agreed to let me continue my daily swims. They sent a doctor with me to study its effect on me, but he tired of watching me swim back and forth and went back to the castle to "write up his findings." I am not sure if his studies ever came to fruition. I was simply glad of my newfound freedom.

Nobody seemed to come to this lake, so I had it to myself. There were more interesting destinations nearby, I imagine, like the town square or the seaside. While the ocean intrigued me, I preferred the solace of my lake hideaway. I was on my fifth day at the lake, expecting solitude as usual, when I heard someone clear their throat and I jumped. As much as a gravity-lacking girl can jump, that is. It was more of a midair shudder.

I was halfway through removing my dress and was too tangled up to turn and see the source of the voice. Rather than clothe myself again, though, I simply removed the dress the rest of the way and held it to my front as I looked over my shoulder. Sure enough, there was a person standing half-hidden by the trees. The first emotion that came to mind was annoyance rather than embarrassment. Who would dare disturb my peace like this? Then the figure stepped forward, and I felt a blush come to my cheeks when I realized it was a man. And I was in a state of undress.

"Excuse me," he said, "I didn't realize anyone was here."

"Clearly someone is here," I retorted. He was still *looking* at me, and I widened my own eyes in indignation. When he realized his faux pas, he averted his gaze.

"It's just that I've never seen anyone at this lake before," he continued. "Please forgive me. I had no idea I would be disturbing your…bathing."

I didn't feel embarrassed because I wasn't doing anything wrong. This was my lake as much as his. More so, probably, because I was the princess. "You aren't disturbing me. You may carry on with your business. Whatever that may be."

I hobbled to the edge of the lake, discarded my dress and lead shoes, and eased myself into the water. When he heard the sounds of splashing, he turned around to watch me. I ignored him and reveled in the watery embrace of the lake.

"Forgive me," he said after a few minutes had passed, "but you're the princess, aren't you?"

"Most people would consider that a foolish question."

"Then you may consider me a fool if you wish, but I didn't recognize you."

I ducked underwater so that his voice faded away and all I could hear was the quiet hum of the lake. When I surfaced, he had taken several steps closer to me. I didn't feel afraid. All I felt was curiosity. "I am sure you look different when you aren't dressed up, too," I said. I hated posing for portraits and having my likeness plastered all over town, because although I was pretty enough with my mother's black hair, brown eyes, and beauty spot beneath my right eye, people didn't like to look at me too long. Something about me made them uncomfortable. Maybe it was the fact that I didn't look away. But this man held my gaze.

"Is this where you come to get away from it all?"

He surprised me into nodding—the first bit of truth I had given him.

"Why do you come to this place?" I asked.

"The same reason as you, I suppose. To escape."

"And what do you have to escape from?"

He shrugged. "Maybe you don't need to be fleeing something to want an escape."

I swam to the edge of the lake so that I could see him

more closely and noticed his leather bag lying nearby. A canvas protruded from it. "You're an artist?"

"Nothing so accomplished as that. I like to paint is all."

He wasn't nearly so intolerable as the other artists who had come to paint me. "What do you like to paint?"

"Anything that stands still long enough."

"I suppose the lake is a worthy candidate, then."

"It depends on the sort of day," he said, removing the canvas from his bag and setting it up against a tree. He then removed a long, slender box that contained paintbrushes, selecting one carefully and testing the bristles against his finger. "Some days the wind is gusting and the water won't hold still. Other days the sun dances across the waves in a pattern I can't keep up with." I was transfixed by how he unpacked his paints, setting them on a flat stone near his workspace. "And other days—like now—it's like the lake is posing for its portrait."

"Except for me," I said quietly. "Too much movement."

"I rather like that movement."

"You would paint me, then? In the lake?"

"I imagine you've had more than your fill of people painting you." I liked the furrow of his eyebrows as he concentrated on his canvas, how his light blonde hair swept over his forehead and cast a shadow on his freckled face.

"You would be the first one I ever wanted to."

And that is how it began. A princess, a pond, and a painter. It would be the first of many afternoons we spent together, always with me in the water, sometimes with him joining me and sometimes with him painting. And over the next few weeks, we would fall in love.

It happens so quickly sometimes. I had read it in storybooks and laughed at the foolishness of it all—saying you knew someone when you had only known them a handful of days. But sometimes that's all the time it takes to catch a glimpse of someone's soul. Like recognizes like, and something within me called to something within him, and the other way around.

I fell in love with Rhi, the painter, and he fell in love with Lillian, the lake girl. We would have picnics and play games and compare childhoods. He would bring me flowers and I would sneak him treats from the kitchen. It didn't matter that all he could get were wildflowers and weeds, because they were all the more precious to me for their wildness.

And that bit of happiness was just too much for Malthea to tolerate.

Three weeks after my eighteenth birthday, a terrible drought came upon the kingdom. While it would normally be approaching the rainy season, there hadn't been so much as a cloud upon the horizon for months. it had been the driest summer in anyone's memory and in any of the royal logbooks. Although the kingdom needed rain more than ever, it looked like it wasn't going to come at all. And that's when my lake, my saving grace, began drying up.

It was during a painting session with Rhi that I made the discovery. When I idly splashed my foot, I noticed that the water line didn't come up to the same part of the rocks that it had the previous day. I will admit that I freaked out completely when I discovered this, when I realized that the drought was beginning to affect my beloved lake. Rhi couldn't calm me down, but he persuaded me to wait until tomorrow and see what had happened, and I went home with worry in every cell of my body.

The next day, when the water level had descended even more, was when I truly began to worry. It was going down at an alarming rate, and at this pace, the entire lake would be drained within a matter of weeks, if not days. This was more than just the weather. This was magic at work again.

Of course, Malthea had kept tabs on me. I wondered why she didn't torment my father instead of me, but then I realized the best way to hurt someone is through the ones they love. My father, for all his faults, would love me until the end of his days. So, to get to him, she went through me.

As my love for Rhi grew, the water in the lake lessened. It seemed an exact correlation. My parents sent divers to investigate and see what was wrong, and they emerged with the news that there was a boulder-sized hole at the bottom of the lake. The most distressing part? A smooth silver stone, engraved with a message, had been pulled from the murky depths.

The lake can be fixed in but one way
A human sacrifice must be made
The body of a willing soul
Is the only way to plug the hole

There was no reason for it to be rhyming except to indicate that it was from Malthea, who had always held a fondness for drama. And her request here was nothing short of insane. A human sacrifice to return the lake to its former glory? On the back of the stone, it went on to detail the method of execution: A willing victim had to give their life, sitting in the hole and letting themselves be drowned, and their body would remain in the lake forever as a reminder of what had to be sacrificed.

There was no way anyone would sacrifice themselves for that. Least of all for me. Everyone hated me because I never showed emotion, so why would they believe that I was even feeling sadness at all?

I would have to resign myself to the lake being emptied and go back to my old life. But I didn't want to go back to the way things were before. It hadn't been a life at all.

Rhi was quiet when I told him what we had discovered. He slid into the lake beside me and pulled me into his strong embrace. I curled into his chest and let him stroke my hair, barely feeling the gentle press of his fingers on my scalp, the grief I felt was so immense.

"We're going to find a way," he murmured. "I'll fix this for you."

"There's no fixing this," I said into his linen shirt.

"There is nothing I wouldn't do for you, Lillian. We'll find a way."

But even I didn't think he would go as far as he did.

The next day, I was awoken before sunrise by my mother shaking me awake. Surprised, I sat up in bed and pulled strands of hair out of my mouth. I pushed aside the silken cord that bound me to the bed by my waist and grabbed the bedpost to keep myself from floating away. "What's wrong?" I asked.

"Lillian, it's the best news," she said.

"Waffles?"

My mother sighed and shook her head. "Could you be serious for once?" No, such was the nature of my curse. "We found someone."

"Could you be any more vague?"

"Someone to plug up the hole for you, sweetheart. Someone has offered himself as a sacrifice."

"What?" I swung my legs over the side of the bed. Who would do that? "Why?"

"He says he only wants to be of service to the crown. That dying for the princess would be his honor."

There were definitely people like that, who wanted to be martyrs. Every once in a while a kingdom requires a blood sacrifice, and you can't exactly be losing members of the royal family every time a witch gets dramatic with her spell ingredients. That being said, I didn't feel great about letting a stranger die for me. Even if I would do anything to get my lake back. "That's…" I said slowly. Something about this didn't feel right. "I don't know about…"

"This is the way for you to be happy, darling. I've never

seen you as happy as you have been these past weeks, swimming there. I would do anything to get it back for you. Please, let the man do this thing."

It's always hard to resist your parents when they ask you to do something—especially when tears are shining in their eyes like they were my mother's. "When will it happen?" I asked.

"Tonight," she said. "We will go to the lake and the sacrifice will happen."

"I want to meet him first," I said.

"No," she said firmly. "That will make things harder for all of us. You will see him tonight, when the sacrifice takes place, and that will be enough."

I shook my head in disbelief. "He's doing so much…we owe him so much."

"We will see that his family is generously compensated," said my mother.

But no amount of compensation could make up for somebody's death. We both knew that; neither of us wanted to say it aloud.

That night I dressed in a dark blue silk gown that brushed just below my knees and my mother French braided my hair. I would go into the water with this stranger and be with him in his last moments. Hardly a time to worry about appearances, but it felt like something I could do, something I could control. My mother tied a cord around my waist to help reel me in when I floated away, and with her and my father, we started for the lake. The entire time my heart pounded in my chest so hard it felt like I was going to be sick.

I must have known, deep down, what I was going to find. I just couldn't admit it. Because I was horrified, but not entirely surprised, to see the face of the man who would give his life for me.

Yes, it was Rhi.

"No." It was the first thing out of my mouth.

"Lillian." His voice was determined. "I had to see you one last time."

"There is no *way* I am letting you do this."

"I don't need your permission. I made this choice myself."

My parents had stepped back to give us privacy, so they couldn't hear our conversation. They didn't know about me and Rhi. But even if they had, I was sure they still would have accepted his sacrifice. They would do anything to make me happy. As would my love, evidenced by the stubborn set of his jaw, the determination in his light blue eyes.

Well, the good news is that I was just as stubborn as he was, if not quite a bit more. "You are not going to die for me."

"I want to see you happy," he said quietly. "After everything you told me about your gravity…You need this lake."

It was true that I needed the lake, that it was the happiest I had been, and yet… "It's not worth dying for."

"But you are worth dying for."

My eyes stung in a way they never had before, and I blinked hard. "I'm not. Not worth that."

"I get to decide that," he said gently. Then he took a step toward the lake.

I grabbed his arm to stop him, but when you don't have a single ounce of gravity, you can't really do much forceful tugging. All this achieved was him dragging me alongside him. We stayed like this for a few steps until we splashed into the water. Oh, the beautiful sensation of the water caressing my calves, and the thought that I would never have this again if Malthea completely drained the lake…I closed my eyes just for a moment. But when I opened them, Rhi had broken free of my grasp and was nearing the center of the lake. The water reached just to his chest.

"No!" I swam to him as fast as I could, swifter in water than I ever had been on land or even in the air.

The water was beginning to form a whirlpool around him as if it knew he was its prize. It pushed me away as I tried to get closer. The water was rising around him, sucking him in, now all the way up to his chin. My chest shuddered with gasping breaths. "RHI! No!"

He met my eyes. I could see the whirlpool reflecting in his pupils. "Lillian," he said with half a smile.

And then he went under.

Nothing could have prepared me for the tidal wave of emotions when his head slipped beneath the surface. The lake didn't matter. Neither did my parents observing from the shore. Nothing mattered except for this precious person whose life was slipping away from him. I let out a guttural scream and hurled myself beneath the water. My arms closed around his torso, and I shot upward with him, kicking harder than I ever had in my life, pleading with the gods, the lake, my own gravityless spirit to give me this one thing. To let him live.

Our heads broke the surface and I coughed up water. His eyes remained closed.

"Please don't die," I whispered. "Please. You are the most important thing to me. Not the lake. It was never the lake as much as it was you. Please don't leave me here alone." I swallowed hard around the lump in my throat. I had never been serious in my life, but I was now. "Rhi, I love you."

My eyes were stinging, and I couldn't breathe, but not because there was water in my lungs. My body shook and I felt something slide down my face. It took me a minute to realize that I was crying for the first time in my life that I could remember. And right as I had that realization, Rhi's eyes flew open and he gasped in a breath.

I sobbed and threw myself into his arms.

We swam to the edge, where I couldn't stop kissing his face, checking to make sure he was still breathing. I didn't care who saw. Let them judge me. They'd been doing it all my life. Now I had something—someone—I cared about, and that mattered more than all the hateful opinions in the world.

"But the lake!" exclaimed my father from the shore.

"Go drown yourself in it!" I shrieked back at him.

I would later apologize for this comment, for I hadn't meant it truly, but in that moment the only thing I could think about was Rhi. My person. My love. For him, I would give up the lake, just like he had been willing to give up his life for me. It wouldn't be easy, but it felt like I could get through anything as long as he was beside me.

"I will never let you go again," I said softly in his ear.

"Good," he replied, and kissed me.

My curse was broken with those three little words: saying "I love you" to someone and meaning it with my whole heart. There's a lot of gravity in those words. And I mean them every time I say them, which I've started doing more often, to my mother, my father, and of course, Rhi. I broke my own curse. It only took me eighteen years.

When I stumbled out of the lake that fateful night, I collapsed onto the ground for the first time in my life. Going from the sky to the earth is an uncomfortable change. I had to learn everything again—how to walk, run, skip, sit, go up and down stairs, dance. But Rhi helped me every step of the way, bandaging the cuts I acquired during these adventures, going on hikes through the woods with me, and of course, swimming. When I broke my curse, something went irreversibly wrong with Malthea's magic. It turned out I didn't have to give up the lake after all. I just needed to break the spell on myself.

Why did I have to give up my magic in order to be accepted by people I didn't care about in the first place? I'll let you in on a secret: My magic is still here. Gravity is something that should be used in moderation. It would never do to be grounded all the time; imagine being with someone who never cracks a smile or tells a joke. That's equally as bad as someone who never takes things seriously, like I was accused of doing. So, I held on to a scrap of that lightness and I never plan to let it go.

My aunt gave me a gift, in a way. Sometimes the things the world views as a curse can actually be your salvation.

Gravity

Here's another secret: The day after I cried for the first time, I went to visit Malthea. I wanted to know why she did what she did. But her home was gone, crushed into oblivion by a freak flood that had come overnight. I found no trace of her body, so I can only assume she got away from there. She was too smart to be killed like that. Not unless she wanted to be, and as I said, I found no body. I hope she got away from this place, where she never got what she wanted. I hope she made something good of her life. I have made something good of mine—and without the curse, I don't know if it would have ended this well. I neither blame nor credit her for how my life ended up. Everyone grows from different circumstances, and if mine were more complicated than someone else's, then that's just the way the cards were dealt.

However, my father doesn't get to make the guest lists anymore. They hire a party planner these days.

I keep my feet on the ground most days. But when I need to get away, I climb to the attic, open the garret window, and let myself float away into the sky. I don't need a tether anymore because Rhi serves as one for me. When I want to come home, I think of him, and it draws me back to where I belong.

After all, gravity is best in small doses.

The Glass Slipper
Doug Rooney

The Prince sighed.

How many houses has it been? Two hundred? Three hundred? You would think the law of averages would mean *someone* in the kingdom would have the same size feet as… whoever she was. And at this point the Prince would take anyone if it just meant he could return to the castle without his dad nagging him. He would even take one of these ugly sisters. Still, at least Jon was allowed to come with him. Small blessings. Come to think of it, if Jon were allowed to join him on his 'quest' that probably meant the king didn't yet suspect—

"Why wouldn't it FIT?!?"

The Prince's attention returned to the scene.

One of the sisters was crushing her foot into the slipper. Or at least trying to. The shoe was clearly three sizes too small. The other sister, already having failed to make the shoe fit, was returning from the kitchen with a stick of butter.

"Look, if you need butter to make the shoe fit, I think it is safe to say the shoe doesn't belong to you," said Jon. He was trying, and failing, to hide his laugh. At least someone was enjoying this.

"No! The shoe is definitely mine. Maybe you washed it and now it has shrunk?"

"How would a glass shoe shrink?" the Prince said as he stood up. God, his back hurt. He would have to ask Jon to rub it later.

"We have to be going, I think. We have many other houses to see before the end of the day. Ladies, I thank you for your… hospitality. Jon, please retrieve the slipper."

Jon stepped forward and gave the over-elaborate bow he sometimes did when they were in company.

"My Prince, I believe there are actually *three* eligible women in this household."

"You can't mean Cinderella…" The sister with the stick of butter hit her sibling over the back of the head.

"Sorry, sometimes my sister forgets her manners when speaking in front of the *Prince*. Bella, why would the Prince want to speak with our *housekeeper?*"

"The king has decreed that all eligible women in the kingdom must be inspected. That would include housekeepers as well, I am afraid."

This was Jon's little joke. The idea of a housekeeper coming to the King's Ball was absurd, but the decree did say *all* eligible women in the kingdom. And Jon did seem to like to see the Prince suffer.

The sisters didn't seem to be any happier than the Prince, but, at Jon's insistence, one eventually huffed her way upstairs to collect this Cinderella. The other stood grinning at the Prince with her stick of butter forgotten and melting in her hand.

"Maybe I could try on the slipper again? I am sure if I just—"

"No—no." The Prince cut her off. "That will not be necessary. We really do have a strict one-woman one-attempt policy."

The three of them stood in awkward silence. The ticking of the grandfather clock and the dripping of the butter as it melted onto the stone flagstone floor the only things marking the passing of time.

"How far away is the housekeeper's room anyway? This really is—"

The Prince trailed off because at that moment Cinderella appeared at the top of the stairs. Even the Prince, never much interested in female beauty, had to admit that this housekeeper was astonishingly attractive. But that wasn't why the Prince was speechless. He was speechless because he recognized the housekeeper. This was the girl from the King's Ball.

Dear God. *This* was the girl from the Ball.

Panic swept over the Prince. If the slipper fit her then this would be it. No more stalling. He would have to get married. Thirty minutes ago, he had convinced himself that he would accept any woman to stop his father nagging. Now, faced with his future bride, this conviction fled. What excuse could he possibly give his father? He had to find a way to—

The slipper.

If the slipper were gone then there would be no way to prove this housekeeper was the mystery girl. That would keep him safe for at least a couple more weeks.

The Prince bent over to pick up the slipper from where one of the sisters had left it. Then, placing one foot on a pool of melted butter, he slipped, making sure the full weight of his body fell on the glass slipper. He heard a satisfactory crunching of glass.

The Prince slowly picked himself up, brushing the shards of glass from his tunic.

"Oh, I am so sorry. This is really tragic." He turned to Jon. "We have *no way* of telling who the mystery girl is now."

Cinderella had reached the foot of the stairs. For a housekeeper who had just seen her chances of becoming a princess shattered she seemed in a very good mood.

"That is okay, my Prince. You see, I still have the other one."

From within the folds of her petticoat she produced a glass slipper.

The Prince fainted.

Later, he would tell people he was overcome with joy.

Nocturne
Emily Barnett Kudeviz

A Sleeping Beauty tale

She learned about the curse through stolen whispers between courtiers in the grand hallways of the castle. When adults thought she was not listening, they would discuss the evil faery, the wicked one who cursed a child for her parents' deeds. And she would hide in the hallways, ducked behind heavy velvet drapes, drinking in their words, trying to hoard anything she could about her mother. She would then talk to her nurses and tutors, courtiers and serving staff, anyone who might share about her mother, drinking in the details of the former Queen, but she never approached her father. Instead, she would spend countless happy hours in her mother's dressing room and library, talking to her about her days, the curse, and her joys and frustrations.

Long before she was born, when her parents married in a grand ceremony celebrated all over the land, the evil faery was not invited. Aurora did not know why that bit of magic was excluded, why her parents decided that that particular magic was not welcome, but when all of the invitations went out, one was not marked for the faery. And later, when her mother carried her in the womb, the land rejoiced. It had been many years without a child, many years without a potential heir. But the birthing was hard on the Queen, and she died in childbirth, leaving behind the King and Princess Aurora.

And the King prepared a grand celebration after the mourning period was complete, sending out invitations to the lords and ladies, Kings and Queens, merchants and faeries, all who had been invited to his wedding. The celebration was for her name day, when the tiny princess would be granted the title of heir, when Princess would be put before her name officially. Again, the evil faery was not invited even though she had caused no problems all of these years.

On the day of the Naming, the King held his daughter, soothing her as she fidgeted, having been separated from her wet nurse. As her head was anointed and the King began to speak, the Great Hall darkened, cracking with lightning that stretched greedy fingers across the ceiling. Screams rose up before being harshly silenced as the evil faery approached. A tall, beautiful woman with blonde hair that tumbled long down her back reached out to touch the princess. "Your Highness," she said to the king, voice velvet. She curtsied deeply. "Your courier must have lost his way, as I never received my invitation to this joyous occasion. Did not the same happen on your Wedding Day?" A smile played at her lips as the King trembled.

The faery swept a large arc around the room with her open hand. "And yet, all of these people from near and far, including some of my brethren, received their invitations." The faery laughed, bells tingling through the room. "I have a gift for the child despite your ill manners." The King tried to speak but the faery had silenced him as well. In fact, only the Princess made any noise. The faery lay her hand on the child's head, so similar to the motion of a priest, and spoke softly, cursing the child with an endless sleep upon pricking her finger on a spindle on the eve of her 17th birthday that could only be broken through the kiss of a prince. It was after this that the King banished all spinning wheels from the country and forbade anyone from talking of the curse.

The courtiers loved telling the story in hushed tones when away from earshot of the King, always becoming overly dramatic when they arrived at the part where the faery entered and left, and the Princess always waited for more, a way to help her combat the sleep that would be hitting her within the year. But they never said more about the faery, never so much as whispered her name. In fact, the King had outlawed magic of any kind, hoping that if he eradicated the root of the problem, then the sleep would not come.

Aurora had studied the ancient tomes in the back section of the library, pouring over arcane script that she didn't quite understand, looking for a way to break the curse. Nothing seemed to give her any clues. She saw segments of words that related to curses and spells, but because she could not read the text fully, she had taken the book and stored it away, believing it might be useful.

And now, nearly a year before her 17th birthday, she stole out of the palace early, before the sun had risen. She tied a small satchel to her saddle and mounted her horse, and she carried the stolen book close to her body. She was going to find a faery to fix the problem, as strong magic can only be broken by equally strong magic, and unfortunately the Princess did not possess any.

Aurora rode for three days, staying to the side roads, away from where the Palace Guard patrolled. She didn't dare stop in public houses along the way, instead picking berries and finding streams from which to drink. Her ride was guided by the book, which contained a small map of the land beyond the Veil, the land where faeries were said to live.

On the morning of the fourth day, she arrived at the in-between place, the place where the world was believed to be split. She waited for hours, but nothing changed, nothing happened, and Aurora began losing hope. She sat on the verdant ground below a gnarled tree, keeping a hand on her horse's reins and resting her head on her knees, knowing that of the days she had left to break the spell, she had wasted four of them and would waste another three getting back. And then she would have to work harder to break free. She sighed deeply, unsure of the next steps to take, unsure if this were even worth it.

As the sun began to settle behind the trees, Aurora heard the breaking of twigs, and her horse startled. Jumping up from where she sat, she drew a short blade, one her father had taught her to carry. "Who's there? Show yourself!" She struggled to keep her voice from wavering.

"Child, have you been waiting here all day?" A woman stepped out of the forest, a bundle of sticks in her arms.

"Yes. I was searching for something," Aurora responded, not willing to reveal her secret.

"I suppose you have not found it, as what you are looking for doesn't appear until dusk," the woman chuckled, waving the girl onward through the glimmery landscape before them.

As they passed between two trees, nothing felt different, and for a moment Aurora felt foolish for believing things would be suddenly altered. The world was the same on the other side of the Veil except for a small cottage that belonged to the woman, a cottage that the Princess had not seen previously. Together the two spoke for hours, the faery nodding sympathetically from time to time, the Princess pointing to different things within the old book. And when the Princess finally left, she clutched a small list in her left hand and an onyx amulet in her right.

For the months remaining until the curse would afflict her, Aurora worked tirelessly, looking for the items on the list, the items which would allow her to break the spell. It would be no kiss that woke her, but rather it would be a piece of ancient magic, magic that needed a sacrifice, a piece of the wicked faery's hair, a piece of thread from her mother's wedding gown, and a gift from her Name-Day. She knew that she would not be able to find some of the items in the short time, but she did gather a small silver locket given to her by her older cousin and a piece of the thread. The remaining items would come later. Now, she just needed to wait.

And, on the eve of her 17th birthday, Aurora pricked her finger on a hidden spindle as she was running her hands along a spinning wheel in the palace treasury. She did not see the spindle, did not know it was there, but that was the way of curses. Despite her father having banished them from the land, one spindle had been tucked away, a relic of her mother's handiwork. Upon pricking her finger, the Princess fell, knocking over items and calling attention to the palace guards.

What followed was an elaborate mourning ceremony, where the women of the court dressed Aurora in her most beautiful dress, a deep purple velvet embellished with silver ermine. They perfumed her, elaborately coifed her hair. Then, they presented her to the King. His face was tear streaked, but he did his duty, honoring his daughter the same way he had honored his wife, and when he had finished, the Princess was brought to a high tower and placed in the upper room. Hopefully, someone would come along, bestow true love's kiss. And then the King went back to his throne room, ruling as he did before, but the land lost its luster.

The Princess' sleep was deep, but on that first night, she woke, the counter spell given to her by the faery she met near the Veil between worlds working. Thankfully, she still had the thread, locket, and onyx necklace. Aurora recalled the faery's words, the spell she had to whisper while holding the onyx necklace against her heart. Carefully, the Princess placed the thread and locket on the ornate dresser. She rose from the bed, her body trembling with life, and she gazed out the window for a moment before clasping the necklace around her neck.

Aurora repeated the spell, words in an old language, a faery language, one that had been lost to humans, even before the faeries were exiled. On the last word, Aurora morphed, arms stretching out into wings, her body shrinking, a transformation that caused her to scream in pain as every bone in her body broke, twisted. No longer was she a princess. Now, she was a raven, the onyx necklace nestled in her feathers.

The faery she had met those months before had given her directions, a path to follow that would lead to the wicked faery. "But remember," the faery had said, "you must return before daybreak, as the curse will once again gain its strength." Aurora flew, enjoying the wind beneath her wings, the lightness of her body. She joined other nocturnal creatures, bats and some owls, joining in their dance.

It took Aurora many nights to make her way into the wicked faery's home, a large stone structure surrounded by thorns. Both time and patience were required to collect the strand of hair, waiting for the right time while she perched at the beautiful faery's window, waiting as the faery moved closer, taking comfort in the warmth of the faery's hearth. She returned to her tower early the night she retrieved the hair, and in those last few hours before she fell back into the sleep, she arranged the three items that she had collected for the counter spell. But, for the sacrifice she didn't understand what to do.

Aurora puzzled, sitting up every evening, staying in her true form, looking at the items and the list. A sacrifice. She grew frustrated, angry. She crumbled the paper, threw the locket across the room, cursed the wicked faery. She cried as well, wishing for her mother, her playmates, her horse. She had been locked up here alone, with only the magic provided to her by the faery. She didn't even know if anyone had tried to rescue her, had attempted to pass the thorny wall that surrounded her tower.

The next night the Princess assumed the raven form and flew to the in-between place, calling out for the faery. When the woman approached, Aurora confronted her, asking what kind of sacrifice was needed.

"It needs to be a personal sacrifice. It needs to come from you," the woman said.

"My life? My title? I don't understand." Aurora was on a precipice, dangling precariously over the edge.

"I cannot tell you exactly what kind, as the spell does not say. But it must be deeply personal, something that is a part of you," the woman returned, stroking the raven's head. "My child, what would you be willing to give up for your life?"

"I don't know. I barely had time to figure out what I had," Aurora said, rising from her perch on the faery's arm, cursing magic as she flew.

For several more nights Aurora gazed out the window, thinking. What did she have? She had her horse, her title, her youth, her ability to have an heir. Small things, big things, personal things, all the trappings of a princess. She didn't feel particularly close to any of them. Eventually, as she watched the night sky, she realized what sacrifice she could give. She would give her memories of her mother. Even though she never knew her mother, the wet nurse's and courtiers' stories of the Queen had been plentiful, vibrant. Aurora had always felt like she knew her mother. She had spoken to her mother out in the gardens when alone, when questioning, when feeling joyful. This, this is what the Princess decided.

A spell had been scrawled quickly on the paper with the list, and as she placed the items together as well as the written-down sacrifice she was willing to make, she began to chant, repeating the words again and again, watching as they created a deep red glow. The Princess stopped chanting, exhausted, and the thin arms of daylight had started reaching out. She wouldn't know if it worked until morning and she sat, waiting, leaning against the wall, tears gathering in her eyes for the loss of something she couldn't quite name.

Aurora had broken the sleeping spell. When she had descended the tower, walked over the crumbled thorny brambles, she heard the trumpets blare loud and sharp. She knew the palace knew she was alive, knew her father would come charging down to find her, gather her up, and take her home. When they found her, there was surprise that she was alone, without a prince, but she was shuttled into the castle and lead to a feast.

The Princess never regained her memories, but when she ascended the throne, she was gifted with the onyx amulet by the faery woman, allowing her to transform at will. Aurora smiled at the freedom and power she gained through magic.

And she lived happily ever after.

Twelve Dancing Princes
Jenny McClay

Once upon a time, there was a king who had twelve beautiful sons, and they lived in a beautiful castle.

Though actually, there are two castles in this story. And two kings. You can't see the other castle right now but it's there… here…in a way. And it's elsewhere in a different kind of way.

It's complicated.

The more normal castle…human normal that is…is down there through the parting wisps of cloud. Its smooth silver-grey turrets twinkle in the afternoon sun, just as the snaking crystal blue river twinkles as it winds around the outer walls. Against the downward flow of the river, the eye flows uphill, tracing the river's path away from the castle through vivid green rolling fields to a loch a little way in the distance that's flat as a mirror. Behind the loch, the river forms again but quickly disappears into dark green forest that covers the hilly land with gnarly old trees like a sheep's fleece covers its back.

There in the distance, riders are galloping out of the forest. One in the lead and more follow. Two, three, four then another four neck and neck, another two, and then two behind. Their laughter echoes through the valley. It's the twelve princes racing home.

They pelt towards the castle, up and down the rolling fields, up the final slope, across the stone bridge, and to the gate. There's a clear winner, but it's not him we're interested in. Well, not so much anyway. It's the tall and slender one with long dark hair tied back, coming in third.

They disappear inside, and the portcullis closes behind them. Inside the castle walls, people are bustling and busying about. Their shouts and laughs, the rattling of carts and the clatter of a blacksmith's hammer on steel ricochet up here to the clouds.

As time goes by, the noises fade with the sun. Without its power, the air returns to its natural northern chill. The silver moonlight is sharp, and the world is all shades of blue now—the distant forest darkest navy, the grass a slightly lighter royal blue, and the castle still twinkles like pale ice. The loch is a little mirror that reflects the starry sky perfectly.

When the silent world reaches midnight blue, there's a thud. It sounds exactly like the sound of someone quite large stumbling and falling onto a hard stone floor cushioned by a heavy velvet cloak. It comes from the castle, the second window from the top on the outermost turret to be exact. Just where we need to be. We swoop down fast as an arrow towards the open window, and in through the thick stone embrasure. It's darker in here, but still moonlit clear enough to see.

There he is, that third prince. Who is in fact the twelfth prince in line of his birth, the youngest of the brothers—Prince Briar.

He stands with his back to us. His long dark hair falls just below his shoulders, and he's draped in beautiful fine brocade that shimmers in the moonlight and delicate heeled dancing shoes of a deep purple.

A shuffling noise comes from the far side of the round turret bedroom, but Briar doesn't seem to hear it. He is staring at the wall. Standing and staring at the curving inner wall of the tower. He raises his hand as if reaching for a handle, but his fingers don't clasp. Instead, he pulls back an open hand. And a door swells out of the wall. The stone door swings into the room. It's easily two-foot thick as the outer wall of a castle turret would be.

Behind the door are stairs curving downwards and a scent of jasmine and pine drifts into the room. And as Briar steps through the doorway, the air stirs behind him. Another figure—an invisible figure who recently stumbled on a hem of thick velvet and had a nasty knock to their left knee—follows. More carefully.

Where's Briar going? And who follows? Well, that story begins some midnights ago.

Prince Briar always had trouble sleeping. He had strange dreams. In fact, he had always been a little strange himself, according to his father. He was strong, agile, and brave, but he was also gentle and kind and more than a little inclined towards books and magic.

The King didn't like magic at all. The Queen occasionally alluded to an incident with a bog witch, but nobody ever talked about exactly what happened. He just didn't like magic. It was banned within the castle walls. And that was that.

And that went largely unnoticed by the magical creatures of the area. They had far more exciting places to be and things to do than sitting about in a boring old human castle. The only ones who were put out at all were folk of the castle who could no longer get magical remedies for boils and warts and digestive issues, at least not legally anyway.

Luckily for Briar, the King wasn't a big reader, so he never noticed or bothered about all the magical books of mythical creatures and wondrous spells in the castle library.

Briar devoured every one of them. Something captivated him about those books that he couldn't put his finger on. Was it the mystery of it all? The excitement of strange places and outlandish creatures? What the something was, it was hard to say.

He poured over spells and learned about bauchans and bodachs, kelpies and selkies, unicorns and wulvers. He found a book of fairie and learned all about their world and the roads that connected it to his. The creatures and their lives that he read about were of all different kinds, big and small, beautiful and ugly—to human eyes that is—but all wild and free, and utterly and completely themselves.

And one day he realised, that was it. If only, he thought, if only—to be wild and free. To be utterly and completely himself. To be who he wanted to be. He wasn't very unhappy. He loved his brothers, he loved to ride, he enjoyed his work helping run the kingdom—repairing walls, building new houses, breaking in horses, and ploughing the fields. He worked hard and was well-loved, though a little strange everyone knew.

He wasn't *intensely* unhappy, he thought. Plenty of people were worse off than him, most in fact. He was just…unfulfilled. Just…not quite whole somehow.

That same day, he read his favourite book once again—the book of fairie. But somewhere close to the middle of the book, he stopped. There was a page he had never seen before. Impossible, he thought, how could he ever have missed this? But there it was.

There was the most beautiful, most detailed and most intricate painting he had ever seen. This one had very little explanation underneath where the others had long paragraphs explaining the otherworldly content in-depth, but this one simply said, "The Goblin King."

And there was a man. He was very clearly not human, but not so far away as most in these pages. A slender figure with a long coat of blue and silver, long silver hair and the most striking eyes, one of blue and one of green…

Eyes that just sparkled from deep in the tired old parchment? They did. There was life in them he was sure of it, somehow. Briar's heart fluttered. He slipped the book under his jacket and took it to his room. He sat on his bed and opened it again, but he couldn't find the page. He flicked through the book quickly, leafed through each page laboriously—it was a very long book—but he couldn't find it. What had he been reading just before? Selkies? Frustrated, and frankly doubting his sanity, the prince eventually lay down exhausted.

Briar had even stranger dreams than usual that night. He dreamed of another castle. It was in their valley, but not, across the loch that wasn't quite the loch he knew. There was a gentle scent of jasmine and pine. He sensed people around him. He heard music. He felt his body move in a dance. A cacophony of bright colours swirled in kaleidoscope blur at the sides of his vision. But all he could see in the centre was the owner of those sparkling eyes, and those eyes were locked onto his. They widened for a second as if asking a question, and Briar heard his voice from far away whisper,

"Yes."

Briar awoke. And the owner of those sparkling eyes, one of blue and one of green, was standing before him. The Goblin King's smile sparkled too, set in a beautiful alabaster face surrounded by shimmering long silver hair. It was as if he were lit by his very own moonbeams from the tip of that silver hair to his fine, heeled midnight blue boots.

The man turned to the wall and waved his hands. A door swelled inwards from the stone and opened. The Goblin King took Briar's shaking hand and led him through, and that night Briar's dreams came true. He followed the Goblin King on the paths he had read about to fairie. He was led to the castle across the loch, not exactly like the loch he knew, to dance with the creatures of his books, The night was magical—both literally, and in his heart. He was free and completely himself. He fell in love with the Goblin King, and they danced together all night.

When he returned, as the sky was blushing with dawn his mind was full of dancing, music, whirling fairies, frolicking sprites, glistening wings, and of course, of sparkling eyes—one of green and one of blue. He had danced through the soles of his shoes. He was exhausted but glowing with happiness and wandered down to breakfast, barely seeing the world around him.

His brothers noticed.

"He's in love!" They laughed.

"I think it's the blacksmith," Biggest Brother sniggered.

They teased him, and he just smiled.

And from then on, every night he danced with his true love, the Goblin King. Each night was as magical as the last.

And every morning he returned, laid his head down on his feather pillow, and then lifted it right back up again. Every day he staggered to breakfast in the Great Hall hours after the others had begun. He lived his life just as he had—working, riding with his brothers, reading when he could, but now counting the hours till moonrise.

It wasn't long until his time in the library was spent with his head literally in his book. The brothers had smiled at the littlest one in love, with a far-off dreamy look in his eyes and the soft smile of someone truly happy. But as days passed, his dreamy eyes grew distant and fluttered with something else, worry? Or was it just tiredness? He smiled less. Each day he faded and began to look nearly as worn as the shoes he discarded every morning.

The glow of happiness within him faded too. Each day he felt more worried and less happy, more tired and less free. He felt a weight growing somehow each day. He felt heavy and torn at the same time and a churning inside that he tried to ignore.

Then one morning he returned and looked out at the sun rising and didn't even go to bed. He dragged himself straight to breakfast. He was so tired that he stumbled and fell just outside the door of the Great Hall. He slowly got to his feet and leaned against the cold stone wall. Inside the hall, the clatter of breakfast and chatter of voices jumbled together like crashing waves of noise. He sighed, and was about to go in when—

"Blacksmith!" Reverberated down the corridor, rattling suits of armour, fluttering tapestries and making Briar jump as the crashing voices of the hall reduced to a gentle frothing.

"Blacksmith!? But he could have his pick of any nobleman or woman, prince or princess in the land!"

"We don't know though!" Biggest Brother's loud voice was nearly as loud as his father's. "Just a theory."

"Maybe he's worried about something," he barely heard his mother's gentle tone.

"Like what?! What on earth could he have to worry about? He needs sorting out!" His father declared, "I mean, just what on earth's going on? What's wrong with him?"

More voices spoke in a quieter hum, and Briar couldn't make out the words. He leaned closer to the door straining to hear. If that's what he says about a blacksmith, Briar thought, imagine what he'd say to the truth. What would he say if he knew?

"Hey!" Biggest Brother's voice came thundering out now. "But I'm the heir! It's my birth right!"

"Well," the King bawled back huffily, "you lot are always telling me I'm too old fashioned. I'm afraid of change. Well, there you are! Change."

What on earth were they talking about?

"You can start right after breakfast." The King orated in his most royally important voice, "And I want an answer by tomorrow. This has gone on long enough. I want to know just what on earth is going on with that boy and whoever tells me can have the throne!…In good time of course."

Briar felt the churning inside him swell and tightness grip his chest. He breathed fast and shallow as he stared at the floor. Footsteps on the stone floor echoed towards him from the kitchens. For a second, he looked around frantically for a way out though he knew well enough there was none. So, he spread on the smile he was so practised in now and walked into the Great Hall.

Because he was so well practised at hiding his thoughts and

his feelings, nobody suspected he had heard a thing. But inside, panic had quickly turned to seething—his life was his own affair he thought, and it wasn't right of them to go snooping around. They hadn't even asked him what was wrong! He might have told them! Not his father, but his brothers at least. Well, he wouldn't tell them now! The family smiled at him, and he smiled back, feeling like an angry fox in a trap.

Biggest Brother felt like a fox in a trap too. He was the only one who wanted to be heir. The others had always been quite relieved it wasn't an option. He *had* wanted to ask Briar what was wrong, but somehow the time just hadn't seemed right. And now he was being pushed into snooping around, and he didn't like it. *And* he didn't know where to start. *And* he was annoyed at his father's power over him, over everything, to just take away something that was his...and actually it was all Briar's fault, whatever it was he was up to!

So, they both smiled on the outside and seethed on the inside. They glared at each other when the other wasn't looking. Each blamed the other for the mess they were in.

So Biggest Brother tried to find out Briar's secret, and he was now far too annoyed to just talk to Briar about it. Though even if he had, Briar was now far too annoyed to have told him anything!

Biggest Brother was many good and worthwhile things, but he wasn't the most clever at deception or at the wheedling out of secrets. The next day he had nothing to tell his father. Or the next, or the next.

He persuaded his brothers to help too, but they were no match for Briar. They waited outside his room to see where he went. Nowhere. They tried to hide inside his room, they searched his papers when he wasn't looking, they searched his room for any clue!

As you can imagine, every morning that Biggest Brother had nothing to tell his father, the King got crankier and crankier. Biggest Brother got more and more resentful of Briar, everyone felt tense, and even the Queen began to get really quite irritated with the whole thing.

Every day that Briar outwitted his family, he felt a little bit worse. And he still didn't realise why. He didn't know that the secret inside him was festering like mould. He had no idea that was the real problem—he was hiding his true self from those he loved. But then, we don't always know what it is that's making us feel wrong, do we? If we did, life would be a whole lot simpler.

Briar kept on telling himself he was just tired. And tired, he certainly was. He was weary not just in body but in heart. Deception is exhausting.

One day he just couldn't stay awake any longer. He was too tired to even try anymore. He went to his room, to his bed, lay down and blissfully fell asleep.

Right at the same time, Biggest Brother had finally had a really good idea! If Briar wasn't leaving the room—and he wasn't Biggest Brother reasoned; that at least they had established—then what was happening must be magic!

And it takes magic to puzzle out the solution to magical problems. So, off the brothers went in search of a witch.

All the magical folk and mythical creatures who chose to live in this realm lived in the deep dark forest.

The brothers rode into the forest. They rode in silence for hours, finding not a whisper of a hare's breath or the crack of a twig.

They rode into the deepest of the deep. There were trees bald and straight as arrows that leapt upwards out of sight. Others were thick and squat with gnarly wrinkled fingers and bark dripping with silver moss. The floor was a carpet of aromatic pine.

They rode on until at last in a clearing ahead, was an old man whistling a high dancing tune and building a fire.

"I say, peasant," said Biggest Brother, "we search for a witch! Where can we find a witch?"

He wasn't usually so rude—or frankly so silly, given that he was speaking to a creature in the deepest of the deep—but it had been a long ride. His new boots were tight, and he had run out of his secret magical remedy for blisters he'd sneaked into the castle.

The old man shifted in his crouch like his knees ached and stared up with surprisingly sparkling eyes, one of green and one of blue.

"I am the wisest witch to be found between the ocean and the sea," he said, "but you must be far more gracious if you want anything from me."

"Um, sorry. Yes, of course. Sorry," said Biggest Brother "I just…well we are all so very worried about Briar."

Biggest Brother felt his eyes welling up with tears. He hadn't realised till he said it that actually, he *was* very worried about his little brother. Now he heard the words from his own mouth he realised how true they were.

"We're desperate. We don't know what's wrong, and we don't know how to help."

The witch turned his eyes to the pile of twigs and logs he had built. He opened them a little wider as if asking a question and as he did, a fire danced up out. He sat quietly for a while looking thoughtfully into flames, muttering.

"I wonder, could I? Is it right? Would he just tell them? He might? The lies are hurting more each day. Perhaps this is the only way. I think a little help is needed to be sure the truth is seeded," Then, he stared in silence onto the dancing flames.

"Very well!" The witch cried out, and the brothers jumped as the seemingly creaky old man sprang to his feet so fast they didn't see him move at all! He was just standing straight-backed and tall, where he had been sitting crouched and staring into the fire.

"Take this cloak of invisibility. Hide and follow, then you'll see."

Then he was gone. Not that he walked away, or even flew. He was just gone.

"Take what cloak?" said Brother Four.

"This one," Biggest Brother whispered, looking down at the heavy velvet in his hand that draped across the pommel of his saddle and down his horse's shoulders. She twitched at the fabric's tickle, and it sparkled just a little. Biggest Brother gathered it up into a bundle and turned for home.

At the castle, he put on the cloak and lay in wait until Briar came to bed. He huddled down beside the wardrobe and fought to stay awake, but he was so tired, his eyes so heavy, and his head thick as swamp water. His chin nodded down onto his chest.

His eyes drifted open sometime later and he drowsily raised his head to see Briar standing across the room and facing the blank stone wall. He remembered suddenly where he was and why and jumped to his feet with a start, tripping on the hem of velvet and crashing down hard on his left knee. He fought not to cry out as he looked up…

A door swells out of the blank stone wall. Briar reaches for the door and without touching it pulls towards him with an open hand. The door that wasn't there before, that *isn't* there Biggest Brother reasons, opens.

Stairs curve down behind it, and Briar steps into the gloom. Biggest Brother stands for a second, looking around the room for an answer that isn't there, then he follows. He steps through a doorway of thick stone. It's disconcerting to be on what seem like castle stairs when the brain knows very well that stairs are not there and the body is somehow outside the castle walls. Or elsewhere.

Briar, who is used to it, easily and eagerly follows the curving stairs that grow less and less like castle stairs with each step. The scent of jasmine and pine grows, tendrils of pale vines creep through the brickwork that gets wilder and more craggy as the steps descend. The neatly cut stones steps get wilder too, now more like descending a rocky hill than a staircase.

Biggest Brother is struck with a sudden unease as to what is outside these craggy stone walls, now almost invisible under the entwining fingers of vines. The air stirs more freely now, new air from above. He daren't look up.

Until he does.

Two moons are dancing—gently waltzing in a deep purple sky thick with glittering stars of every colour that swirl in currents around them. Then there is blackness as he steps on the corner of the cloak, stumbles, flails for the walls that are gone and falls flat on his face into thick pine smelling moss.

Briar looks back for whatever made the strange scrabbling sound. He is sure he heard something behind him and feels something. But there is nothing to see.

Biggest Brother lies frozen—not on purpose to be quiet though it has that effect—but because of what he sees above and behind Briar's head. The dancing constellations in the purple sky are dizzying, and below them is a shimmering loch of pale lavender bordered with leafy trees of royal blue. The still water reflects the trees and sky above it perfectly so that both above and below, everything's dancing.

And there is a boat on the dancing mirror-loch, a little rowboat without oars gently floating towards them. Briar turns and walks towards it. He follows the river that flows slightly uphill into the loch. Only as Briar—and the rowboat—nearly reach the shore does Biggest Brother remember himself and scramble after him, the odd hand and leg visible for seconds as he bumbles along under the cloak, dizzy with the movement of the stars in the sky and the water.

Biggest Brother catches up and creeps behind. As Briar gets in the boat, he throws himself in at the same time. The boat doesn't tip too much. It should have; Biggest Brother should never have gotten away with that clumsy move. It's as if the loch held the boat steady for him, though even it couldn't compensate for him tripping and head-butting the side. He grunts and Briar looks back, but there's nothing to see and the boat creaks slightly like someone coughing to cover a laugh.

The boat sails through the loch. Or does the loch carry it to the other side? Either way, it gets there. To the foot of a castle that wasn't there a moment ago. Now it is. It's silver, tall, and bright. And loud! It's overflowing with music, laughter, and the clattering of feet on a hard floor. Light streams from hundreds of windows from the bottom to the dizzying heights of the tallest towers. Cavernous doors are open in front of them and warm air drifts out into the night with the music and laughter.

Briar hurries in and the crowds greet him, whirling him into the centre of the dance—the centre of the floor where his true love waits. Biggest Brother follows and here too, everything's dancing.

Everything you could imagine. Beautiful fairies with slender golden limbs and gossamer wings, hulking giant creatures that look to be made of earth and boulders, and everything in between, some with two legs some with eight, some with two eyes, some less and some more. All singing and dancing, smiling and laughing, eating and drinking happily together.

The walls are woven with glistening spider-webs and the roof held up by tall old trees with kind, sleepy faces, like old ladies and gentlemen watching the young ones and remembering when they capered around like that before their joints stiffened.

The dance is everywhere so the whole castle is a shifting sea of whirlpools, with the fastest dancers in their centres dragging creatures in and spitting them out, while currents and eddies and tides shift all around them.

A wizened little goblin woman with a back so hunched her chin is at her knees reaches up and grabs Biggest Brother's hands, hauling him into the fastest whirling centre of the dance. They join a group of fairies and a mossy creature who is actually seven small mossy creatures standing on heads and holding arms and legs to make a figure the height of the fairies.

Biggest Brother remembers he must find Briar at some point. And tell him he understands now why he comes here every night.

But after this dance. Just one more. And Briar looks too happy to be disturbed right now anyway. Biggest Brother smiles to know he was right about one thing—Briar is clearly very much in love. Across the room, Briar is dancing in his true love's arms with eyes only for The Goblin King.

Who knows how long they dance. Eventually, Biggest Brother's laugh echoes across the hall to Briar. When Briar turns to see his brother, he laughs too, to see Biggest Brother frolicking with the fairies and the hag. Briar forgets to even wonder how Biggest Brother came there in the first place. His brother is here and having a magical night. They come together and stay that way, dancing until the clock chimes and it's time for the boat to carry them home, back across the lavender lake, back up the winding stairs, back through the heavy stone door, and back to morning.

They sit on Briar's bed looking sleepily down, their shoes in tatters.

"Please don't tell father," Briar's mouth is dry and his body shaky. He's tired of course but it's more than that. He's scared. He doesn't know why. He just. He isn't ready. He can't. Not yet.

Biggest Brother squeezes Briar hand and smiles,

"Come on, I'm starving. And I won't say a word."

On wobbly legs, they follow down the neatly hewn stone steps that curve with the inner wall of the turret and towards the hum of the Great Hall.

Biggest Brother looks more nervous than Briar. He isn't so adept at hiding his feelings and 'something's wrong' is written all over his face. The King looks expectant already and all the other brothers are at the table. They must have told the King, not about the witch, but something—that today was the day and Biggest Brother had found the truth.

The King looks between the two brothers and frowns. Something is amiss here; he is sure. And he has lost all patience waiting. He stands and puffs out his ample chest. He takes a deep breath as if about to dive underwater, he takes it in deep and wide to prepare for the most sonorous and important tones he can muster.

"Before you start," Biggest Brother says, and the King deflates like a whoopee cushion, "I'm done with this. I won't do it anymore."

The King eyes Briar who eyes the floor. The King, of course, thinks that Briar has no idea what has been going on these last weeks, and what they are speaking of now.

He draws the breath again and aims for a sombre tone.

"If you resign, you will never reign."

"Fine," Biggest Brother doesn't intend to sound quite as huffy, but it had been a long night. Briar reaches for his brother's hand, and Biggest Brother looks back at him and smiles.

"Fine."

And he means it.

"Some things are more important."

Biggest Brother turns towards the breakfast table, but Briar hesitates, standing alone.

"No," he says, "I can't let him. I…"

Briar falters a little and looks unsure. Biggest Brother turns as if to go back to him, but just then the air stirs with jasmine and soft pine. Briar smiles and the uncertainty melts from his face.

"I have something to tell you, Father. But, well I don't know where to start…"

Then, sudden as a twig snap, the Goblin King stands beside Briar. And he takes Briar's hand smiling like moonbeams. There is silence, for a long moment of utter confusion. Then,

"Magic!" roars the King. "That's what's poisoned you. I told you magic always leads to trouble, I told you!"

"No," says the Goblin King calmly. "It's not the magic that hurt him, it's the hiding of his truth. Look. Look at him already and there's your proof!"

It's clear as a starry sky the Goblin King is quite right. The colour rushes back into Briar's cheeks, he stands taller, his eyes brighten, and he breathes deeply like he hasn't taken a breath properly in a long while. Whatever his father may say, Briar has done what he has to do, and he feels free—utterly and completely himself.

"I didn't know how to tell you. I'm sorry, Father. But I need magic in my life. And when I found it, I found my true love."

The King looks flabbergasted as the Queen smiles. She gets up from her chair, walks to Briar and hugs him close,

"Oh, my dear, I was so worried. I'm so sorry you felt like you had to hide."

She looks lovingly at her son, then turns to the Goblin King with a warm and welcome smile and says,

"I am very pleased to meet you, Your Majesty."

The King shuffles nervously and walks to stand beside the Queen. She does well not to glare at him too much.

"Well. Well, it's true I've never liked magic all that much. And the thing with the bog-witch…well…that's by the by."

The Queen coughs gently.

"Ah yes. I'm sorry, son."

And *'If this man is what you want and who you love, I will learn about his world and the world you have been living in because you mean the world to me.'*

The King doesn't actually say this—instead, he gruffly mumbles something like, "being happy son, what matters," and gives him a very regal, manly back slap and sniffs, looking at his boots—but that is what he means. Briar beams because he knows his father well enough to know that.

"Welcome, Sir," the King barks at the Goblin King so suddenly he makes them all jump.

So, the castle bustles into life as breakfast ends, and it is an especially noisy day. Not only full of talk about the drama and excitement of a Goblin King within the castle walls but what

that means—magical remedies for their boils and bunions! And the blacksmith's hammer sounds loudly with a very special task from the Queen. Fourteen metal-soled shoes must be made that very day to be ready for moonrise. One for each prince and for the King and Queen. They have a very special night ahead of them.

As the sun sets behind the forest the castle turrets dim from bright silver to pale icy blue. The snaking crystal blue river sparkles in the dimming light and beyond the rolling green fields, the loch in the distance mirrors the sunset.

The other castle is waiting.

Hunger
Sarah Dropek

They don't call us witches at first. When we emerge from the woods, they don't yet have words for what they think of us. But I can tell they're anxious to give us a name, a category, some epithet to stick onto us to give their trembling hearts solace.

I want to give them one, but I don't remember anything. And neither does the boy who was with me, holding my hand before I yanked it away when we left the forest and broke whatever spell we had been under. Our minds are empty of what has happened or who we are to each other. All I know is he must be a little older than me when the shadow of a beard begins to grow along his jaw as we are held captive together.

For three days, the villagers torture us, trying to goad magic or evil from our bodies, anything to give them cause to kill us that their God would forgive. And though we are half-drowned, starved, and exhausted, our suspicion for each other never flags. We watch each other from the corners of the cell we are kept in, both unsure one of us isn't the monster. But I am sure of myself, sure of the voice that filters through the gray haze of my mind and tells me to survive.

Cut your tangled hair. Clean up. Smile.

Her voice is warm like a mother I must have but can't

remember. She keeps me company as I weather the villagers' distrust and the boy's stare. She is all I have.

At the end of the third day, the people relent. They move us from our cell to the outbuilding by the church at the edge of the trees. They lock us in together. They call us witches. They leave.

They don't know the real threat. Stay strong. I will keep you safe from him, child.

An old woman is sent to pass food through our locked door every evening.

The first night she comes, she brings bread and milk that is more sour than sweet. She names us Niv and Vymra. "Night and Death," she says before running from our door.

The second night she comes, I catch her before she can scuttle away, "Why name us and feed us if we're kept in here to wait out death?" I beg.

Behind the thin wooden door, she says nothing, but she does not walk away.

"I wish no harm to this village, only to be freed and allowed whatever meager life I can make. Give me a job. Anything, please," I whine, pressing my forehead to the gap where door meets wall and feeling the cool air slip in over my lips that are hungry for more than just bread. If I could make money, I could buy some real food, something worth eating.

Niv says nothing but sits near the fire with a blank stare as if my attempts to win the woman over are pathetic. All he has done every morning since we awoke is ask me the same question; "What do you remember?" His eyes dart more frantically around our prison when my answer does not change.

I remember nothing.

He is afraid you will remember what you already know, that he is evil and must be killed.

But the voice I have decided must be my mother reaching out to me through all I have forgotten does not tell me how to kill him, and I cannot stand his silence and furtive glances anymore. I wait for the old woman's answer to my question, hoping if I am freed, she will keep Niv here.

Her whisper is as rough as the wind beating against the door, "What did you see in the woods?"

"Nothing. I swear nothing. I was under some sort of spell, I don't know. I just want out, please."

She sighs deeply and I catch the scents of honey and lavender on her breath. I yearn for a taste of something so decadent.

"Get yourself washed and cleaned tonight. You and Niv, both. I'll bring my grandson by in the morning. He may have work for you."

She begins to shuffle off.

"Wait," I yelp. "Please, may I have a pair of shears or a blade? I can clean my hair but there won't be any brushing through the knots it's tied into."

She lets out a harrumph of disapproval, but after a moment, I see a flash of metal drop into the basket. She shoves it through the small hole in the door, and I reach past the bread and milk to find the blade. It is barely as long as my middle finger and has been yanked out of its hilt, so the end is difficult to hold and I nearly slice myself. But it's more protection than I've had for the last three days, and I tuck it into my skirt pocket, ignoring the strange warmth it left in my hand.

"I suppose if you kill yourselves, it saves us any more trouble," she says before checking the lock on our door and leaving.

Behind me, I hear Niv begin to fill water into the large iron pot to heat for a bath.

"You don't trust me," he says, catching me in his dark gaze when I turn around.

"I don't know you," I reply, bringing the old woman's bread to the table.

He walks to it after stoking the fire and presses his portion to his face, taking a deep inhale of it before he bites down.

The knife in my pocket feels suddenly too small.

"I have every reason to be as suspicious of you," he says through his full mouth. "But if you're determined to gain their approval then we're going to have to work together. What story do you want to create for us? Everyone enjoys a good romance," he suggests, giving me a wink as he chews the tough crust of the bread.

"I will not pretend to be promised to you."

The old woman told us both that the demons of the forest enjoy the thrill of the chase sometimes as much as the satisfaction of the kill when she locked us up. I thought she was trying to scare us away from attempting escape, but what if she was trying to warn me. Who knows what evil could possess me from his lips if we were forced to kiss to keep up with such a charade?

Good girl. Don't let him get close until you're ready for the kill.

I want to beg the voice in my mind to tell me when and how. To ask why she makes me linger in fear, living with the devil. But Niv continues talking. I will have to wait until he sleeps to pray and plead to her.

"Brother and sister, then," he says. "Our parents separated, tore us apart. But we saw it coming and made a plan to walk through the forest to be reunited in spite of them and live together, fending for ourselves."

"Right. Clever," I say, worried the pretense that could get me away from him will first bring me deathly close. "Do you think they'll believe it?"

"I think they have made up their mind about us and it's almost impossible to convince someone out of that," he tips his chair back on two legs and narrows his eyes at me. "Have you made up your mind about me, yet?"

Say yes, daughter. Let him think he's safe so he will let down his guard.

I open my mouth, then close it again. I do not want him safe and comfortable, edging closer to my side of our cage. I do not want him to expect I will return his smile with one of my own.

"No," I manage. "No, but I can play along."

I hear her scratching scream in my mind before I am frozen in pain. My blood feels as if it boils in my veins and I cry out in agony. My skin crackles and chars like I have been set on fire. It only lasts long enough for one tear to squeeze out from my eyes shut tight, but it feels like eternity.

When I open my eyes, Niv looks at me no differently than a moment ago.

"Good," he says, frowning as he turns back at the fire. "Play along well enough and you won't need to trust me. We'll be free of each other if the lie convinces them we're harmless."

"Yes," I murmur.

He takes the boiling water off the flame to cool for cleaning ourselves. I look around the room. Nothing is amiss. The fire I felt raging over my skin only moments ago has left no marks. It's as if I didn't just feel like I was on the edge of death. But I reach a fearful hand to my face and wipe away a tear that tells me I was.

Niv knows what the knife is the moment he sees its shimmering flash. The glint of the metal in Vymra's hand reminds him of the gifts their mother used to bring him from the forest. Blood red flowers in the dead of winter, a perfect butterfly wing long after their migration had ended, things that only existed because she had made them. He could always see her magical mark on the presents when he held them to the sun and tilted just so, making the light tremble on the thing as if it might disappear.

Niv sees the same magic in the knife the old woman gave to Vymra, only he can't tell what its purpose might be. Their mother had died before she could teach him how to read or harness the magic of things for himself more than a few tricks. Murdered, Niv reminds himself, as he watches the steam rise from the cooling water.

Like milk poured into black tea, Niv's memories only reveal themselves as they are stirred up by the world around him. And though he could never prove it, he knows in his heart his father killed his mother for discovering her magic. Even if her magic had kept them alive so near the forest all that time, letting his father eke out a living selling timber that he would have died chopping down without her, he killed her out of fear. And cast his children out to die in the forest from the same fear.

Niv reaches for the memory of how they survived but finds only a gray blankness in his mind where it should be. He swallows back tears knowing his sister's mind is an entire void of gray nothingness. Since they walked out of the trees, she has remembered nothing and treats him more and more like a threat. She mutters and whispers to herself, and he hopes it is something coming back to her. But then she looks at him with the same scared mousy eyes of their father, and he knows she is still lost. Maybe a bath tonight, a shave, anything to make him look more like himself will remind her who he is. He wishes the purpose of the dazzling knife could be to wake her from her daze. He wishes for his sister to come back from the forest.

Niv lets me bathe first. My limbs shake as I undress. I am afraid of my own body and the pain that rushed through it. Why would she hurt me?

To protect you, my sweet one. I know his kind. You must listen to me.

Then tell me how to kill him. Why do you make me wait in fear?

Evil is weakest when it feels in control. You must make him think you are fooled, then deliver death.

I do not know how good of a liar I can be. I do not remember a childhood where I might have kept secrets or hidden away treasures.

You have always been exceptional. You will be perfect now, too, my love.

I unclench my jaw.

Yes. There, there.

I swirl my fingers in the water to test it before getting in, wary of how long his dark eyes watched it cool, worried he has set it as a trap.

You are safe with me, child.

I take the warm blade from my skirt pocket and sink into the hot water. I hack at hair that has grown too long.

Since you left me.

I will be pristine. I will look like the savior I am. When I finally kill the evil in Niv, the village will know who to thank.

Clean and dry, I wrap my shorn hair around the small knife that has become too hot to touch and put it safely back into my skirt.

When I return from the bath, I try my hand at pretending.

"I'm sorry. It's gone cold," I say, pulling my brows together in demure concern.

His laugh is hesitant, "Are you sure we aren't siblings? Seems very much like a younger sister to hog all the hot water for herself."

What does he—

"Do you remember something?" I ask, clasping my hands together with excitement, though my heart stutters in fear.

"Nothing. Not even myself," he breathes, giving me a wide berth as he walks past me to the bath. He stops short with his hand on the curtain and turns back to me. "I like the trim by the way. Any chance I can borrow the blade for a shave?"

I freeze in terror at the thought of him slitting my throat so easily in the night.

"Didn't think so," he says before disappearing behind the sheet.

Niv barely hears the soft knock at the door over the crackling of the logs he has been feeding the fire all night. His sister finally fell asleep in the pitch blackness of early morning, but he still couldn't rest listening to her smacking lips and muttered words.

He stands and goes to the door wishing it was his to unlock and open.

The old woman's grandson is barely visible beneath his winter clothes, but tufts of jet black hair peek out beneath his woolen hat. He says nothing at first but looks over Niv as if searching for something.

"Please," Niv whispers, not quite sure of how to put words to what he fears has happened to his sister.

"Did she use the knife?" he asks, his voice urgent but hushed.

"On her hair," Niv replies. "What magic does it have?"

His eyes widen with surprise, "You can see it?"

Niv checks that Vymra still sleeps, "Our mother taught me some of what she knew."

"Mine too, and Goma before her. I'm Adrik."

"But the village has feared us to be witches since we arrived," Niv says, confusion and anger churning in his chest.

"My Goma lived in this room for ten years after she left the forest. My mother for two years after her magic came in. I stayed for a week. It has taken three generations for them to trust our magic. And Goma didn't arrive with a demon holding her hand."

Niv shakes his head, but he knows it is true.

Adrik pulls his scarf down so Niv can hear him better when he whispers, "The knife was enchanted for evil to covet. It will bind her here every night to cut hair that won't stop growing. It will give us time to get you ready to kill her."

"She's my sister," Niv breathes.

"And the demon has taken hold. If you don't do it…" Adrik's voice grows tender when he says the words that ended every fairytale Niv's mother ever told him as a boy, "The hunted must kill the hunter—"

"—for the final rest of lasting death," Niv finishes. "I know. But I can't…"

"I will teach you. You won't be alone in this," Adrik promises.

Then he looks past Niv and concern disappears from his eyes, replaced with the same wary suspicion that every villager has had for them since they arrived.

"I hope you weren't thinking of leaving without me," Vymra chirps.

Niv's chest grows tight again with a torrent of fear and sadness until it feels like he cannot breathe. But the smallest nod from Adrik gives him strength, and he turns to face the demon.

His mouth drops at the sight of her long curls that have grown back past her shoulders overnight. Niv can't help but stare and Vymra follows his eyes, her hand trembling as she picks the hair up as if it is a dead rat.

Niv watches goosebumps blossom over her skin before she knots it back at the nape of her neck and laughs.

"Curls more once it dries," she says quickly. "Where are we working?"

"A roof burned down last week," Adrik replies. "We need good wood and since you've already been through the forest…"

"The village won't mind if we go back and don't come out again," Vymra says as she itches her neck red. "But won't they miss you?"

Her flushed cheeks and too-wide grin make her question even more sinister, but Adrik only smiles.

"We'll end work well before dark, and I have a few tricks to keep us safe."

"A witch," Vymra gasps.

"A boy," Adrik corrects, quick with his lie, "who spent enough time growing up by the forest to know some ways to tame it. A witch wouldn't survive long here."

"Then we will prove our innocence by staying alive, won't we brother?" Vymra steps forward and rests her arm on Niv's like she's his sister again and they are walking together on an errand to town.

"Yes, we will," Niv says, barely able to get the words out.

"Thank you, Adrik. For helping us."

Adrik nods to them both.

Niv marvels at how he stares darkness in its eyes and does not flinch. A memory rises to the surface of his mother staring down his father with the same confidence, telling him to leave the house and never return. Niv had cowered behind the bed with his sister, watching them fight. He had hidden from his father's cruelty since he was a boy. His mother had died for it and his sister was lost to darkness because of it. He would not hide from evil anymore.

My hair.

Will be cut tonight, no matter. Watch him. Fool him.

I yearn to reach up and scratch at my neck, but my arm is trapped in Niv's as we begin our walk to the forest. We stay locked together for a while. I shuffle to keep up, taking two steps for every one of his while Adrik charts a path through the trees ahead of us. But I can only force myself to hold him so close for so long.

"Do you think he believes us?" I ask, dropping my arm away. I shove my hand in my pocket, away from the cold to the reassuring heat of the knife.

"I think it's enough for today," Niv says.

The gap between us widens. Niv stays close to Adrik, casting cautious glances back to me. He trips over the heel of Adrik's boot once before taking a place at his side.

He thirsts for your soul, but he sniffs out his next kill.

Tell me how to end him.

His heart must want yours. He must invite us in. Be the sister you know he craves, and I will take care of the rest.

Niv settles into a tense charade for the next few days of work, pretending to fall for Vymra's stilted attempts at sisterly love. But all he can find in his heart when she jokes with him or laughs too loud at something he has said is a piercing fear and sadness. It reminds him of every time he has been weak before and how he cannot fail her again, letting this demon have her body.

As they move through the forest each day, Niv is in awe of Adrik's magic that protects them. Before their axes ever begin working, Adrik oils both of his palms and touches them to the bark of three trees that are so close their roots twine over and under the earth like strands of hair. He moves his hands over each of them in large silent circles.

Niv watches how the oil shimmers on the bark before it begins to peel away of its own accord. He thinks of his mother who taught him the words and motions to shave without a blade before his father ever noticed he was becoming a man. He lifts a hand to where she had made small circles along his jaw and mourns how much strength her magic must have had that she never got the chance to teach him. Niv wonders if his sister would have been just as strong when she came into her magic. He wonders how long it will be until he can kill the father that took away his chance to find out.

In short snippets and whispers, Adrik teaches Niv how to feel his own magic and what gods to call on to ask for what he needs. They speak only when Vymra is far enough away to be a dark smudge against the pale sky, only when her ax flies through the air too quickly for her to hear them.

It is two days until Vymra strays far enough while they work that Adrik can put his hand over Niv's and show him what he will have to do.

"Your hands are the place where all magic enters and exits," Adrik instructs, holding his palms up close enough that Niv can see the scars from where he has waged battles with his own power. "It's why enchanted objects are powerful to use and difficult to fight. It's how the demon first came to your sister.

It gave her what she wanted, and she took it with an open hand and open heart."

"Sweets," Niv says, remembering the cloying scent of it on his sister's breath when she ate the old woman's candy before Niv could stop her.

"The young and the old are the easiest to steal away. I'm sorry," Adrik replies. "Evil offers candy with a smidge of freedom or hot chocolate with a dash of warm love, and desperate children devour it."

"My father was never kind to any of us," Niv says, pretending the shake of his voice is from the cold. "But my sister, she was younger, and he expected too much from her after Mother died. It made her crave love and approval long after I had learned to stop looking for it. He left us in the forest after he found out about my magic. An old woman came upon us, took us to her cottage and fed my sister's cravings. I remember eating until it hurt, then being hungry, and then I don't remember. But why… why us?"

Adrik takes Niv's hand and places their palms together as he speaks, "You're looking for blame where there isn't any to be had. Demons hunt because they hunt. A weak or needy soul can help them wheedle in easier, yes. But mostly they are hungry. Like all of us."

A warmth flows into Niv from where Adrik's calloused hands rest against his skin and his chest unwinds until he feels like he can breathe again.

"It convinced your sister to let it in, and it won't stop until it has your soul, too. And everyone who shares your blood. I've heard of entire generations of extended families being devoured before a demon moves on. You think you failed your sister or that you can still save her. But she's gone. And you only fail now if you don't keep going and make it right. Even if to keep going means you have to leave things behind," Adrik says.

"My sister," Niv heaves a sobbing breath.

"And your guilt," Adrik says gently.

When Niv falls into his arms, Adrik holds him for a moment before they must pull away and pretend again.

It is a week until Niv knows how to end the demon. A week that Niv measures in the moments he and Adrik are alone, and he feels safe with their hands touching, learning magic and each other. And in that week, Adrik's grandmother fashions the blade for his sister, one last lie he will have to tell her.

I am the perfect sister. Love and warmth and hope and light radiate from Niv's skin more and more every day. He relaxes. He is ready to let me in. He asks Adrik for better food. I lick the honey from my lips long after breakfast. He brings me an early spring blossom and tells me I am the sister he wishes he could remember.

Today we break from work early. He gifts me a new knife, tells me I deserve it. The hilt of blue glass glitters in the sun and snow. It is cool in my hand as I test it on my hair.

I hold on as tightly as I can.

My fingers freeze.

It's just the cold.

Vymra cries out in rage, but the knife stays in her hand as her finger turn from ice-white to pale blue.

The demon knows their betrayal. Adrik whispers to Niv he must be strong while they wait for the magic to freeze the demon enough so he can get close and finish it off.

And Niv does feel stronger. With Adrik at his side, he is ready to use the magic he has learned and to say goodbye. He is ready for everything except the sound of his father's voice coming from his sister's body.

"You will pay for your trickery with a more painful death," the demon says, staring down Adrik before turning to Niv.

His sister's face contorts into a snarling, smiling rage, and Niv understands. It was never his sister or his mother who were weak and let the demon take hold in his family. It had been his father all along.

The demon gives out a low growl and smacks its lips, watching Niv.

"And you, I will savor you for as long as your sniveling soul will stay alive for me."

"Alive?" Niv stammers, gulping down fear.

Vymra cackles, "Demon's don't feast on the dead, silly boy."

"She's still alive?" Niv yells looking to Adrik.

But Adrik's gaze is locked on Vymra, hands up, palms open, ready for a fight.

"Oh my," the demon coos. "How fine. The witch has told you your sister was dead in here. He must think you're too weak to kill me if you knew. You could keep her alive, you know. There are trades. Bargains that can be made."

"Niv, do not listen to it," Adrik spits. "Whatever it offers, there's not enough left of your sister for her to be your sister. If you don't kill the creature, the death won't ever stop."

"I assure you she's still here, begging for every morsel of love I give her," the demon says, Vymra's eyes glowing brightly with hunger. "But I'll leave her be for a better meal. I won't make the same mistake of lingering too long like I almost did with your mother. She was so delicious and stayed alive so long trying to fight me to protect you. I almost forgot how to move on by the time she ran dry. Thankfully, scared children are easily tricked. Your sister welcomed me with open arms."

The demon hums in satisfaction, though Niv can see its body growing rigid from the magic of the gifted knife. He clutches at the other blade in his pocket. His fingers run nervously over the smooth, gray-glassed hilt of it, the sister knife to the one the demon still holds onto that will begin its death.

Adrik clears his throat next to him. Niv knows he should not wait any longer. The demon could catch onto the charade

Adrik and Niv are playing to give their magic time to work. At any moment, the demon could overpower the pieces of Niv's sister that he knows are left. His sister that is more powerful than he ever could have imagined, gripping the knife with all of her strength to let Niv end the demon and herself.

"Let her rest," Adrik whispers.

Vymra smiles, "You would murder your own—"

The soft thud of Niv's knife sinking into the demon's stomach cuts it off. The matching blade falls from Vymra's hand, but it's too late.

Niv and Adrik watch silently as a blue brighter than the afternoon sky snakes through the veins of his sister's body until it reaches her eyes and covers over the blackness that had grown there. Her body falls and Niv sinks down into the soft snow with it.

Adrik's hand slips into Niv's and stills his shivering breaths.

"Just a little more strength now," he whispers.

Niv moves to crouch over the body, placing shaking palms over blue eyes. But as he makes small circles with silent prayers, as Adrik taught, he knows it is not just a little more strength to let her go. It will be a lifetime of strength, summoning what he can every day to keep going with the knowledge of what he has done and what he can never allow himself to become.

Author Bios

Laurel Beckley is a writer, Marine Corps veteran, and librarian. She is from Oregon and currently lives in northern Virginia with her wife, fur creatures, and a collection of gently neglected houseplants. Her debut novel, *That Distant Dream*, is available from NineStar Press and Amazon. She can be found on twitter @laurelthereader and her blog, The Suspected Bibliophile (*https://thesuspectedbibliophile.home.blog/*).

David Costa was born in the beautiful city of Lisbon where he grew up daydreaming about knights and dragons. Throughout his life he kept nurturing his love for books, movies, and videogames, and after becoming a researcher in the field of Health Psychology he decided to pursue his dream of becoming a writer. When he is not working on his next novel, he can be found glued to a screen, working out, or playing electric guitar.

Helen De Cruz is a philosophy professor who lives in Saint Louis, Missouri. They also enjoy playing Renaissance lute and archlute, and dabble in fiction and illustration.

Sarah Dropek writes poetry and fiction in Texas. Her work has appeared in HerStry, Solana, and Mic, with a forthcoming story in Wyldblood Magazine. You can find her sporadically on twitter @Dropek. And in the offline world, she's usually found digging in the garden dirt for worms and roly polies with her toddler.

Sonia Focke is an an author and Egyptologist, and has drawn on elements of Ancient Egypt in this story, including the Mesolithic and Neolithic cultures of the Nile Valley. She has published stories in The Were-Traveller's "Women Destroy [Retro-] Sci-Fi" issue (a fun Galaxy-Quest-meets-Lower-Decks-style romp), Wolfsinger Press' dragon-themed anthology "Crunchy With Ketchup" (with the 5102 World Flaming Championships with your favourite dragon commentators, Carol and Bob) and has twice participated in the Munich literary exhibition Arcana.

Her other accomplishments include building a Prehistoric Egyptian horn bow, cosplaying Queen Amidala with only her own hair, moving house in a VW Polo, and inventing the word "turtlet" (the proper term is "hatchling" and she has zero regrets.)

She lives in Germany with a blacksmith and two Padawans. You can find her on Facebook, Instagram and Twitter, and occasionally on her homepage *soniafocke.wordpress.com*.

Betsie Flynn lives in a council estate in mid-Wales with her husband, children, and cats. A long-time lover of fairytales and folk stories, she couldn't be happier that this anthology houses her first short story publication. She tweets @betsieflynn

Claire Olivia Golden likes books, yarn, and the Oxford comma. She graduated summa cum laude from Portland State University with a B.A. in French and English and now works as a copywriter and professional crochet designer. She is the author of *Unraveled*, *The Lost Girl of Goose Creek*, and *The Button Jar: A Poetry Parody*. Her short stories, creative nonfiction, and poetry have been published in several anthologies and literary magazines. Claire lives in the Pacific Northwest USA with her husband and her emotional support cat Persephone.

Cliff Jones Jr. is a rising star in the world of dreampunk/ irrealist literature, though he has quite a ways yet to rise. In both his writing career and his day job as a software developer, he leans heavily on his background in linguistics and the years he spent teaching English at home and abroad. Autism has been ever-present in Cliff's life, being on the spectrum himself and dealing with it in his family. This may be why he places such a high value on internal worlds and alternative modes of experience. Cliff is surviving with his wife Tina, their two daughters, and the family cat Baloo. Find him online at *CliffJonesJr.com*.

Emily Barnett Kudeviz lives in Tennessee with her people and two ~~gremlins~~ cats. She is a writer, publisher, and teacher of college-aged and third-grade students, and she travels every chance she gets. This is her first publication. She tweets at @conjurestars.

Jennifer Jeanne McArdle grew up in New York State, where she now lives, along with her partner and an agent of chaos made flesh (her dog) and now works in animal conservation. She previously lived in South Korea for four years and served in the Peace Corps in Indonesia. You can find some of her other work in the following anthologies/magazines: *ParAbnormal* September 2019 issue, *Whigmaleeries and Wives' Tales*, *Lovecraft in a Time of Madness*, and the upcoming *Mesozoic Reader Volume 1*. Follow her on Twitter @mcardlejeanne or Instagram @aerocrystal.

Jenny McClay is a psychologist from Glasgow, now living on the northeast coast of Scotland with her husband and four kids.

She writes everything she has time to write and has a special soft spot for Scottish mythology. When not working or writing, she spends her time in or on the beautiful North Sea pretending she's a Selkie and keeping one eye out for the local dolphins.

Toni Mobley is a reader, writer, and ardent connoisseur of mythology. Raised in Australia and Japan, she currently lives in California with her two cats, who she can't disprove aren't vengeful deities. Hobbies include long drives up the coast, playing video games, and enjoying the same five television shows as background noise.

Doug Rooney is a lecturer in English Language and Literature at the Capital University of Economics and Business in Beijing and the co-host of the podcast *Speaking to the Dead*.

Lucy Zhang writes, codes and watches anime. Her work has appeared in *Black Warrior Review*, *The Cincinnati Review*, *DIAGRAM*, *West Branch* and elsewhere. Her work is included in *Best Microfiction 2021* and *Best Small Fictions 2021*, was a finalist in Best of the Net 2020, and long listed in the Wigleaf Top 50. Find her at *https://kowaretasekai.wordpress.com/* or on Twitter @Dango_Ramen.